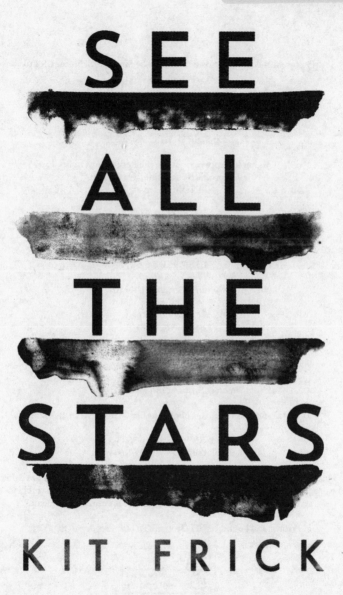

SEE
ALL
THE
STARS

KIT FRICK

SIMON & SCHUSTER

First published in Great Britain in 2019 by Simon & Schuster UK Ltd
A CBS COMPANY

First published in the USA in 2018 by Margaret K. McElderry Books,
an imprint of Simon & Schuster Children's Publishing Division

1 3 5 7 9 10 8 6 4 2

Simon & Schuster UK Ltd
1st Floor,
222 Gray's Inn Road
London WC1X 8HB

www.simonandschuster.co.uk

Simon & Schuster Australia, Sydney
Simon & Schuster India, New Delhi

A CIP catalogue record for this book is available from the British Library.

PB ISBN 978-1-4711-8603-5
eBook ISBN 978-1-4711-8604-2

Printed and bound by CPI Group (UK) Ltd, Croydon, CR0 4YY

SEE

ALL

THE

STARS

For the best friends who make it through
the beautiful, the messy, the thorns.
For the best friends who don't.

DON'T CRY WHEN THE SUN IS GONE,

BECAUSE THE TEARS WON'T LET YOU SEE THE STARS.

—VIOLETA PARRA

THE PAST IS NEVER DEAD. IT'S NOT EVEN PAST.

—WILLIAM FAULKNER

JUNE, SOPHOMORE SUMMER
(THEN)

We went to the party because Ret insisted. I was perfectly happy right where we were: lying on our backs in Jenni's sprawling front yard, building our best-ever summer playlist, telling time by the dandelion clocks until the sky was a white haze of down. We were idle and airy. We had perfected the summer loaf.

But Ret was bored with our listless and lovely string of afternoons. Always the four of us—Ret, Jenni, Bex, and me. Always at Jenni's big and typically parentless house. Always the same.

I liked it that way.

Ret was there. I was there. Did the setting really matter?

Jenni ran back and forth between the lawn and kitchen, bringing us a container of oil-cured olives, then a loaf of carrot bread to try while I scoured Spotify, the iPad raised above my head like a sunshade. The Ramones ("Rockaway Beach"), The Smiths ("Ask"), and Katy Perry ("California Gurls"), just to see if anyone was paying attention. Ret lounged back next to me, half watching Bex rehearse the newest dance team combination on the porch. I pressed play and put the iPad down in the grass. Five slender fingers threaded their way through my own. Ret squeezed. *You are mine.*

I wanted only this, the four of us together, but Ret said nothing ever happened, and Ret Johnston was the sun. Hot, bright, at the center of our universe. That we revolved around her was simply a fact. Ret said the whole sophomore class would be at Dave Franklin's party, which was exactly why I didn't want to go. But Ret was sitting up, latching and relatching the buckles on her tall black boots, and I was the one with a car.

"Who cares about some boring party?" Jenni plopped down next to us and plucked a fuzzy globe from the grass, puffing out her cheeks. Jenni Randall was the Earth, the gravitational force anchoring us to her yard, to her house, tempting us to stay. She was also Ret's oldest friend, a fact she made sure I'd never forget. "What does Dave Franklin have that we don't?" she asked.

"A bathtub full of coke," Ret answered. She swiveled around until she was kneeling behind us, then gathered Jenni's thick red hair between her fingers and began to braid.

"You know that's crap." Bex squinted at the three of us across the porch railing, which she'd been using as a ballet barre. Her torso and arms formed one long arc, all smooth lines and taut muscle. "Are you seriously considering crashing Dave's?"

I shrugged and popped an olive in my mouth, then waved the

container toward Jenni. If Ret was set on going, I guess you'd call my consideration serious. "The coke stuff's just a rumor," I said, but really, who knew.

"No, it's true," Ret insisted, her fingers deftly pulling lock after lock into place. Jenni sat still and let her hair be tamed. "I heard you can get a contact high from licking the walls in Dave Franklin's bedroom, and I plan to find out. Anyway, we're not crashing. Dave invited me."

Invited Ret, not me. But if Dave asked Ret, the rest of us were part of the package. Dave knew that. Everyone knew.

"Just watch out, okay?" Bex hopped off the porch and settled down next to Jenni, grabbing the olives. "Something's up with that guy. I said 'hey' in the Starbucks lot last week, and he literally jumped. I swear he was hiding a dead body in his trunk."

"Finally, something newsworthy on the West Shore. What are we waiting for?" Ret released Jenni's hair, letting the half-finished braid fall heavy against her back, and motioned toward my car with her chin.

"Yeah, no thanks," Bex said. "Rich people's houses freak me out. Besides, our playlist needs some serious work." Her eyes flickered across the abandoned iPad, the three songs I'd managed to add in the past hour. She was a transplant from Montreal and the newest addition to our solar system. French on her dad's side and Moroccan on her mom's, Bex was our Venus: headstrong and free willed, rotating opposite the rest of the planets. Opposite Ret.

"Suit yourself, but don't blame me if you die an old maid." Bex didn't flinch, and Ret turned to Jenni and me. Her eyes were a liquid, lapis lazuli kind of blue. You could fall down those eyes like a well. No return. "Ladies?" she asked.

"Pass." Jenni threw us a look that said she had *feelings* about the afternoon's development. The only parties Jenni liked were the ones she hosted herself, and she wasn't happy about me taking Ret away. Which was clearly how she saw things, even though this plan was all Ret's. Her back stiffened as she reached around to tuck a stray strand of hair into her braid.

I groaned and pushed myself up off the grass. "Let's order Rosa's for dinner?" I asked, angling to keep the peace. "Just the four of us."

Jenni's shoulders visibly relaxed. "Taco night," she agreed. "Get your asses back by seven if you expect chips and queso."

Bex glanced up from the iPad. "Have fun, dears."

Ret ignored her and ran toward my car, leaving me to follow in her wake. Then we climbed inside my dad's old Subaru and left the others behind.

I could have said no. I could have let the sweetness of carrot bread melting on my tongue and the lull of the breeze on my face keep me anchored to the grass. I could have let the trill of the iPad drown Ret out. Everything that came next might have been different.

No Matthias. No lies. No hot, bright surge of rage that flung us all apart, lodging galaxies between us by senior year until we were planets orbiting no one. Ret, Jenni, Bex, and me.

But that day I was the moon, dark and cold without the sun's light. Ellory Holland—constant satellite. So I went. Ret went, and I followed.

It was about a mile and a half between Jenni's and Dave's. We all lived on the West Shore of the Susquehanna River, home to

Panera and Starbucks and the Crestview Mall. Like everywhere else along the Rust Belt, the capital took a nosedive after the factories shut down, and my parents were part of the wave of people who moved across the river, to the suburbs. And there we stayed. Most of us West Shore kids had the same story to tell.

On the other side of the river, across the Market Street Bridge, the East Shore was the compressed gleam of our tiny downtown, the government buildings, and then not a whole lot beyond them. Downtown quickly faded into auto lots and the crappy mall and little houses hemmed in by chain-link fences. You went to the East Shore to paw through the same tired selection at the same two record shops and go thrifting at Salvation Army. You got dinner with your parents on the three blocks of Second Street we called "restaurant row" because it was the only strip of restaurants in town. It was hardly a thrilling departure from the West Shore, but anything beat the mall. Or parties at Dave's.

I glanced over at Ret next to me in the passenger's seat. I wondered how long it would take her to notice if I turned the car around, headed toward the bridge. She had the window all the way down, her ear pressed against the headrest, her face turned into the wind. Ret was never happier than when she was in motion. And I was happiest when I was with Ret. She turned to me, catching my gaze.

"Two roads diverged in a wood, and I—"

It was our call and response, the famous line from the Frost poem our whole English class had memorized freshman year. It started as a joke because Maria Hidelman flubbed it when it was her turn to recite, saying, "I took the one more traveled by," which was pretty much Maria Hidelman in a nutshell. Over the next week, Ret and I made up wilder and wilder call-back lines, one-upping each other. *I took the one to the darkest corners of your heart. I took the one to heaven's gate. I took the one to the deep end of the Arctic Ocean.* More than a year later, we were still going. Whoever didn't start it had to finish. It was like a dare; you had to come up with something new each time.

"I took the one to Dave Franklin's giant-ass house because Her Majesty wished to make an appearance among the commoners."

Ret scowled, but her lips soon turned into a smile. I held my hands steady on the wheel and kept driving toward Dave's.

Ret and I found each other in freshman English, in the weeks before Robert Frost. My best friend—the only girl who knew all my secrets, who'd been my other half since second grade—had moved that summer to the middle-of-nowhere, Georgia, and I'd been floating through the first weeks of ninth grade without her. How dare she leave me to face high school alone? But then Ret appeared like an angel in red lip gloss, flannel, and vintage Betsey Johnson, and I was saved.

She started talking to me one day like we knew each other. I was wearing my new Nirvana T-shirt, which I'd just ordered online. "I like your shirt," she'd said. "But it's a knock-off. See?" Her finger traced a line across my back, and I wondered if she could feel me shiver. "Their slogan should be here, that stuff about being corporate rock whores? It was half celebration, half call-out after the band signed with Geffen in ninety." I swiveled back to face her, turning red. This girl was the real thing, and I was an imposter.

But the look she gave me was curious, kind. She didn't see a fake. Beneath the knock-off T-shirt, the red cheeks, the lost look in my eyes, somehow she saw down to the real Ellory. The girl hidden beneath layers of ninth-grade insecurity, itching to be set free.

"I'll lend you mine, if you want. One hundred percent Kurt approved." She'd said it like it was no big deal, like we were already friends. And then we were. Her taste was impeccable—personally tailored to what she knew I would like, who she knew I longed to be. She made me playlists: The Ramones. Dead Kennedys. Blondie. She encouraged my metalworking (it was hard core) and steered me clear of black-and-white photography (so passé). Little by little, she drew me to the surface.

Soon Ret's world was my world, her friends my friends. It was like it had always been that way. Everything Ret touched felt electric, exciting, a little bit dangerous. Including me.

Before Ret, I was basically invisible.

With Ret, I was *somebody*.

Ten minutes later, I maneuvered into a sloppy but passable parallel parking job across the street from Dave's and killed the engine. Ret was right, as she was about most things. The whole Pine Brook sophomore class did seem to be there, along with some enterprising freshmen and a few upperclassmen too. Technically, we still had three more days of school next week, but they were half days, finals. Classes were over and no one was studying. Everyone was crushing cans of Narragansett and PBR into the Franklins' impeccably manicured lawn and testing out the first cannonballs of the season in the pool around back.

The thought of making small talk over a clove and a Solo cup made my chest feel tight. I longed for the safe monotony of Jenni's, the familiar circle of our friends. Ret could talk to literally anyone, but parties made me feel naked, exposed. All I wanted was Ret and me. The rest was just noise, and this party was sure to serve up an especially obnoxious roar.

"We could still go back." My voice came out loud and choked with nerves. I flinched, waiting for Ret to pounce.

"Ellory May. You're not serious." Ret had a way of telling, not asking. She also had a way of invoking my middle name to make a point, an infuriating practice she'd picked up from my mother.

"Margaret." Her name rolled off my tongue in three fully enunciated syllables. Two could play at the mother game. "We are not friends with these people."

Ret screwed up her lips and glared at me. "I hate it when you call me Margaret."

In the moment I'd been looking away, she had applied a fresh coat of gloss, something called Three Alarm Fire she'd picked up at CVS. She was not about to turn back.

"We will mingle. We will expand our nascent adolescent horizons. Tonight may even be Dave Franklin's lucky night. Now come on." She needed me, but she needed all this too. To make an appearance, to be seen. So I gave in, like I always gave in to Ret, and unlatched my seat belt.

"One hour. Tops."

"All right, Ellory. Don't have a good time or anything."

Ret threw open the car door and stepped into the street. She looped her arm through mine, and just like that, we were fused again, two girls against the world. We took off toward Dave's lawn and our bracelets—matching black enamel bands I'd made in shop earlier that year—flashed in the sun. We were night and day. Her firecracker to my liquid gold. As we walked, I could feel the flutter of my hair down my back, yellow waves against my blue dress. Next to me, Ret was fierce and petite, all sharp black bob and Ultra Violet streaks in her bangs. We were Snow White and Sleeping Beauty. Serena and Blair. *Two roads diverged in a wood, and I—I took the one with Ret.*

For a moment, I felt powerful. I took a deep breath.

Inside, I waited for my eyes to adjust to the dim light. The Franklins lived in one of the new developments, the West Shore's own little enclave of wealth. Stainless steel appliances gleamed from the kitchen. A universal sound system blasted Tupac or maybe Dre into each room. Everything was expensive looking and probably breakable.

Ret pulled off her shades and placed the red plastic frames on top of her head. We walked into the kitchen, where a few guys from the lacrosse team lingered around a keg. Everyone else was out front or out back, enjoying the late afternoon heat. One of the boys waved a cup in our direction, but Ret turned up her nose. She liked her guys edgy, older, and tragically flawed. Or maybe just rich and flawed, in Dave Franklin's case.

"Let's check out the scene at the pool."

"I'll meet you out there in five," I promised. I didn't want to leave Ret's side, but the thought of going anywhere near that pool—and possibly ending up in it, because isn't that what happened at this kind of party?—was making my stomach churn. "I need to find a bathroom."

"You'd better not bail on me, Ellory May." I watched her fingers close around her bracelet. *Our* bracelet. She needed me as much as I needed her. Or maybe she just wanted me to think so.

"Scout's honor, okay? I just need a few."

"If I'm not at the pool, check Dave's room." Ret grinned. A minute later, she had disappeared through the sliding glass doors that led onto the deck. Ret would be fine. Ret could handle herself.

It was me that I needed to worry about.

I turned away from the kitchen to check out the rest of the downstairs. Maybe I could find an empty room to hide out in for a while. I folded my arms across my chest and tried to look small, which is not so easy when you're all arms and legs and sharp angles everywhere.

I took my time walking down the hall, deeper into the house. The Franklins had a series of family portraits hanging on the wall, Dave and his little brother front and center in every one, flashing the same winning grins. Dave's hair got longer and his face got gaunter frame by frame, the latter either a product of puberty or too much coke. If you believed Ret. I'd probably never exchanged more than ten words with Dave at school. I could hear the slurred shout of his voice from the pool, something about Kylie Jenner and Jägerbombs. It was weird being alone in his house, but it would be much weirder to go say *hi*. I'd let Ret take care of that for both of us.

At the end of the hall, I stepped through a wide arch into a big, sunny room. It was nice in there. Peaceful. So far, my classmates had managed to leave the drapes untorn and the carpet stain free. The boy sitting on the couch was so quiet that at first, I almost didn't notice him.

If I hadn't, I might have kept walking.

If I hadn't, I might have turned back around, toward Ret.

Somewhere, there's an alternate reality version of Ellory. She never fell in love, or she met a different guy. She's surrounded by friends, happy, naive. I think about that girl sometimes, until the wanting gets too big, and I have to stop. In my reality, there's only the aftermath, the nights when all I can hear are the scraps of his voice. *I'm sorry, Ellory*, over and over. *I'm so sorry*, like a Jeff Buckley song forever snared on the same damaged note.

In my reality, I noticed him. Against the wall, in front of the big window, Matthias Cole was sitting alone on the couch. He looked tousled and tired—and seriously beautiful.

"I was looking for the bathroom," I blurted. Not that he'd asked. Not that he cared. I started to turn back toward the hallway.

"You probably want to skip the one down here," he suggested. "There is another, shall we say, more hygienic option on the second floor."

I froze. Matthias Cole was talking to me. The time he asked if there were curly fries in the cafeteria freshman year did not count as conversation. But I still remembered. He'd touched my elbow. He'd asked me like my answer really mattered. And that was it. Yes, there were curly fries. No, we never spoke again.

After all this time, I knew just three solid facts about Matthias:

1. His hair was a color exactly between dark blond and light brown, and he wore it either flopping down over his eyes or combed up into a messy peak.
2. He worked as a line cook at a Thai restaurant downtown, which was way more professional than everyone else's after school jobs at Panera or the mall.

3. He was always dozing off during Comparative
   Religions, the one class we shared sophomore year.

It wasn't a lot to go on. About once a week, I tried to talk
myself into waking him up, or passing him my notes, or asking
what kept him up so late at night that he couldn't keep his eyes
open by fourth period. But I never had the guts.

"You're still here."

Still standing frozen in the middle of the living room, at least
thirty seconds later. *Well-played, Ellory. Very smooth*.

"I guess I don't really need to find a bathroom," I admitted. "It
just seemed like a good excuse to avoid the pool."

"Then I think we can combine forces in that mission. Because
I have absolutely no intention of leaving this couch. And I can
tell you right now that there is nothing worth seeing out by the
pool. Unless you count the Smurf's bare ass, because he is lousy
at strip poker and loves to show off for the ladies."

The Smurf was Steve Murphy, a generally lovable doofus and
the third star in the Matthias-Dave-Smurf constellation. That
Steve would be there was basically a given. But I hadn't taken
Matthias for the house party type, even if the house in question
was Dave's.

"I think I'll take a rain check on the strip poker action." I
smiled, picturing Ret accepting an offer to deal her in. Ret never
could turn down a dare.

He hovered an empty hand above the seat cushion next to
him. "What do you say, Ellory Holland? Sit?"

My breath caught. "I didn't know you knew my name."

"We have fourth together."

"You're always asleep," I countered.

For a second, I thought I'd pushed a button, pushed too hard. But then his face broke into a wide, easy smile.

I sat next to Matthias on the nice white couch in the Franklin's living room, and I was feeling everything all at once. His breath barely stirring my hair. The faint mix of bar soap and mint lingering around his clothes and skin. All the scuff marks on his loafers, because that's where my eyes were fixed until he put his hand lightly, hesitantly on top of my hand on the couch.

For a moment, it was like everything shut down and then kind of rebooted. There was a giant splash and shouting out by the pool, but it sounded really far away. In there, it was just me and Matthias, at our own private party.

"You okay?" He was looking at me, his head tilted to one side.

I breathed in and I breathed out, and I was still there. Still at a random house party, on a random day at the end of sophomore year. Sitting next to Matthias Cole. I thought about Ret. She was going to be pissed, but this was worth it. Matthias was worth it.

"Definitely okay."

"You know, I was actually thinking about you the other day."

"Yeah?" I kept my voice casual.

"I was in a store downtown with my sister. She's in this ankle bracelet phase. Anyway. They had a necklace in the display case, big metal triangles with that shiny coating?"

"Enamel?"

"Yeah, enamel. It reminded me of that bracelet you always wear, and your earrings with all the colors sort of melted together."

He'd noticed my earrings. He'd *seen* me.

"You do work in the metal shop, right? For Mr. Michaels?"

"Yeah, that's me. After school, five days a week. Mostly cleaning and stuff, but I get to use all the equipment. I'm into sculpting too. I'm trying this new thing where I paint on the scrap when it's still hot from the kiln. Kills the brushes, but it looks awesome."

"That is seriously amazing, Ellory." He looked straight into my eyes. "You should show me sometime."

My insides melted, lead under a butane torch.

Then I pulled myself together and we kept talking. Metal shop, school, the guys Matthias worked with in the kitchen at Fit to Be Thai'ed. What we talked about didn't really matter. What mattered was that we were there, together. What mattered was that I was laughing, and then he was laughing, and then his fingers were laced through my fingers. Our hands were the beginning of a spectacular, bright promise.

AUGUST, JUNIOR SUMMER
(NOW)

"Ellory, telephone!" My mom's voice blasts down the hall and through the closed door, rupturing the shrine of perfect silence in my bedroom. I can't remember the last time I got a call on our home phone. It doesn't matter who it is; I don't want to talk to anyone. Tomorrow is the first day of school, the start of senior year, and by my count I have twelve more hours of solitude before I have to speak to anyone aside from Bruiser, the gray and white fluff ball of a feline who loves no one but me.

I pat the comforter, and Bruiser jumps up on my bed and rubs his soft kitty cheek against my leg.

"Ellory May?"

I sigh. *Do what's expected. Do what you need to do.*

"Who is it?"

"It's Bex, honey. She said she tried your phone earlier."

Bex has been blowing up my phone for the past week, ever since I got back to the West Shore. She's the only one. I press my palms against my eyelids until I see a bright burst of stars. I'm not ready to talk to her, but school starts tomorrow. I can't hide forever.

It was my choice, returning to Pine Brook for senior year. My mom calls what happened *the fall*. It's a kindness, a shortcut, a way of taking something hard and shaping it into two little words that can slip off your tongue. My brain riffs on the possibilities: fallout, fall from grace, fall guy, fall apart. There's a piece of truth in each and every variation. I could have transferred. Even now, it's probably not too late. Every molecule in my being is screaming *run away*, and that's exactly why I have to stay. Running away means not dealing with the truth. Running away means giving myself an easy out, and I don't deserve an easy out.

Tomorrow, whether I want to or not, I'll see everyone. I think about Bex, waiting it out on the other line. Might as well rip the Band-Aid off.

"Okay, Mom. I'll get it up here." My hand is shaking just a little as I pick up the phone from the desk in the spare room. I've always loved the wallpaper in here. Swirls of cream and lavender, from another era. Like a glimpse back in time. Like rich custard cream.

"Hello?"

"Ellory! I've been trying you all week. I ran into your dad at Wegmans. He told me you were back." Her voice is cheery, filled with best intentions.

My voice is flat. "Hey, Bex."

There's a short stretch of silence on the other end. I wander across the hall, back into my room, and sink into the warm folds of my bed.

"I didn't even know you'd gone to Philadelphia. You just . . . disappeared."

She is accusing me, or she feels left out. I don't need to ask to figure out that Bex spent the last three months right here, sweating through another summer at the West Shore's mediocre ballet academy. She's too good for that place. Why should I get a summer of art camp, a summer away? Why should I get to disappear? If she thinks that I didn't deserve an escape, she's probably right.

"Yeah," I say slowly. "Not telling anyone was kind of the point." But now I'm back. No more escape for Ellory.

I can hear a sharp intake of breath on the other end. It's okay. It's not like we're friends anymore. We haven't spoken in months, which is entirely my doing. I shut down my Instagram and Snapchat and everything else. I turned off my phone and let the battery drain until I got back from camp. I went dark.

When I charged my phone back up this week, I had a backlog of messages from Bex and one solitary text from Jenni: I'm praying for you. I can't be sure without reactivating my social media accounts to snoop, but I'd bet anything she finally took her aunt and uncle—the ones she always called "the born-again Randalls"—up on their offer to spend the summer in Tennessee. I guess I wasn't the only one who needed a summer away.

Jenni's text was easy to ignore. Whatever prayers she's sending my way, they're not the forgiving kind. Bex's persistence is throwing me off, though. It's not like we were ever super tight, not in a one-on-one kind of way.

My thoughts drift back to sophomore year, spring. Bex had been living on the West Shore since middle school, but Ret had just recently drawn her into our group, making our triangle a square. Having Bex around immediately made things easier. When it was just the three of us, Jenni and I were constantly chafing at each other. Ret fed off our spats, but Bex diffused things. She wasn't about to compete for a spot as Ret's favorite. We still had our moments, but she balanced Jenni and me out.

So when Ret set us up on a kind of "friend date," I didn't know what to expect. Bex had been part of our group for a couple months, but we'd never hung out without Ret there. We met for coffee at Starbucks, Bex's choice. I preferred the Roaster, but Bex was on an espresso macchiato kick and swore Starbucks did it best.

Without Ret, we grasped for stuff we had in common. I asked about her dance lessons, and she quickly turned the conversation to metal shop. *I hate talking about my art. It sounds so . . . pretentious, or something.* Yeah, me too. *Are you thinking about studio programs?* What, for college? *Yeah.* Sure, but I don't want to jinx it. *Right, me either.*

The conversation quickly died out. We ended up talking about Ret, our common denominator. She and Bex had just come back from Canada, a spring break trip to visit her grandparents. Bex said it was the first time she'd brought an American friend to Montreal, how cool it had been to show off her hometown to someone who really cared about language and art. I almost choked on my latte. You could have fooled me that Ret cared about art—aside from giving it her blessing, she'd never shown any interest in my metalworking. I always figured it just wasn't her thing, but maybe art wasn't her thing *with me*. She'd saved it all for Bex.

We talked about their trip until we'd drained our coffees, and then I dropped Bex at home and texted Ret: **That was kind of weird.** I'm sure Bex sent her a version of the same text. Ret acted bummed for days, like we'd let her down. Inside, she was gloating. I could see it in the spark of her eye, feel it in the brush of her fingertips across the inside of my wrist. *You need me.* Without Ret, none of us worked. We were her solar system, her creation.

My brain snaps back to the present. Four months after *the fall*, no one even remembers how Ret broke all of us apart. The facts—what she did, how she lied—were immediately lost in what followed. In the end, who hurt who didn't matter. The result was the same: the four of us split down the seams and a world of pain in my heart.

I needed this summer away, and not just because I couldn't face them. At camp, I poured everything I had into taking my sculpture and metalworking to the next level. I put together the portfolio that's going to get me into college, get me out of the West Shore forever.

I'm not going to spend senior year navigating the waters, playing nice. Making it through to graduation is the only thing I care about. Bex has dance team at school and the girls at her studio. She'll be just fine without me, like I'm sure she has been all summer. And the truth is, I'll be better off without her sympathy spiked with blame, her careful words, her eyes that hold all the memories I don't want to relive.

I may be going back to Pine Brook tomorrow, but I don't have to go back to Bex or anyone else. I'm going back alone.

"Listen, Ellory. I'm happy you got away from the West Shore for a while. I really am. But school starts tomorrow, and look. It's our senior year. And I'm Switzerland, got it?"

"What?"

I can hear her breath soften against the phone. "Switzerland. It's a neutral country? I just mean it was nobody's fault, or everyone's fault. I don't blame you, okay? We've all had a few months to put it behind us, and it would be nice . . ."

I mentally complete Bex's sentence. *If we could all be friends again. If we could just go back to the way things were.* Yeah, that would be nice. But nice and real are two separate things.

It must have taken a lot of guts to call me, I'll give Bex that. To go against Jenni, her steadfast adherence to Ret's interests, to Ret's never-ending demands. What would she think, if she knew Bex was on the phone with me right now?

I shift aside to make room for Bruiser. His soft kitty face nestles into the spot in the center of the bed where the sun has been beating down all afternoon. I move too fast. My insides crackle as I scoot over. *Crack, crack, pop.* If you cut me open, split me apart, you'd find a blackened cavity. Charred. Nothing but ash. A burned-out wasteland of a girl where a living, breathing human being used to be.

"Yeah, got it," I say, suddenly exhausted. "But I don't need your pity."

"This isn't pity. It's . . ." But she can't finish the sentence.

"Save it," I say, too sharp. "You don't want to be seen with me. Believe me, your senior year will be much better without me in it." I'm being mean, and I kind of hate myself for it, but it's the truth. I'm sparing her. And besides, I can't be friends with Bex, not anymore. It's too hard.

"Fine." Her voice falters. She tried to make an offering, and I threw it back in her face. Now she's not sure which Ellory she'll encounter tomorrow in the halls. Will it be angry Ellory? Fake-nice Ellory? Bitter, acidic Ellory? Sobbing and screaming and wracked-with-guilt Ellory?

The truth is, she has nothing to be scared of. I don't have any of those things left in me. The Ellory who's starting senior year tomorrow would rather curl up and die than have any sort of confrontation in the halls—saccharine sweet or acid burn or otherwise. The Ellory who's starting senior year tomorrow had all the fight burned out of her last spring.

But they don't know how much I've changed—Bex, and everyone else. They haven't seen me in four months. They don't know that the Ellory returning to Pine Brook tomorrow wants nothing more than to keep her head down and get through her classes and escape to the metal shop after school where she doesn't have to talk to anyone. If it were possible, if the teachers wouldn't fail me, I'd drift through the next nine months until graduation without saying a single, solitary word.

It took Matthias three days to text me. Four days after that, he had a night off from Fit to Be Thai'ed. The distance between Dave Franklin's party and our first date felt epic, but by the time we were starting our second loop around the upper tier of the Crestview Mall, cold smoothie cups in hand, the space was shrinking fast. When his gaze fell on me, I felt myself transform—black and white to color, two-dimensional to three. I was fully, wildly alive. I slipped my free hand into his, and he closed his fingers around mine.

As we walked, I snuck a glance at our filmy forms in a store window. Boy, girl. Together, apart. Long stride matched to long stride. For a moment, I was transfixed by our doubles, gliding easily through the stiff mannequins in their pencil skirts and pastel cardigans. In the window, the top of his head bobbed just above mine. He wasn't exactly basketball material, but the boy had impressive posture.

I turned away from the glass and let my hair fall back, away from my face. I wore it down, always, covering my long arms and sharp shoulders. At five foot ten, I towered over most of my classmates. But standing next to Matthias, walking past the racks of sneakers and the dark suits on their wooden hangers and the rainbow of little bottles on the nail salon wall, I felt confident. The right proportion of legs to torso to hair. The right outfit—tank top, jeans that flared over my sandals, green and gold enamel teardrops dangling from my ears.

Only one thing about tonight was less than perfect—the setting. It was the bright fluorescent lights and the smell of wild cherry that swirled out through the vents. The mall was maybe the West Shore's least romantic destination, but this is where he had brought me. My confidence flickered.

"If you weren't here with me, what would a Friday night in the life of Matthias Cole look like?"

His eyes—brown with tiny, dark green flecks—latched onto mine. "You are aware that everyone on the West Shore, including teachers and old babysitters, calls me Matty?" he asked.

"I prefer Matthias. You hate it?"

"Not exactly. It's just so . . ."

"Formal? Biblical?" I suggested.

"Let's just say my parents were . . . aspirational when they had me. Matthias does not say 'music writer.' Or 'person under forty,' for that matter."

"Music writer?"

"I run a website. Concert write-ups, album reviews, new bands. That sort of stuff."

I fought an inward groan. Writer? Hot. Audiophile? Not so hot. I could see my future stretch out before me like an unending track list. Creating playlists with my friends was one thing, but I was not down for the preaching and preening, the reverent silence for the not-yet-released single from the next greatest indie band in central Pennsylvania. The fly sound system. The dark, poster-plastered bedroom.

"I see your face, Ellory Holland, and I am not that guy, promise. You can listen to stuff or not. It's kind of something I do on my own. And since you asked, that's what I'd be doing on a regular Friday. Hang out with Dave and the Smurf for a while, stop in at home to tuck my little sis into bed and borrow the truck, then head downtown and find a show. I review concerts, local music scene stuff." He shrugged, take it or leave it.

"It's just, I never knew that about you."

"To be fair, we've never talked about much of anything before."

I could feel the live feed of regret flash across my face. We started to speak at the same time.

"I didn't mean—"

"I promise—"

"I'm sorry, you go," I offered.

"I was just going to say, I promise my conversational abilities range beyond my animal obsession with indie bands. Stick with me, and I will never subject you to a Purling Hiss deep cut. You have my word."

My lips twitched up at the corners. "You know I have no idea who or what that is, right?"

"And I swear I will keep it that way." He grinned, quick and easy, and my stomach did a little flip.

"I'm going to hold you to that." We stopped in front of the elevator in the center of the floor, and I suddenly realized that we were here for my benefit. Music was his thing, private. He wasn't looking for a copilot for his regular Friday plans, so he'd brought me here because doesn't every girl like the mall?

"You know," I said, "I think this is a first. I've never been on a mall date before."

"Really?" He seemed genuinely surprised. Suspicions confirmed. "Yeah, me either."

"But here we are. Exploring new territory." I gestured in front of us with my smoothie cup.

"Cultivating a fledgling interest in the American Mall Hang."

"Which we have now confirmed is officially not our scene."

We both laughed. He wrapped his arm around my waist, and we leaned back against a giant beige column to survey our surroundings: all the mall stores, the eighth-grade girls shrieking and skipping down the corridor, the moms and dads weaving strollers around the guys slouched in front of Game Stop. Groups of girls, groups of guys, other duos on meandering dates armed with sodas and hot pretzels.

"I have to admit," he said, "this classic artificial citrus drink is kind of growing on me." He raised his cup into the air. "So here's to the first of many nights of exploration. To be continued at an expanded range of venues."

"Cheers." I clinked his cup to mine with a wet paper tap. *The first of many nights.*

Matthias gestured toward a bench beside an oversized

terra-cotta planter. "Let's hit the pause button on this whole mall walk?"

We settled down on the bench, and I thought he was going to kiss me. I wanted him to, just a little, just to confirm that what I thought was happening was really happening. That we had more than just cold hands and good banter. That he really saw me.

But instead of kissing me, he said, "I think you're beautiful."

"What?"

"I've been wanting to tell you all year."

"You're lying." He was lying.

"No, really. I just figured you thought . . . I don't know. I'm not exactly a model student or whatever."

"You mean how you're always sleeping in class?"

"Yeah, that. Sometimes I work in the kitchen late. Sometimes I go to shows even later. I'm not very good at this whole sleeping at night thing."

"Your parents don't care?"

"They might care if they noticed. My mom would."

"But they don't notice."

Matthias shrugged. "They have other stuff going on."

I looked at him hard, waiting for him to explain. After a pause that stretched on a beat too long, he said, "My dad installs audio equipment, the kind rich people buy for their homes. He used to play, though. He was a really good bassist."

"He was in a band?"

"The Rocket Pops." For a moment, his face lit up, and I could see him drift far away. I pictured Matthias as a little kid, his dad teaching him how to hold his instrument, where to place his fingers on the strings.

"They still play?" I asked.

He shook his head, the faraway look gone. "I have some of their old recordings. But they fell apart a long time ago."

"Oh." I wanted to know more, but I could see Matthias closing back up. "And your mom?" I asked instead.

"She's a writer. She put out a book of nature poems in the nineties, but I guess there isn't a big market for that stuff now. Cordelia's a big fan, though."

"Your sister?"

His face broke into another quick grin. "Yeah, she's nine."

"Ankle bracelet phase?"

"That's her." He reached for his phone and pulled up a photo of a smiling girl in soccer shorts and a grass-stained T-shirt, her long hair pulled back into a ponytail, the same brown-blond as her brother's.

"She does soccer, ballet, gymnastics, and she's super smart. She's basically destined for rocket science. If you want to meet her, I'll have to schedule you in."

"I'd like that."

He stared at his phone for a minute more. When he clicked it off, his eyes stayed fixed on the black screen. Finally, he said, "Look, Ricky and Rebecca aren't exactly winning any parent of the year awards. My dad drinks. A lot. My mom spends all day locked in her office. So now you know, okay?" There was a hard edge to his words that I couldn't quite grasp onto.

I nodded, my eyes searching for his, but they were still locked on his screen. Finally, he looked up.

"But Cordelia's got me. She's going to be fine." He said it like he had something to prove. As if I thought he might let his sister down.

I reached over and touched his arm just above the elbow. I wasn't sure if I was supposed to comfort him or offer to call child services. I was an only child. My parents were annoyingly present. I didn't know what taking care of your little sister might mean. I pictured homework, rides, haircuts. I was sure it was a lot to keep track of, but my mental image didn't quite line up with the gravity of his tone. I couldn't find the right words, so I dropped my hand and ran it back and forth along the leg of my jeans.

"Sorry, I didn't mean to get into all that." He shook his head softly, as if he were trying to clear the air. "We were talking about you."

"We were?" I asked.

"About how beautiful you are."

I watched him click his phone on and off, then rest it face down on his knee. For a moment, I didn't say anything.

"Thank you."

"What for?"

"For saying I'm beautiful. I'm not the best with compliments, but word on the street is you should say 'thank you.'"

"You're welcome." The grin was back. He reached out and ran his fingertips very, very lightly through my hair. They stopped at the tip of my earlobe, and he traced the outline of the enamel teardrop dangling there. "Sorry it took me so long to tell you."

I let him melt me. I was full-color, three-dimensional, in-focus Ellory. I was *alive*.

He leaned his head back against the mall railing behind us. "If you want out, I totally get it. I probably would."

My phone chirped, *ki-ka-ri*, three quick notes. It was the signal for our group chat, the one that the four of us pretty much always had going when we weren't together. That week, it was titled Hot Days & Kewl Nights.

"Because of your parents?" I asked. "No way." My phone chirped again, and I reached into my bag for it. "Sorry, one sec."

"No worries, I should check in with Cordelia." He flipped his phone back over and clicked it on.

I opened our chat.

JENNI RANDALL
How's the hot date? Any ooh la la?

ELLORY HOLLAND
All the ooh and all the la.

JENNI RANDALL
I can totally see you with the tortured
cutie type.

BEX LANDRY
Ellory! We're so bored, there's
nowhere to go. Get over here right
now.

I could picture them. Bex sprawled out on the Randalls' couch, her legs perpetually turned out at the hips. Jenni fussing over something in the kitchen, her stepmom's cooking magazines spread out on the counter. Where was Ret?

ELLORY HOLLAND
You just love me for my car.
Promise next Friday I'm all yours.

JENNI RANDALL
No way. Your face is not welcome
around here until there are stories.

I frowned into my screen. Jenni was enjoying my absence a little too much. Before I could come up with something good to say, Ret's words filled up the screen. There she was.

RET JOHNSTON
Drop it, Jenni. Jealous, much?

She didn't have to type it into the chat; they were no further than a room away. But Ret wanted me to see. Ret was Jenni's for tonight, but her gloating wasn't scoring any points. This was how Ret kept us on our toes. This was how Ret kept us.

I typed back quickly, keeping it light.

ELLORY HOLLAND
Stories galore coming up.

Tonight, I was not playing Ret's games.

RET JOHNSTON
I expect a full report, missy.

Every part of you is mine. Even the parts that are his.

"Everything okay?" Matthias asked, clicking off his phone again.

"Yeah. The girls are just making sure you're not a serial killer." I gave him a light shove in case he thought I was serious. Then I closed the chat, giving Ret the last word. She could have it. I was sitting on a wooden mall bench with Matthias Cole. He thought I was beautiful.

When he kissed me twenty minutes later in the only slightly more romantic mall parking lot, it was my third kiss total, but the first one that really mattered. The kiss was short, but warm, and slightly citrusy, and quick pulses of heat flashed against my lips and tongue and then across my face and down my neck, until every inch of my skin was lit up by a fiery wave. We were oxygen and fuel. A deep, slow burn.

And then it was over. He pressed his cheek against mine and whispered, "That was okay, right? That I kissed you?" We were half sitting, half leaning against the bumper of my dad's car.

"That was absolutely okay." I pulled my cheek away to find those tiny green flecks in his eyes. I was brave. "As long as you plan to do it again."

A second later, his lips were crashing back into mine, the heat spiking up again beneath my skin. I wanted more.

SEPTEMBER, SENIOR YEAR
(NOW)

When we were in fifth grade, Maria Hidelman swore up and down that our elementary school was infested with mice—in the insulation and pipes, under the floors, lurking in the curled-up scroll of the projector screen—we just couldn't see them. She said they came in through the vents at night, that mice could squeeze through the tiniest spaces because they had collapsible bones.

It was complete bullshit, of course. Her house had just been exterminated or something, and the pest control guys had probably been messing with her. It was way too easy to pull a fast one on prissy Maria Hidelman. But even now, years after freshman bio taught us that mice do not, in fact, come equipped with a collapsible skeleton, the image has stayed with me.

Collapsible bones. I sit in my seat in AP English, my long legs folded up as small as possible beneath the tiny desk. If I could have one superpower, that's what it would be. The ability to fold myself in two, slink between tiny spaces, vanish inside walls.

The old Ellory wanted to be seen, known inside and out. I can feel my classmates' eyes wash over me, wanting to get a good look. *Ellory's back.* Now I feel too visible, on display, and it's only day five of senior year. My nine-month sentence until graduation has only just begun.

I take a long, slow breath and remind myself that I chose this. I'm alone because I don't deserve anything different. It was Ret's fault first, and my fault last, and now I have to live with the consequences. But now that I'm back at Pine Brook, totally exposed and no one to run to, I'm not sure I'm going to make it.

I glance up at the clock, careful to move only my eyes. It's the game I've been playing in English this year. How many class minutes can Ellory get through without moving a muscle? It's 2:26. Fourteen down, thirty-four to go. I tell myself I'm honing my listening skills. Who needs to take notes when your ears are tuned in to every word?

I can get through most of the day okay. I know these hallways. I have my routes. But whoever designed my senior year schedule, slotting English into eighth period, must be some kind of sadist. They could have taken pity on me. Scheduled the class early in the day. But no. Instead, I am guaranteed to spend every hour of senior year dreading eighth, blazing bright at the end of the day like a house fire I just keep walking into.

I force my eyes to drop from the face of the clock straight down to the face of the girl at the desk directly across the room. She is the reason this class is such hell, but she's also the reason I can't leave. I refuse to give myself an easy out. Or her the satisfaction.

Ret. I'm prepared to look immediately away, but she doesn't look up, doesn't notice my eyes burning holes through her skin. She's completely focused on the book open on the desk in front of her. With a shiny purple pen, she underlines some key passage, something meaningful only to her. If I let myself lean forward, even just a little, I could get a look at the page.

But I can't.

I won't.

We used to sit next to each other. We used to share books. Ret & Ellory. Ellory & Ret. We used to share everything. Now, eighth period is a daily reminder of English classes past. Ret and me passing notes, secret smart, laughing at the book nerds. Ret and me against the world.

Now she sits across from me, taunting me with her silence.

My eyes wander over her ivory skin, her hair just brushing the tops of her shoulder blades. She's let it get long over the summer. The glossy, black strands are streaked bubblegum pink, and her lips are coated in a faint, nude gloss. For Ret, it's shockingly demure.

Before she can catch me looking, I tear my eyes away, feeling both like a trespasser and somehow violated at the same time. Dr. Marsha would say I need to stop fixating. I need to live in the present. In the present, Ret and I are not friends. In the present, we do not share secrets or books or long afternoons on Jenni's front lawn. In the present, we're moving on to chapter three. I'll have to give up my game and turn the page in a minute.

I wait until the last possible second, until I'm sure Ms. Halim is going to ask me if I care to join the rest of the class, and then I reach in front of me and flip the page. My arm floats over the desk, weightless because it's empty inside. Hollow.

As Ms. Halim draws our attention to the use of foreshadowing in the text, I close my eyes and a soft, deep voice fills up the dark. *I think you're beautiful.* I can almost smell him—smoke from somebody else's cigarettes, bar soap, mint. I can almost feel his arm slide around my waist, pull me close. I give my head a firm shake, *no*, forcing my eyes back open. I will not let myself do this. I do not have a boyfriend, this is not last year. I'm not that Ellory anymore. I may look the same on the outside, but like we've always been taught, it's what's inside that counts: Burned-up girl. Wasteland.

My eyes drift back to the clock. It's 2:47, and the class is debating the merit of authorial intent. Ms. Halim suggests that critical analysis supersedes intentionality. Maria Hidelman is arguing, saying *just to play devil's advocate* in her clipped, whiny voice, but she doesn't have a case. Ms. Halim is so, so right. Best intentions, worst intentions. Planned, unplanned. All that matters about last spring is what went down. Who cares what I meant to happen, what I meant to say. Intentionality is so clearly meaningless when you run it up against the facts.

I keep my eyes fixed on the second hand for the next thirteen minutes until the bell finally rings. My classmates are out the door with a squeal of chairs and a stampede of sneakers before I can even get my bag zipped up. I keep my head down and take my time. It's Friday. They all have places to be, people to meet, but I'm only going down to the metal shop like every other afternoon of my life. And to be honest, I've felt a little off my game all week. I was on fire at camp this summer, but I haven't felt inspired to make anything since I got back to school. Regardless, I still have cleaning to do and materials to pull for Mr. Michaels's classes on Monday.

I'm almost to the door when her hand closes around my wrist, digging my bracelet—our bracelet, the one I still wear—into my skin.

"Ellory May."

I flinch. I didn't see her hanging back, waiting for me. After a week of silence, Ret wants to talk. Has she been reading my thoughts, the ones that scream I can't hack it alone?

"It's not a good time," I hiss.

Ms. Halim turns from the whiteboard where she's erasing today's key words. "Did you have a question, Ellory?" she asks.

I shake my head and drag Ret out of the classroom, into the hall. It's clearing out fast like it always does after the dismissal bell rings, but there are still plenty of people around. People who will see us. I give my arm a shake, and she lets go. My wrist is sore where the bracelet pinched the skin, and I know she felt it too. How I still wear mine. How her wrist is bare.

"We can't do this here." My voice is barely a whisper. Whatever we have to say to each other, it's no one else's business.

She doesn't say anything right away. Her hair smells like campfire and bleach. People are staring. I look away from the banging lockers and scuffling feet, right into Ret's eyes. Bad move. I'm falling hard and fast; I can't breathe.

"Meet me by the river," Ret says, her voice low but clear, pulling me up for air. "After you're done in the shop. The patch of bank where the guardrail's missing."

I know where she means. We used to go there sometimes freshman year, Ret and Jenni and me. You could scramble down the embankment toward the water, where no one could see you from the road. It was a hideaway right out in the open, and for a while it was ours. As soon as I got my license sophomore year—I was the oldest, the first—we packed into my car when we got the itch to explore. I haven't been back to our spot by the river in years.

My mind spins back to the first time Ret took us there, a March afternoon that still felt more like winter than spring. She'd discovered it, of course, led us through the break in the guardrail like she was taking us to Narnia. Nestled into the tall grass along the bank, we all wrote our darkest secrets on sheets of notebook paper and folded them into swans to sail on the surface of the water. Ret said it would be like an act of absolution, a letting go. But before we could set them free, she stopped us. *It only works if you read them out loud first.*

She was playing with a stacked deck. She'd written something just incriminating enough, but still safe to share. Before we could stop her—and didn't we want to know what she'd done?—she unfolded her paper and started to read. *After my dad left, I made a list of all the ways my mom had driven him away. Then I left it on my dresser for her to find. I laughed after she read it, when she locked herself in her room and cried.*

"That's really low," I'd said.

Ret tossed back her hair. "The split was my dad's fault, one hundred percent. But he wasn't around, so I needed to take it out on someone. I was ten, sue me. Who's next?"

Jenni and I balked, but Ret played hurt. She'd gone first after all, now we *had* to do it. Didn't we trust her?

Jenni told a story from elementary school, how she'd gotten some kid—a nose-picker, an easy target—in trouble for something she'd done. It was bad, but not as bad as mine. I'd written my real feelings about Jenni: that I thought she tried too hard, how I put up with her for Ret's sake.

I refused to read it, choosing Ret's ridicule and Jenni's scorn over the alternative. But somehow, Jenni knew. Whatever I'd written, she knew it was about her. The damage was done.

"I can't," I say to Ret, her expectant face drawing me back into the present. "Not today." It's tempting, but I'm not ready for whatever she wants to talk about. For whatever game she's playing.

She's quiet for a moment, shifting her bag against her shoulder and studying my face. "Okay, Ellory," she says finally. "Some other time then. I'm there most days after school. Come find me." Without waiting for my response, she takes off toward the nearest stairwell. I watch her retreat down the hall, her hair fluttering against the back of her neck in a fan of black and pink.

Alone again, I slump against the wall and close my eyes. I can feel my muscles let go, my body sliding down the cool paint like a marionette clipped from its strings. Somewhere down the hall, I hear a boy's voice shout, "Better keep it together, Holland!" followed by a chorus of giggles and slamming locker doors. When the laughter dies down, I can almost swear I hear a softer voice say, "Leave her alone," but that might be wishful thinking.

From the instant I saw her in class on the first day back, I knew. She could sense the cracks in my resolve. She knew I still needed her, after everything. *Come find me.* The echo of her words in my ears starts as an invitation that swiftly becomes a rush of river water, pummeling and loud, until all I can hear is the greedy, deafening roar.

5

"You seem nervous." Matthias turned his gaze on me from the driver's seat. He, on the other hand, looked almost too relaxed. His eyes lit on my hands, which I'd been clasping and unclasping on top of my cutoffs for the last five blocks. I shoved them underneath my legs.

"This is just kind of new," I said. "It's like worlds colliding."

"So quiz me," he said. "Ret, Jenni, the girl from Canada. How'd I do?"

"Not bad. Bex. You really haven't had class with any of them?"

He shrugged. "Ret, I think, freshman year. I kind of keep my head down, remember?"

Four weeks ago, Matthias had been an idea, a pretty star in a faraway galaxy. Now he coursed beneath my skin, wet ink, a heady drug. For four weeks, I had kept him close. Mine and mine alone. But Ret was getting antsy. *Is there something wrong with him?* I told myself I didn't need her approval, but of course that wasn't true.

In my defense, my time with Matthias was measured out in small doses. He was almost always working or substitute parenting or away on mysterious Cordelia-related missions about which he'd tell me little. I fantasized about lifting the burdens from his life, taking them for my own, but they weren't mine to take. Instead, I lived for the time we had together, wrapped my whole body around it, held fast. I was greedy. I didn't love the idea of sharing Matthias today, but it was a party. It was time.

So we were on our way to Jenni's. My parents were grilling with the neighbors, a family event that had not been so easy to wriggle out of. I'd never had a boyfriend before. They weren't sure what to do with this new, consuming presence in my life. In the end, they'd agreed to release us to Jenni's on the condition that Matthias come by the house first so they could bestow their approval.

He looked over at me in the car. "I think I can handle it. Your parents loved me."

I pressed my lips together. My parents were easily charmed. Ret was not so easy.

"Seriously though," he said. "It's cool that your parents care. Really cool."

Cool was not a word I used to describe anything related to my parents, but I bit back the thought. Of course it would mean something to Matthias that they gave a shit. I was a jerk for even thinking otherwise.

"Consider my alternative," he went on. "Babysit Ricky's drunk ass while Rebecca takes Cordelia to the pool? Hard pass."

"That's good about your mom, though. That she's out with Cordelia." I gave myself a mental high five for holding my tongue.

"The holidays always bring out her parental instincts. Good timing though, because now I get to spend the Fourth of July with my gorgeous, only slightly nervous girlfriend."

"Girlfriend?"

"I was thinking girlfriend. That okay with you?"

The word echoed inside my head like a beautiful secret. "Definitely."

He grinned, that quick flash of joy I was growing to crave, and it hit me that Matthias wasn't searching deep inside me, scouring my depths for the girl I was trying to be. He liked me for the girl I was already. He thought I was beautiful. He liked my jewelry, wanted to know more about the art I made in shop. He even liked my parents, their profound lack of chill. I was so freaking *lucky*.

By the time we pulled up to Jenni's street, I forgot to feel nervous. "It's the third house on the right, the big blue one."

Jenni's house was an anomaly in our neighborhood of little ranch homes—an old brick two-story at the end of a cul-de-sac with a big yard in the front and back. The party was in full swing when Matthias and I rounded the corner to the back of the house. Jenni was grilling hot dogs and burgers on the patio, and there were kids sprawled out on the lawn, drinking beer, bouncing on the trampoline. There were more people here than I'd ever seen at Jenni's. More people than I *knew*. Pine Brook was a big school; no one knew everyone. Jenni may have been hosting, but the guests—mostly upperclassmen from the look of it—were all Ret's doing. I slipped my hand into Matthias's just as Jenni turned to deliver a heaping plate of burgers and buns to the picnic table. When she spotted us, she raised a pair of aviator shades and waved.

From across the patio, the sun at her back, Jenni looked aloof and terribly cool. Empress of her domain. Her thick red hair was twisted up into a knotted braid, and her apron hid the front of a gauzy shirt and patched bell-bottoms. She looked plucked from an earlier time, an era when finding yourself mattered more and being a high achiever in all things academic and extracurricular wasn't practically mandatory at sixteen.

Without Ret, we might have actually relaxed into one another, appreciated the good stuff. And there was a lot of good stuff about Jenni. She was a consummate hostess, a style queen. She cared about making the people around her happy. Her dad and his new, young wife were preoccupied with their ten-month-old, leaving Jenni basically alone to cultivate obsessions with vintage fashion and ambitious recipes. I was a little jealous of Jenni's freedom, a fact I'd never admit to her face.

Burgers turned over to the hungry masses, she strolled our way.

"Welcome to our little soiree." Her voice was a purr. "We're all so glad Ellory finally brought you around."

For the past four weeks, I'd been at Jenni's less and less. Now I was back, bearing the reason for my absence. Of course Jenni loved my boyfriend. *Boyfriend.* Sure, she was probably genuinely charmed, but it wasn't lost on either of us that Matthias was her ticket to more and more of Ret.

"Matthias, meet Jenni, our hostess."

"Hey there." He extended one hand to shake hers and in the other, he held up a six-pack of some craft beer I'd never heard of. "Brought some brews." I wondered if Ricky had bought them for his son, but decided against asking.

Jenni gave Matthias an approving smile, then turned to me. "Matty is welcome here any time."

She was the only one of us who had ever had a regular boyfriend, but Jenni and Mark had broken up in March, and Ret never brought her string of guys around. Being here with Matthias felt good, even if Jenni's approval was a little self-serving.

She took him by the arm to give him the rundown: "Food's over here, drinks in the coolers by the door, swing set, tire swing, trampoline, and there's a bathroom down in the basement."

"Is Ret here yet?" I asked.

Either Jenni actually didn't hear me over the music suddenly pumping from the little speakers on the picnic table, or she pretended not to. Still holding Matthias by the arm, she continued. "Two rules: no puking on the trampoline, and the upstairs is off limits. Also, don't forget to hydrate. That's not a rule, just common sense. Otherwise, go wild."

Jenni glanced back toward the grill, which was starting to smoke, and turned on a platform heel, ushering us off into the party. Matthias strolled over to the coolers to add his beer to the collection, and I took a look around. Older kids, rising seniors, abounded. I recognized a group of guys from our year jumping on the trampoline in the back, and across the lawn, through the haze of grill smoke and incense, I could see Bex and another girl passing a clove back and forth.

Abigail? For a second, all I could see were dark curls floating down to frame round, rouged cheeks. But she couldn't be here. Ret would never, ever allow it. Then the girl plucked the clove from Bex's hand and tilted her head toward the sky. The grill smoke cleared. Not Abigail, of course not. Just some girl from dance team.

My heartbeat slowed, and I realized it had been racing. I lifted my hand to wave, and Bex waved back.

Rebecca Landry. Rebex. Bex. Her family moved here in eighth grade, which is a terrible time to move anywhere. Her mom was a professor of Black Atlantic history, and when Professor Landry got a new job at a college nearby, the whole family left Montreal to settle on the West Shore. It must have been pretty rough. Bex grew up speaking Quebecois French and eating things with exotic names like coq au vin and tourtière. I guess her accent and extensive knowledge of ice hockey didn't endear her to the few other black kids at Pine Brook, and she spent a lot of eighth and ninth on the social outskirts—not exactly an outcast, just displaced, alone. Like the rest of us, until Ret drew us into her fold.

When she first started bringing Bex around, I saw her how Ret saw her: vulnerable, serious, the new girl who still hadn't found her place. But Bex had no interest in being anyone's charity case. She knew who she was; she needed friends, not pity or advice.

Bex was ballet (which Ret quickly insisted she'd always admired, after initially throwing shade at Bex's place on dance team) and French romance novels (which Ret adored—*so* much more sultry than American erotica) and a complete unwillingness to compete with Jenni or me (which despite Ret's persistent baits, I think she respected more than anything else).

I wanted to be closer to Bex. I did. But three months after

our wobbly coffee date, I let Ret keep us at arm's length because it seemed to be what she wanted. Another stage direction in the never-ending performance of our lives in which Ret was writer, director, and star. We knew our parts; only Ret knew where the plot would lead.

Matthias returned from the cooler with two beers, jolting me back into the present. I tore my eyes away from Bex and not-Abigail to fill two plates with hot dogs and potato salad at the picnic table. We had just settled down on the patio stones when the back door swung open revealing Lizza Kendrick, one of Pine Brook's most rabid gossips. Of course she was there, trolling for scraps. Behind Lizza was Ret, holding hands with none other than Jonathan Gaines. Jonathan had fine, white-blond hair, an all-American smile, and Abercrombie catalogue abs. Jonathan played varsity lacrosse, did community service with his church youth group, and helped old ladies cross the street. Jonathan was about as far from Ret's type—scruffy, slightly dangerous, and usually college-aged—as I could possibly imagine.

Yet here he was at Jenni's party for indie kids and emo queens, fingers intertwined with Ret's, grinning that perfectly straight and sparkling grin as he walked through the screen door and onto the patio. I may have kept Matthias close for the past month, but I had told Ret everything. And she hadn't mentioned Jonathan once. I almost choked on a chunk of red skin potato.

"Hey, lady!" Ret called, breaking away from Jonathan to run over and give me a big, sprawling hug. "About time you showed up."

She flung herself down next to us and swiveled toward Matthias, extending her hand. "Ret, Ellory May's best friend. If you don't play nice, you'll have me to answer to."

Matthias took her hand and gave it a firm shake. "Yes, ma'am." His voice was perfectly even.

She tilted her head to one side and looked him up and down. There was nothing subtle about Ret. She wanted him to know she was giving him the once-over, that she was watching him. I silently promised to forgive her for neglecting to tell me about Jonathan as long as she blessed Matthias with her approval. Even though I was still a little pissed.

"So, what's the deal with—" I started to ask, but Ret was already back on her feet and waltzing over to Jonathan, who was waiting just outside the back door. He hooked his thumb around the back of her studded belt and pulled her in close. I raised my eyebrows at Ret. She grinned and gave Jonathan a kiss on the cheek. Her eyes were open, fixed on me. I wasn't sure what game she was playing, but it hit me that it was somehow my fault that I didn't know about Jonathan. This wasn't neglect, this was a deliberate omission. And Ret was rubbing it in.

I turned toward the grill for backup, but Jenni was staring straight at me, smirking. So I was the last to know.

I must have been making a face because Matthias reached over to squeeze my hand. "Your friend has nothing worry about," he said, mistaking my look for nerves. "I always play nice."

But I had moved past nerves. I squeezed his hand back, but my eyes were on Ret, who was nuzzling into the collar of Jonathan's polo shirt across the patio. Ret had introduced a plot twist, and she was waiting to see how I'd react.

Twenty minutes later, while Matthias was dissecting pop covers of rock classics with Jenni, I went off in search of Bex.

"How long?" I asked, when she'd drifted away from the rest of the dance team and I had her to myself. She knew exactly what I was asking, but it still took her a full thirty seconds to answer. Bex made a habit of steering clear of Ret's drama, but right now, I needed her. I gave her my most pleading look.

"A few weeks." She leaned back in the grass, crossing one long leg over the other.

I pulled my own legs into my chest. I felt a little ill. "And she really likes him?"

Bex laughed, quick and sharp, then rolled over and lit another clove. "You want?" She held the pack out toward me.

I shook my head, no.

She took her time drawing the smoke between her lips, then putting away her lighter before responding. "She seems entertained. He's so normal, he's different." Then she pulled out her phone and started scrolling.

I nodded, shoving myself up off the grass. So Ret had been bringing Jonathan around. I wanted to press her for more, but Bex's fingers were already flying across her screen. I tucked my hands into the pockets of my cutoffs instead and started to walk away.

"You hurt her feelings, you know?" Her words caught me off guard. I spun back around and waited for an explanation. Bex took another drag, then said, "You're either with Matty, or you're thinking about him. You know how Ret is. She misses you."

"Thanks," I mumbled. My eyes traveled across the backyard, searching for Ret. There she was. Jenni was back at the grill, putting on a round of corn on the cob, and Ret was standing behind her, her arms wrapped around Jenni's waist. She leaned over to whisper something in her ear, and I watched Jenni's face light up. I wondered how long it had been since Jenni's dad had given her a hug, made her eyes sparkle like that. How long since her mom had remembered to pick up the phone. I stared at them until Ret looked up, her eyes meeting mine. Then I turned away and walked toward the tire swing.

Five minutes later, Ret came to meet me.

"So Jonathan?" I asked.

She sat down on the swing and kicked off her flip-flops, letting her bare feet drag in the dirt.

"Push me?" she said. It was more statement than question.

I pressed the tips of my fingers into her shoulder blades and pushed. Ret kicked her legs up and let out a whoop like a little kid. She was going to make me ask again. I started to count backward from ten.

When I got to three, she said, "We started hanging out at that party last month. While you were making googly eyes at Matty, I had to entertain myself somehow by the pool."

So this went all the way back to Dave Franklin's party. This was punishment for picking Matthias over her. For abandoning her at the pool. *You'd better not bail on me, Ellory May.* Ret had been with Jonathan since the day I'd been with Matthias, and she had made sure I was the last to know. I pushed her again and again, sending her sailing higher and higher.

"Easy, tiger." She spun around to look at me, a warning. I stood back and let the motion of the ropes run their course. "I was talking to Dave for a while," she said when the swing had slowed to an almost-stop. "But he was so wasted. Like a six-pack and two bumps of coke wasted. The Smurf and some freshman had to drag him up to his room like an hour after we got there. Remember?"

I didn't. An hour after we got there, I was still on the Franklins' couch, totally absorbed in Matthias Cole. And Ret knew it.

I shook my head.

"Right. Well, Dave was out for the count, so I started talking to Jonathan. I always thought he was a total snooze, but there's something beneath the surface. I'm going to unpeel every single layer."

"I've told you everything about Matthias!" I blurted. I couldn't help it. She was under my skin, pulsing, jabbing. "What the hell, Ret?"

She tossed back her hair, the fine strands of her bob flying up in the air, then falling right back in place. I'd been kept in the dark. I'd let my anger bubble to the surface. Bex was right: I'd hurt her, so she'd hurt me.

Ret examined my face, doing the math. An eye for an eye, a heart for a heart. Then, her face softened. "We're not like you and Matty," she said. "We're just hanging out." She jumped off the swing and settled in the grass. "Two roads diverged in the wood, and I—"

I sank down next to her. We were Ret & Ellory again. Secrets buzzing in the air between us.

"I took the one across stark, wind-swept moors to Heathcliff's farmhouse manor."

Ret smiled, satisfied. I leaned my shoulder into her shoulder; her skin was impossibly cool in the summer heat.

"That didn't look like *just hanging out* before," I said. "He seems cool. And he's basically a male model."

Ret cracked a grin. "Let's be real, Ellory. Guys like Jonathan

Gaines may slum it with girls like me for a few weeks over the summer, but he'll be sexting with some wide-eyed freshman by the first week of school, promise. You know the type. Homecoming potential. Prime candidate for dinner with Mom and Dad."

I blew a stream of air slowly through my lips and leaned back in the grass. Ret was needy, and cruel, and a giant pain in my ass. But I loved her. "All I'm saying is don't count yourself out. You're Ret Freaking Johnston."

She laughed and tossed back her head. "I'm Ret Freaking Johnston!" she yelled at the top of her lungs. A sea of heads turned to stare, and Ret threw her arms around me, pulling me down, and then we were rolling, laughing, feeling the bright glow of a million eyes on us, curious, jealous.

And then Ret was off, her pleather skirt and ribbed tank top flashing across the lawn to the trampoline, where Jonathan was taking his turn launching himself into the air, looking every inch an ad for designer jeans against the backdrop of a perfect summer sky. I had won Ret back. I was released.

At nine, when the community fireworks lit up the almost-darkness, I held hands with Matthias at the top of the hill in the far back of Jenni's yard while bursts of white and blue and red flashed and faded over our heads. His hand was warm and dry. A half-empty beer dangled from his other hand, and his breath was hot and thick. I offered to drive home, and he nuzzled his head into my neck.

I glanced over at Jonathan and Ret, sitting a little ways to our left. Ret caught my gaze, blew me a kiss. *I shouldn't have ditched you at Dave's party. I'll be better. I am already better.*

I turned back to Matthias, felt his breath slow down against my skin. He was falling asleep. The bottle slipped out of his hand, then rolled down the hill, the beer soaking the grass. I eased us back on the lawn, and he burrowed into my side. I burrowed back. His skin radiated a steady, soft heat even after the air was cool, even in the complete, after-fireworks dark.

I forget to grab my Spanish book before homeroom, so I have to make an unscheduled stop by my locker after second. It's a detour from my meticulously planned daily route. Three weeks into the semester, I may as well have a Marauder's Map of the school—minus all the magical stuff. I know which hallways are safe between which classes, which bathrooms I can never use, and exactly how early I have to pull into the parking lot each morning to guarantee a clear path to my locker before homeroom. But today I messed up, and all bets are off.

I breathe in, and I can feel the air knocking against the cavity inside me, tearing loose big flakes of ash. I weigh the pros and cons as I duck out of physics the instant the bell rings. I could just go to class and hope someone will take pity and let me share their book. But with my luck, Señora Martinez will have us doing exercises from the text all period. I've been struggling as it is. Showing up without my book invites attention, which is the last thing I want.

I turn left down the hall, making a beeline for the closest stairwell, the one that will take me up one flight directly to my locker. It's a stairwell I never use, that on any other day, I'd avoid like the plague. It's been two weeks, and I still haven't taken Ret up on her invitation. *Come find me*. Her eyes follow me in English—she hasn't given up. But the halls are mine. As long as I stick to my route, there's no Ret, no Jenni, no Bex to find me. No Matthias either.

I stand in front of the stairwell door. I tell myself I'm just running upstairs to my locker. This is not a big, dramatic thing. There's no showdown coming, no screaming match, no repeat of last spring. Dr. Marsha is right; I need to stop fixating on things I can't possibly change.

I steel myself and push through the heavy door. A steady stream of kids rushes up and down the stairs, but no one notices me. I take the stairs two at a time. The sooner I'm out of here, the better. If I don't get it together, I'm going to be late to class.

After years of French, I'm the only senior in first-year Spanish. I fed my parents some line about diversifying my language skills until I almost believed it. But they caved pretty fast. The truth is, they're terrified of pushing me too hard. Would two AP classes be too big a strain for Ellory? Would it push her back into dicey territory? Could it be a trigger? It's a series of questions they never would have considered asking a year ago. Of course I would take two APs in my senior year. Some kids take five. Of course I could handle it. Now, they're all about treading lightly. Considering my mental state.

My French is pretty good. I always planned to take it all the way through. I might still sign up for the AP test in the spring. But this year is all about making new plans. AP French was not an option. Not given everyone else who's in that class. My former friends. Reconsider, redirect. Living through senior year at Pine Brook is one thing. Facing them is another.

So Spanish it is, with all the Pine Brook freshmen. I like the freshmen. They have short memories.

I get to the top of the stairs and reach toward the door, but before I can push it open, three sophomore girls shove past me onto the landing. One brushes against my sleeve, and I flinch. "What's her deal?" I hear her ask her friends. She starts down the stairs, and my eyes follow her hand as it runs down the railing. The wood shines with a fresh coat of glossy, white paint. Everything used to be pink in this stairwell, the color of poached salmon. It was pretty tasteless, but now it looks like the stairway to heaven, or a mental institution, depending on your frame of mind.

Clearly, I'm in no frame of mind to hang out here.

The sophomore's words reverberate inside my head. *What's her deal?* That's the question on everyone's mind—if I indulge the voice that says everyone is talking about me, pitying me, dissecting my every move. *I can't believe she came back.* The other voice says that no one feels anything close to pity. *Not after what she did.* I'm not sure which voice is worse.

I shut them both out and force my feet to march into the hall. Get the book, get to class, get it together. I haven't gone more than two steps before I see her leaning against my locker.

Dark curls floating down to frame round, rouged cheeks. Books hugged to her chest, nails painted seashell pink. All curves and bounce and sugar and spice.

Abigail Lin, leaning against the wall. Against my locker. What the hell is she doing here?

I know I should be working on separating the past from the present. But Abigail was never even my past. She was Ret's.

I dart back into the stairwell and grab my phone from my bag, pretend to check for new posts on the Instagram account I don't have. Buy myself a minute to think. I've hardly spoken to Abigail since eighth grade, and even then, our paths barely crossed. But I knew *of* her. Before Bex, before me, there was Abigail.

And then over winter break our last year of middle school, Ret froze Abigail out. When we came back in January, it was impossible not to know about it. *Did you hear?* I heard Ret dropped Abigail. *I heard Abigail couldn't take it anymore.* Take what, exactly? *You know.*

Years later, all I knew for sure was that Abigail had crossed Ret in some unforgivable way. Whatever shape her betrayal had taken, Ret took it personally. Even well into high school, she refused to talk about Abigail, to acknowledge her existence. And I knew better than to ask.

Abigail's a senior now, like the rest of us, but I can't stop seeing her face the day she broke down in the girls' locker room after that winter break. I'd never really understood how Abigail fit in with the other girls. They were vintage shops and punk rock; she was Taylor Swift and *Teen Vogue*. Peach-berry lipstick and too much rouge. But Ret saw something in her, like she saw something in the rest of us.

Until she didn't anymore. That day in the locker room,

Abigail just lost it. I can still see her collapsing into the mouth of the little gym locker, then sliding down to the concrete floor, red faced, her makeup streaming, her mouth stretched wide into these ugly, gulping sobs. In that moment, she didn't look trendy or flawless or lucky. She just looked like a vulnerable girl who couldn't hack it without her friends. Without Ret. I felt bad for her, but I was embarrassed for her too. We all were. No one said anything. We just left her there, alone and half dressed in gym shorts and a tank top while we finished changing and filed into the gymnasium.

When I slipped quietly into Abigail's place freshman year, I swore I'd never end up like her. Can you define irony?

I peek through the small window in the stairway door, craning to get a better look. She's still there. Alone. Not talking to anyone, not doing anything. Just leaning against *my* locker door.

Because we're the same now. Because she feels sorry for me. Because she thinks she has something to say. I may not be ready to go back to Ret, but I'm not ready to seek solace in Abigail either.

The first bell rings for third period. Thirty seconds until the second bell. I'm going to be late. Two senior guys I barely know push through the door, on their way upstairs, and I move out of the way, flattening myself back against the wall.

"Don't trip, Holland!" One of the guys, broad forehead to match his broad shoulders, steps forward to intentionally body-check me into the wall. My shoulder hits brick.

His just slightly smaller, no less Neanderthalian buddy holds up his hand for a high five. Bigger slams his open palm against Smaller's skin, and they disappear up the stairs, howling.

No one checks to see if I'm okay. The second bell rings.

I rub my shoulder and blink back the tears stinging my eyes. I will not cry in school. I stare down at my phone, my shield, my defense until the stairway is empty. Then I take a deep breath and peek back out through the window at my locker. Abigail is gone.

I dash into the hallway and spin the dial for my combination fast, too fast. I'm now officially late to Spanish. I get my locker open on the second try and grab my book. I'm about to slam the door shut and make a run for it when something white on the locker floor, balanced right on top of my gym bag and a practically rust-free carburetor I found on a recent scavenging trip, catches my eye. It's a piece of notebook paper, folded into a careful triangle. I reach down and pick it up; my name is printed on one side in neat block letters. It's handwriting I haven't seen in months, but I'd recognize it anywhere.

Has everyone been haunting my locker today?

I close the door and slide down the wall until I'm crouched over, butt resting on my heels. I'm already late to Spanish, what's another minute? I shouldn't even read it; I should just throw the note away. But I can't help myself. I unfold the triangle and my eyes skim across the words. *I was so selfish.* It's an apology of sorts, an explanation that doesn't really explain much of anything. *If anyone is to blame, blame me.*

I shove the note into my backpack, force myself to stand back up. *Don't worry. I already do.* Then I hurry down the hall, toward the farthest set of stairs, the ones that will take me to verb conjugations and mindless freshmen chatter and a perfectly boring present I can lose myself in for a while.

The restaurant where Matthias spent thirty hours a week in the summer was a casual, sixty-seat modern Thai joint wedged between a gastro pub famous for its tabletop mini-kegs and a take-out pizza window on the East Shore's small restaurant row. Jenni gave it a solid B plus, which was a decently high mark from the culinary queen.

It had been open for a couple years now, but somehow I'd never been inside, until tonight. I waited while Matthias locked the back door and flicked on the lights, illuminating the very shiny and very still kitchen.

"It's like a ghost town in here," I said. "I feel like we're trespassing."

"Nah, come on." He took my hand, and we slipped between the stove and prep stations. The kitchen was small and clean and filled with banged-up appliances and worn metal surfaces. Most importantly, it was closed. Tonight, it was only me and Matthias Cole. Tonight I was a VIP, but I couldn't shake the feeling we were being watched. It was Monday, the kitchen's off night, but I looked over my shoulder, just in case.

"Live a little, Bonnie Parker." Matthias pulled me toward him. Bar soap. Cigarettes and mint. Then his hands were around my waist, spinning me in a circle. My skirt billowed out into a wave of blue and green as I twirled faster, faster. I was beautiful, dangerous. In glorious Technicolor.

A minute later, I collapsed back against a worktable, dizzy and gasping for breath. We were Ellory & Matthias. Bonnie & Clyde. When I could stand up straight again, I patted the imaginary holsters at my hips and cocked my head to the side. "Bang bang."

He grinned and I grinned back. We were outlaws together. Nothing in the whole world could compete with what we had. His hands on my waist, twirling me. My hair flying out like yellow streamers around a maypole. The green flecks in his eyes flashing like marble glass, signaling *yes, yes, yes*.

In that moment, I swear the whole world was *yes*.

"Ellory Holland, consider this your official backstage tour. Sauté, Grill, Fry, Veg. And this is my station." He led me across the kitchen, guiding me to a small segment of counter toward the front. His hand on the small of my back. His voice in my ear. "Garde-manger."

"You're the guard of eating?"

"Well, that's the literal translation. Don't you take French?"

"I think culinary vocab is a little too advanced for French Two. I'll take it up with Madame Clement in the fall."

He grinned again, quick and bright. "It basically means the pantry. It's the station for salads and cold apps. Someday they'll move me up to Fish or Grill, but for now it's rice paper spring rolls and green papaya salad."

"Sounds good to me."

"It will be. Here." He dragged a chair from the dining room in through the kitchen doors. "You sit, I'll cook."

"I can help," I offered. Not that my culinary skills extended much beyond grilled cheese, but it was weird just sitting there. Even if it was my birthday—sweet and spicy seventeen.

"Actually, yeah." He motioned behind me toward a wall shelf with an ancient boom box and a stack of CDs. "See if you can find us something decent to listen to."

While I sorted through the stack of cracked jewel cases, he began arranging his station. Little metal tubs appeared from below the counter, which were soon joined by plastic squeeze bottles and an assortment of produce and chilled, precooked shrimp and chicken from the walk-in refrigerator. Proteins, according to Matthias. Veg. Kitchen-speak.

"Aren't you even a little bit worried we'll get caught?"

"I'm not messing with anyone else's stuff. We're good." He spread four rice paper wrappers on the cutting board in front of him and began to fill them with thin strips of cucumber and carrot. "Unless Joel swings by to check his email, in which case we're totally screwed."

My eyes were wide, my feet poised to run. I was not a model outlaw.

"I'm just playing with you." He turned around long enough to snap a white dish towel at my back, then returned to his wrappers and shrimp.

Once I checked my nerves and let myself relax into the rhythm of the kitchen, it was pretty freaking cool to be there—back in the restaurant's heart while the dining room was dark and silent. It was fun watching Matthias work. Sexy. It made me think about Jenni's ex, who played bass in a really terrible prog rock band. When they were dating, Jenni went to every show. She was always talking about how sexy it was to see him onstage. How he was in his element. How he was more himself. I never got it. I couldn't get past the fact that I really hated the music, but Jenni thought Mark was so talented. I mean, maybe he was. That's not the point. The point was that I got it now. Watching Matthias move deftly around the kitchen, not questioning, not thinking, just doing. It didn't matter that he was preparing more than he was actually cooking. Or that I hadn't even tasted the food. He was clearly talented. Confident. Sexy.

"Your first course, Miss Holland." He turned away from his station to set two small plates on the counter beside my chair. "Rice paper spring rolls with two dipping sauces: spicy plum on the left and sweet chili-carrot on the right. Did you find anything?"

"Yeah." I closed the boom box lid and pressed play. "Prince. A diamond among lumps of coal. Your coworkers have weird taste."

"Excellent choice. You've passed with flying colors."

"I didn't realize this was a test." I narrowed my eyes, slightly annoyed, slightly proud that I had proven myself in some critical way.

"Hardly. Most of these CDs are junk someone's parents didn't want anymore or shit that didn't move in a summer of 2010 garage sale. There are only three acceptable albums in the Fit to Be Thai'ed collection: Prince, *1999*, now playing. Talking Heads, *Speaking in Tongues*. And KMFDM, *Symbols*."

"KM-what?"

"German industrial rock—probably not your thing. But it's awesome to cook to." He gestured toward my plate of spring rolls. "Have a seat, birthday girl."

His lips on my forehead. His eyelashes against my cheek.

"But you're still working." I glanced down at the little plates. "Besides, it's not like they're going to get cold."

"No, seriously. Your birthday meal will be served in a series of small courses. A tasting portion of every salad and cold app on the menu, prepared especially for Ellory Holland, on the first day of her seventeenth year. May it be filled with good food, good music, and good company."

"I think we're off to a very good start." I picked up a spring roll and popped it in my mouth.

"Which reminds me, we should have a proper toast." He disappeared into the back of the walk-in, and my phone chirped, *ki-ka-ri*. I swiped it on, and the screen filled up with a series of texts.

RET JOHNSTON
Hey birthday lady.

BEX LANDRY
We're over at Jenni's drinking wine coolers in your honor.

JENNI RANDALL
Not that you like wine coolers.

BEX LANDRY
It's all we could find in Jenni's
basement.

ELLORY HOLLAND
Don't have too much fun
without me!

RET JOHNSTON
Jinx.

A second later, my Insta dinged, and I opened the app. Ret had posted a picture of the three of them huddled together in Jenni's living room, holding up a sign: GIRLS' NIGHT IN ON ELLORY'S BIG NIGHT OUT. HAVE FUN & HAPPY SEVENTEEN!

Matthias emerged from the walk-in with a bottle of Prosecco and two champagne flutes before I could fully dissect the subtext of Ret's post. I'd spent all weekend with her—Saturday at her house and Sunday birthday brunch with the girls. But the night itself had gone to Matthias, and Ret wanted me to know that she loved me, but she noticed.

I fixed a smile on my lips and turned to my boyfriend. "Where'd this come from?"

"Ricky, where else? He's a beer and whiskey guy, this must have been a gift. He'll never miss it."

I stared down at the table. Suddenly everything was a little off.

Ret was being passive-aggressive, and I was having flashbacks to the beer Matthias had brought to Jenni's party.

"What's wrong?"

I shook my head, shaking it off. Maybe I was reading too much into Ret's post. And was I seriously upset that my boyfriend had brought me champagne? *Live a little, Bonnie Parker.*

"Let's celebrate," I said, grinning until I felt as excited as I looked.

He grabbed a dish towel and popped the cork with a loud hiss. "To my beautiful girlfriend on her birthday."

The spicy plum sauce was cool and hot at the same time, and the little bubbles in the Prosecco burst brightly against my tongue and lips. I refused to worry, and then I forgot that there was anything to worry about. I was happy. I was exactly, precisely happy.

I wanted to remember that moment. Capture it. It felt so secret and perfect to be there, in the center of Matthias's special light. I closed my eyes and recorded the night in a series of movie stills across the back of my eyelids:

> *Me, grinning.*
> *Me, with plum sauce on the corner of my mouth, still grinning.*
> *My arms in the air, head tilted back, singing "Little Red Corvette."*
> *A stack of empty white plates.*
> *Pale yellow bubbles bursting against my lips.*
> *His lips against the mouth of the glass. His lips against my lips.*

Matthias wouldn't let me help with the cleanup either. I gave up protesting. I sat in the kitchen, stuffed on appetizers and a little tipsy, watching him move between the counter, the walk-in, and the sink. Swift, precise, confident. Sexy. He locked up and we emerged onto Second Street. I'd promised my parents I'd be home in time to open presents, but it was still early.

"Want to walk down by the water?" I asked.

"Okay if I make a quick stop first? I just have to duck into Sally's." He jutted his chin toward a formerly white sign across the street that read SALLY'S PUB.

"Sure, no problem." I took his hand and started to walk toward the street.

"This is going to sound kind of weird, but would you mind waiting here for me?"

I stopped. "Oh. Okay." So he was embarrassed to bring me inside. I dropped his hand and wrapped my arms around my waist.

"It's just, it's twenty-one plus, and I didn't tell them I was bringing anyone. They know me, but I . . . it could be awkward."

"Sure, I get it," I said quickly. That sounded totally reasonable. I felt like an outsider in his world.

I waited for Matthias for five minutes that became ten. I leaned against a parked car and stared across the street at the flickering pub sign. Nothing. I checked my phone. Nothing. What had he said he was doing inside? Getting tickets for a show?

He hadn't said. Was he meeting someone? Another girl? Should I text him? I shouldn't text him. I shivered, even though the night air was muggy and warm against my skin. I waited.

Finally, Matthias emerged and ran across the street. "So, so, so sorry." His lips moved light and quick across my cheekbones, my lips, my hair. It felt like I was being covered by a kaleidoscope of butterflies. "Those bastards made me wait." He kissed me again, a hundred times, and soon I was laughing, and we were both laughing, and he was pulling me down the sidewalk toward the river.

The lights of the capitol building sparkled out across the water, and the ground was hot beneath the streetlamps. His hand in my hand, my feet on the pavement. Solid, real, good. The dogwood trees. The white stone law offices. Two ducks out for a night swim, chasing each other, wings flapping. Familiar, real, ours. What had he been doing for so long at that bar? He didn't tell me. It didn't matter. What mattered was the late July air that refused to cool, not ever, not even at night. The slight mist lifting off the water, settling on our skin. The sense that tonight would go on into tomorrow, and everything would still feel new and special and wonderful. That all the tomorrows were ours for the taking.

We paused at the top of a set of stone stairs that would take us down to the water's edge, deeper into the night. Matthias pressed his lips into my hair, his breath warm against my ear.

"Forgive me?"

"For what?" I asked, and I meant it.

"I love you, Ellory."

His voice was low, catching just slightly on the night air like a door on a rusty hinge, then swinging wide open, inviting me through.

I didn't hesitate. I stepped inside those three words, and I didn't look back.

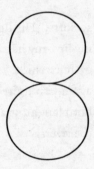

Two more weeks go by until I get up the nerve to go find her. Or before I cave, depending on how you look at it. I see Abigail twice more in that time—again at my locker, one day after school. Then hanging around outside the metal shop, just before lunch. I avoid her.

The notes don't stop either. Now there are three—one for each week since they started. Always folded into neat triangles, always at the bottom of my locker. The words rise off the page, float in front of my eyes, then sink into a meaningless puzzle. *I'm afraid. Paralyzed by indecision.* I take them home, keep them in a shoe box at the back of my closet. *I wanted to tell you. I wanted.*

But I don't go down to the river because of Abigail, or the notes. I go because therapy stopped working.

It's not Dr. Marsha's fault. At first, I lived for our sessions. It was part of the arrangement when I left Pine Brook last April. Mom took a work hiatus to supervise my at-home lessons for the remaining weeks of the spring semester. I went to yoga on Fridays. I saw Dr. Marsha three times a week that eventually became one by the fall. I only had to go back to school for finals, and they let me take those in an empty classroom, away from all the other students. Let me or made me. It's all a matter of perspective.

When Principal Keegan determined I wasn't a good candidate for Pine Brook's "Restorative Justice Teen Up" program, finishing out the rest of my junior year at home was the only other option aside from transferring, which I refused to do. I didn't need restoration, or justice. And I wasn't a runner. I just needed time to heal. Principal Keegan called it long-term suspension. My parents agreed on the terms that it wasn't expulsion, that I'd be allowed to return to Pine Brook for my senior year, and that it would appear on my transcript as a medical leave of absence.

For four months, I clung to therapy like a lifeline. Dr. Marsha was the only person I could really talk to, the only one who never judged, never tried to scrub me clean with pitying looks. When I left for art camp in Philadelphia, we continued our sessions over Skype. I wasn't magically cured, but I was managing the cocktail of emotions she called "an experiential sense of loss." I was coping.

Then I returned to Pine Brook. Then Ret sat across from me in AP English like everything was totally normal. Then I knew that everything I thought I'd worked through in therapy was a giant, glaring lie. *Hi, my name is Ellory. I've been lying to myself.*

I go to the river because it's time to face her. It's time to face myself.

When I finish in the shop after school, I drop my stuff off at home and tell my mom I'm going to the mall with Bex. She's thrilled, cooing about how happy she is to see Bex and me making plans again. I get in the car before I can feel bad about lying to her too. I can walk to the river from our house, but I need the car to keep up my mall ruse. I park on a side street right around the corner and walk the rest of the way. It's unusually warm for early October; the capital is in the middle of an autumn heat wave. The beads of sweat that break out across my skin feel feverish, sticky. I think about turning back and actually driving to the mall.

When I get to the river, I take three deep breaths, in through my nose and out through my mouth. I can feel my insides crackle as I slip through the break in the guardrail. *Crack, crack, pop.*

At first I think she's not here. I scramble down the hill to the base of the bank, but there's no one. "Ret?" I say softly.

I look first to my right, but the strip of grass and dirt is empty save for the occasional soda can and dirty T-shirt. Farther down, the stretch of ground that runs beneath the bridge is heavily spackled with debris. Ret's nowhere in sight, and I can't imagine her hanging out with the beer bottles and dirty diapers, so I start walking in the opposite direction. As the bank extends away from the bridge, the grass gets taller and the shore more uneven. I lose my footing on a patch of wet rocks, and my hands slam into the ground. A thin red line appears on one palm where a rock bit into me, and I bring the skin to my mouth.

"Ellory?"

I press through a rough tangle of weeds, and there she is, tucked back into a hollow in the bank, earbuds in, cracked copy of *Jesus' Son* in her hands.

"I thought you'd never come." She pops the earbuds out.

I sink down next to her, and she takes my bleeding hand in both of hers like a concerned nursemaid.

"You cut yourself."

I jerk my hand away, and her lips twitch down.

"I'm fine." It's the first thing I've said to her since the day she pulled me aside after English class, over a month ago. It's a complete and utter lie.

For a moment, we sit side by side on the bank, letting the river sounds fill the silence between us. But silence sucks, and soon we're passing a bottle of amaretto back and forth.

"Better than a Band-Aid," Ret says. My hand throbs in response. I lift the bottle to my nose and inhale. The liqueur smells syrupy sweet, like toasted almonds and maraschino cherries. The scent reminds me of my mom; she likes to pour a tablespoon into her evening coffee on winter Sundays, one of her few little luxuries. I take another long gulp; I don't want to think about my mom.

Ret raises her eyebrows and takes the bottle back again.

"Didn't peg you for an amaretto drinker," I say, because it's better than more silence.

"Ever since Veronica joined AA, I've been working through the liquor cabinet. I'll drink whatever." She tilts the bottle back and takes a drink, then passes it back to me.

Now it's my turn to raise my eyebrows. "Your mother is an alcoholic?"

It clicks then that I've seen Veronica a few evenings this fall, coming out of the United Methodist next to Wegmans. The older brother of my childhood best friend—the one who'd moved to Georgia before the start of ninth grade—had attended meetings there. The thought that Veronica was there for the same reason has been hovering at the back of my mind for weeks, and now the pieces fall into place.

Ret shakes her head. "Not exactly. It's the third group she's tried since April. She hates them all. It's hard to find the perfect support group for her niche brand of parental remorse. But she likes AA the best. Everyone's pretty fucked up."

I nod and take another drink. Aside from the United Methodist sightings, I've seen Veronica only one other time this year, at the gas station by the mall. She was sitting in the passenger's seat, burrowed deep into an overcoat despite the late summer heat, while a man in his forties stood outside her car and filled up the tank. I slouched down in the Subaru's driver's seat and watched, making sure they couldn't see me. Ret's dad split years before we became friends, but I knew it was him. This man had Ret's lapis eyes, her pale skin. I barely breathed until they finished and drove off.

"I heard your dad was in town," I say, attributing my sighting to the Pine Brook rumor mill. "Did he move back in?"

Ret's face clouds over, and she leans into the bank. She clearly doesn't want to talk about it, and I decide to let it go. Her business.

"What were you listening to?" I ask, changing the subject. I want to ask what she does this year when she's not here, drinking alone. I want to ask if she ever brings Jenni, or Bex. But a part of me already knows that she doesn't. There's no cosmos, not anymore. We're all scattered, spinning off into space.

"Oh." Ret brightens up, and I slip one of her earbuds into my ear. "Listen."

I recognize the music immediately. It's the third track on *Adios*, KMFDM's studio album immediately following *Symbols*. Old Ellory spent too much time listening to their entire catalogue the summer before last, trying to impress Matthias, or Ret, or both.

"You know this was their breakup album," I tell her.

Ret closes her eyes and doesn't speak for a minute. "They got back together," she says.

I slip the earbud out and hand it back.

"You don't want to listen? I thought you were *so into* them."

"Things change."

She turns off the music and slips her phone into her bag. I take another drink, and by now I'm feeling warm and relaxed inside, like soft cashmere sweaters and mugs of hot cocoa. Now I'm ready to really talk.

"I didn't come here to rehash the past," I say.

"No?" Ret straightens up, tilts her chin toward me. "Why did you come here, Ellory May?"

Because you invited me. Because I couldn't stay away. Because I still hate you. Because you destroyed everything. Because I still love you. Because I still hate myself. Because I'm dying without you.

"Because I need you to promise me something," I finally say. I glance down at her wrist, bare and pale where the black band still hugs mine. "You can't talk to me in school," I tell her. "No more chats after English. If you see me in the halls, you ignore me."

"You don't want to be seen with me." Ret's voice radiates hurt.

I force myself to look her right in the eyes. "You know what would happen."

"I need you, Ellory," she says. This time I let her take my hand, hold it tight. "Now more than ever."

She's manipulating me, but she's also right. She *does* need me. "We keep things private," I say.

"You, me, and the river," Ret agrees.

"And no more KMFDM. No wallowing in the past."

"I'll drink to that." Ret holds the bottle to the sky, then tilts it back, taking a long swallow. She hands it to me, and I take another drink.

"Two roads diverged in a wood, and I—"

"I took the one to the river," Ret says. Then she hits me right back. "Two roads diverged in a wood, and I—"

"I took the one back to you." I say it because it's the only thing that's felt truly honest in a while. I say it because it's what she needs to hear. And even now, a part of me needs to make her happy.

Then I push myself up to my feet. The world rushes up at me, and I stumble, catching myself against the side of the bank. "I have to get home."

She nods but doesn't make a move to stand up. "Come back any time. You're always welcome."

I walk along the bank to where I can see the break in the guard-rail, then scramble up the hill to the road. Good thing I walked here, left the car around the corner from the house. I wrap my arms around my waist and walk quickly, trying to sober up. I need to pee. I need to think. Dr. Marsha would not be pleased to hear about my afternoon activities: drinking, hanging out with Ret. Dr. Marsha thinks okay-ness is a destination, that all I need to do is keep walking in a straight line.

I know she cares. But she's still full of shit.

I keep walking and think about our next session. I should tell her everything, but at least for now, I want Ret for myself. I'm not ready to share her with Dr. Marsha or anyone else. I slip in through the back door and announce that I need to take a shower before dinner, that some kid spilled soda on me at the mall. I'll go back out and move the car into the driveway later; hopefully my parents won't notice I'm back, but it's still gone.

I step into the shower and let the hot water cascade down around me. I can see Dr. Marsha's approving face as I tell her about my college applications, how I'm getting straight As, how my healthy, drama-free fall is going so well. Her smile is a kind trick; it says that there is forgiveness in the world and sunshine and moving on. It says I can have these things if I want them. After today, I'm not sure I want them.

The inside of Ret's bedroom was dark, as always, and stifling in the late summer heat. The heavy blackout curtain drawn across the room's one small window kept the sun out, but the standing fan whirring near the door was fighting a losing battle. Time seemed to operate under its own special logic there. It always felt like midnight, no matter what time it was outside. It had something to do with the candles flickering from every open inch of windowsill and bureau. And the boa draped from her mirror's gilt frame, ready for a late-night show.

I loved YouTube deep dives and pints of Ben & Jerry's at Jenni's, and I loved midnight drives in the Subaru, Bex singing along to Imogen Heap, the notes spilling across the dark streets that wound down along the river.

But I loved being at Ret's, just the two of us, best.

The first time I came over freshman year, I remember thinking Ret's room looked like it belonged to the love child of a burlesque dancer and a punk rocker. The decor was all black and silver and the walls were covered with posters of seventies punk bands, *Sid and Nancy*, London's Leicester Square. They were mostly from Hot Topic, where Ret checked her morals at the door for a paycheck. Whenever anyone asked about her job, she would say, "It's a store full of poser shit, but it's better than the Gap."

Ret rolled over on her stomach and fished a bottle of blue glitter polish from underneath the bed. "I've been looking for this."

It was Sunday afternoon, and Ret and I were killing time. There were a very specific number of hours that needed killing: three, until I had to be home for dinner. Then twelve more until my alarm would signal the start of junior year.

"First day statement?"

Ret considered the bottle carefully. "Not if I go with the leather skirt we picked up at Salvation Army. I'm thinking neon yellow, maybe a red accent nail."

I was listening, but the other half of my brain was with Matthias. He was at the restaurant, working his last lunch shift of the summer. Next week he'd switch back to his part-time, school year schedule, and they'd promote one of the dishwashers to take over his daytime garde-manger hours. As Ret contemplated her outfit options, I leaned back on her bed and imagined his hands chopping tiny slivers of lemongrass at his station, the length of his torso and back arched over the cutting board, wiry arm muscles showing through his T-shirt sleeves.

I picked up my phone and shot him a quick text: We on for grocery run at 5?

"Gotcha."

"Huh?" Ret's voice snapped me back to her bedroom.

"You're texting him again."

I tossed my phone to the end of the bed and held up my hands in surrender. "Just confirming a plan. I'm back now."

A slow smile played across her lips. "Tall, brooding, good with kids, loves to cook . . . I'm not sure what you see in him, Ellory May."

"Shut up, you're just jealous." I tossed a black pillow covered with silver and pink sequins at Ret's shoulder.

"Hey!" She grabbed the projectile before it could make contact. "I've got Jonathan to keep me warm, remember?" She lowered her lashes across the deep pools of her eyes and fluttered. She was ravish and flash.

"I might remember if you ever talked about him."

Ret's eyes snapped open. "You're right," she said. "I'm going to text him right now and end things."

"That's not—" I started to say.

"He should have broken up with me by now, but I guess I have to do everything." She reached for her phone but didn't turn it on.

"He's with you because he's *into* you, Ret. Low self-confidence much?"

Around us, Ret was nothing but confidence. But around guys, she was pink and raw. Tender and bruised. She never brought them around because a leader is never vulnerable. A leader never exposes her belly.

"Screw self-confidence. That's a bunch of bull-crap for only children."

"I'm an only child. *You're* an only child!"

"And mercifully, Veronica skipped self-confidence day in How to Screw Up Your Kid class. Anyway, we're not talking about me, we're talking about you."

"Whatever." I reached down and picked up the blue bottle of polish from the floor. "You have any red?"

Ret twisted her lips to one side and examined my face. "Not red. You need something cool, a sea-foam green maybe. Oh, I know!" She pushed herself up from the floor and opened a metal tin on her dresser. "This teal will really bring out the summer highlights in your hair."

I wasn't entirely sure about teal, but Ret's excitement was infectious. Plus, she knew more about this stuff than I did.

"Teal it is."

She tossed me the bottle and sank into the big red armchair in the corner of her bedroom, and I started on my left hand.

"The important thing to consider is what kind of entrance you plan to make tomorrow." Her bangs were freshly trimmed and streaked with Electric Banana, and her skin seemed to smolder in the room's low light.

"Entrance? I plan to park in the student lot and make the grand hike to the main doors like every other day of our lives. What are you even talking about?"

"You and Matty, of course."

The polish was smooth and pearly. The color was a little loud, but Ret was right; it would bring out the natural sun-streaks I always had in my hair by the end of the summer. I kept painting until all ten nails glistened.

"Top coat?" I asked.

Ret dug back into the metal tin and produced a clear bottle. "Seche Vite, only the best. Come sit."

I walked over to Ret's dresser and sat down in front of her burlesque hall mirror. She placed her hands on my shoulders and leaned back, taking me in.

"Matty's been good for you," she mused. "You're positively glowing."

I fought a smile. "It would be hard not to glow in all this candlelight."

She ran her fingers through my hair, smoothing it back. "Hmm-mm. It's more than that. You're so beautiful, Ellory."

I folded her words up tight and tucked them into my heart. Then she unscrewed the cap and started on my left hand.

"That stuff smells like cancer," I said, breaking the mood.

"As long as you don't eat it, I'm sure you'll be fine. And don't think I don't know you're avoiding the question."

I sighed. "We're not making some grand couple-y entrance tomorrow, if that's what you're asking. All I need is Lizza Kendrick asking if we came from his house or mine."

"Not before school," Ret said like it was obvious. "I mean at lunch. You do have fourth in the sky dome, right?"

The sky dome was what everyone called the upperclassman cafeteria. It was on the eighth floor of the school, and instead of a solid roof overhead, there was a big open skylight cut into the center of the ceiling. It wasn't as nice as it sounds. It leaked in the winter, and by spring, the glass was always smeared with grime and bird shit. Eventually, the school would throw a big tarp on top, blacking it out. The only really good thing about the sky dome was that it was reserved exclusively for juniors and seniors, which meant that this year, we finally got to eat there.

"Yeah, we both have lunch fourth."

"And?" Ret's line of inquiry was innocent enough on the surface, but underneath it all, she was testing me.

"And nothing. I'm not sitting with his indie dude-bros. I will meet you in front of the east doors, and we'll go in together."

Ret smiled, satisfied. "Just checking."

"You don't want to eat with Jonathan and the varsity lacrosse team?" I asked.

"Hell no. I just thought you and Matty might have your own plans, now that you're all serious."

"And you wouldn't disown me?" I asked. I already knew the answer. *You are mine.*

"I would totally disown you."

"Fascist." I said it to call her out, but the truth was I needed her to care. I needed her to need me.

"That's me. There, all done." Ret dropped the bottle of top coat back into the metal tin and blew across the tops of my nails. "Give it ten, and you're good to go."

She grabbed her phone from the floor and wrapped her arm around me, then angled the screen at the mirror. "Say *senior belles.*"

But I didn't say anything. I tilted my chin down, letting my hair fall forward over my eyes, and curled my lips into my sultriest smile while Ret pressed her lips against my cheek. *Snap.*

There was a quick knock on the door, and Ret's mom poked her head in. "Hi, girls."

"Why even knock?" Ret asked.

Ms. Johnston stepped inside, looking flustered despite her business suit and heels. Her blouse was unbuttoned about two buttons too many, and her lipstick looked like something she'd borrowed from Ret. "You don't want me to knock?"

"It's rhetorical. Never mind."

"Hi, Ms. Johnston." I held up my right hand and began blowing lightly across my nails.

"Ellory, please. It's Veronica." She turned to her daughter. "Margaret, I have a showing in Carlisle this evening. You remember?"

"Sure." Ret shrugged. She hadn't remembered, or didn't care. When did Ms. Johnston—Veronica—not have an open house to run or a date that might go all night? I felt a little bad for her. Sure, she was kind of a flake, but it's not like she had it easy raising Ret on her own. It's not like Ret made things easy for anyone, least of all her mom.

"I'll be back by ten."

"Sure."

She started to back out of the doorway, then stopped. "Have you eaten dinner yet?"

"Mom, it's like hours until dinnertime."

"Oh, right." She frowned. "Well, there might still be Chinese in the fridge. Or you can call for pizza, okay?"

"Sure, whatever."

"It was really nice to see you, Veronica." I smiled extra sweetly. I don't know why I felt the need to be nice on Ret's behalf, but I did. Ret didn't say anything, and in a minute Ms. Johnston turned and closed the door behind her.

"Ugh, anyway." Ret scowled into the mirror in front of us. "Back to you and Matty."

I closed my eyes and pictured myself pulling into the lot tomorrow morning, making that first walk of the semester across the pavement and down to the main doors. I was itching to get back to the metal shop. I wanted to make a series of sheet metal postcards and an ankle bracelet for Cordelia. I wanted to walk the halls with Matthias, holding his hand for everyone to see. I wanted to take over a window table in the sky dome with Ret, Jenni, and Bex. Everything was lining up, coming into sharp and brilliant focus.

Ret picked up her phone again and clicked it over to our group chat, which was currently titled Boys of Summer, and was the reason I'd had that corny eighties song stuck in my head all week. I leaned over to get a look. While we'd been talking to her mom, Ret had posted the picture of the two of us in the mirror to our chat. Bex had responded with a series of blurry, faraway shots of some Usher look-alike she'd spotted at the mall, but Jenni was radio silent. Either she hadn't seen the latest chats, or she was sulking, feeling left out. I grimaced. Ret couldn't pass up the opportunity to draw blood.

"I'd better go," I said. "I have to go to Wegmans for my mom before dinner, and the list is epic."

Ret gave me a kiss on the cheek and handed me the bottle of teal polish. "In case you chip. Sky dome before fourth?"

"East doors." I kissed Ret back and grabbed my phone and bag.

As soon as I walked outside, the late afternoon sun smacked my skin in a bright blaze. If possible, it was even hotter out there than it had been in Ret's room. I fished my sunglasses and phone out of my bag and leaned back against the car. The metal burned through my cotton tank top.

It was 4:55, and Matthias had been done with his shift for almost an hour. He should have texted me back by now. I clicked on my phone, but the only new messages were from our group chat. I opened up my conversation with Matthias, just to make sure my last text had gone through. Even though I already knew it had.

I could swing by his house, but wasn't that a little needy? He'd said he *might* need to go to Wegmans, that he'd let me know. But he hadn't.

It wasn't a big deal. It was just groceries. But it wouldn't have been a big deal to text me back, either.

I tossed my phone in my bag and slid into the driver's seat, putting the windows down and cranking up the AC. The icy blast hit my chest, and I sucked in my breath. I was probably going to rot in hell for wasting energy, but I was in no mood to care. *He's just busy. His battery died.* It wasn't the first time Matthias had forgotten to text me, or forgotten a plan. But he always had a good excuse; Cordelia had needed something, or he'd had to pick up an extra shift. He had responsibilities. It wasn't like he didn't care. I backed out of Ret's driveway with the AC blasting and the windows down, and I headed to the store. *It's not a big deal. It's not a big deal.*

OCTOBER, SENIOR YEAR
(NOW)

At lunch, I head down to the metal shop like I do every day at the start of fifth. The thing about scheduling your lunch period to avoid everyone you know is that then you have lunch with no one you know. The sky dome is a right but not an obligation. I take my usual route from math on the sixth floor down to the art wing, all the way across the school. A blocky sandstone addition that was tacked on sometime in the nineties, the art wing is home to the wood shop, metal shop, art studio, dance studio, and theater. It stands out like a sore thumb next to the redbrick, ivy-trimmed main building. It's the best part of Pine Brook.

As I round the corner into the haphazardly diagonal hallway that connects the two buildings, two witches brush past me, followed by Ariana Grande and a goblin.

At Pine Brook, only seniors dress up for Halloween because only seniors attend the Zombie Smash in the sky dome after school. Funded entirely by the annual Senior Council cheesecake drive, the Zombie Smash has always been and will always be a senior class event. Wearing a costume to school is a mark of seniority, a privilege. Some Pine Brookians spend four years planning their outfit.

We were going to go as Pussy Riot. As the Golden Girls. As the Pretty Little Liars. We were going to go together.

Now, it seems so pointless. An exclusive dance for exclusivity's sake. This senior will be avoiding the sky dome today like the plague. Now. After school. This senior is not wearing a costume. This morning, it felt like an act of protest, but now I feel the nakedness of my slouchy jeans and cardigan. No costume, no friends. No date for the dance.

As I walk, I listen for my name. *Don't get mad, Holland. Don't rage out.* Any one of the burns I've had hurled my way from across the parking lot, down the hall, inside the locker room this fall. But today, no one says anything. Everyone's too wrapped up in the spooky fun to notice me shuffling down the hallway to the shop corridor.

But I notice them. Among the stream of plainclothes underclassmen, I spy three cats. Kobe Bryant. A sexy nurse who is definitely getting sent home before eighth period. And then, all the way down at the end of the corridor, three girls in short leather skirts, high heels, and identical black wigs bobbed neatly at their chins. As I squint toward them, hoping my eyes are playing tricks on me, one girl tilts her head back and raises her hand in the air. I watch as a stream of what must be water flows down from a flask into her mouth, and the other girls shriek. Are they actually dressed up *as Ret*? Are they some kind of baby minions?

Before I can even diagnose what I'm feeling—angry, ill, betrayed?—someone much closer catches my eye. I duck into a doorway, but it's too late. He sees me.

"You don't have to hide. I don't bite, you know?"

Dave's practically in my face, coming at me with a low, oily chuckle that makes my skin crawl.

"Maybe *I* do." I snap my teeth into the air between us. "Bite."

He takes a step back, surprised. Roving eyes, flushed cheeks, slight twitch at the corner of his lips. Dave Franklin may not be the last person I want to have a heart-to-heart with today, but he's definitely high on the list. I crane my neck around him, down the corridor toward the Ret Johnston Fan Club, but they're gone, if they were ever really there at all.

I turn my attention back to Dave. He's wearing a trucker hat that says *Cool Story Bro*, which I guess is his idea of a costume. Not that I'm one to talk.

"Jesus, Holland. Just jokes, okay?" He holds up his hands defensively.

I sigh and step out from the doorway, back into the hall. "What do you want, Franklin?"

"I'm not going to hassle you, okay? It's just . . . there's some-thing that's been on my mind."

My stomach sinks. Whatever Dave's selling, I'm not buying.

"It's not a good time." I start walking toward the metal shop.

"It's about Ret."

I freeze.

"It's something she said last winter, while we were hanging out downtown. I can't get it out of my head. She said she didn't deserve you. That you were too good for the rest of us."

His words form a knot somewhere deep in my gut, stirring the ash. "She was probably drunk."

"Doesn't mean she didn't mean it." He shifts his weight back and forth, back and forth, his expensive sneakers squeaking against the Pine Brook floor. Does he want me to thank him? Is this his way of waving a white flag?

I don't say anything and Dave doesn't say anything, and for a minute we stand there silent in the hall while the last bell rings and classroom doors close.

"You're late," I say finally. "To wherever you're going."

He shrugs. "It's no big."

I stand there until Dave gets the picture and turns back toward the main building. "See you, Holland."

When I step through the door, the crisp, tangy smell of the shop hits me right away. Everything about being in here is familiar, comforting. I immediately feel the knot in my stomach loosen a notch. Mr. Michaels is at his desk, eating a sandwich out of a white paper bag. He looks up at me, taking in my regular Ellory outfit.

"I get it. It's meta, right?" he asks. Mr. Michaels is cool. Easy to talk to. He makes fun of his age all the time, but then he'll surprise you by quoting Miley Cyrus or the new Shailene Woodley movie. Someone in his family subscribes to *US Weekly*.

"Yeah," I say. "I'm going as a junior. Totally meta."

"You are going to the Goblin Gala, right? I assume I won't see you after school."

I slide my bag off my shoulder and walk over to the shelves in the back where my assorted unfinished projects are stashed.

"Zombie Smash. And no, you'll see me." Dave's words are still ringing in my ears, and I can feel my insides crackle. I lift my sculpture-in-progress up onto a worktable and try to shake it off. "Faux-spooky decor and football players dressed as hipsters—it's not exactly my scene."

"Hmm." Mr. Michaels regards me coolly. "I thought the dance was every senior's scene."

I shrug, and he lets it go, returning to his sandwich. That's what I like about Mr. Michaels. He takes an interest, but knows when to butt out. He's one of the only teachers who isn't all over me with concerned eyes and down-turned lips this year.

I slip my earbuds in and try to get to work. This sculpture is the first thing I've made any headway on since school started, but something's still off. The proportion, the mix of materials, I don't know. Thank god I got so much done over the summer, because ever since I returned to Pine Brook, my work has been shit. I can't figure out why nothing's coming together; I'm used to being in my element in here.

I took shop freshman year along with everyone else, but while my classmates packed up their metal roses and never set foot in the shop again, I couldn't get enough. I begged Mr. Michaels to hire me as his assistant so I'd get to keep working on my own stuff after I cleaned up and pulled materials after school. It's not like I see myself joining the Future Welders of Pennsylvania, but there are so many possibilities in the metal.

I'm not interested in making things that are beautiful, although sometimes there is a beauty in what I create. I'm interested in making things that are strong. I start with metal scraps—whatever I can scrounge from abandoned lots on the East Shore and down by the river. They're discarded things, broken and beat-up pieces of metal that nobody wants anymore. Except me. I look for the relationships between the parts, the ways they sing to each other. I bring them together. Alone, they're just scraps, useless junk, but when I'm done, they're part of something strong, unbreakable, unrecognizable. Something new.

When I can make myself focus, that is. Which hasn't been much ever since I got back to school. I grab a curved, triangular piece of scrap—something that used to belong to a playground set—and hold it up, trying to concentrate, but I can't get Dave Franklin's voice out of my head. I remember that day, or a day just like it. By February, Ret had been spending more and more time downtown with the guys. *I'm so bored, Ellory. I just want an adventure.* I'd left school late, as always, after finishing up in the shop. When I drove out of the lot and pulled up at the first red light, I realized the car stopped ahead of me was Dave's. There were only so many black Mustangs in town, and I could see Matthias in the passenger's seat, his arm hanging out the open window despite the cold.

I followed them. It wasn't my coolest move, but by then, I had no chill to spare. I had to know where they were going. If Matthias wasn't going to tell me, wasn't going to let me in, I had to find out for myself.

They drove to Ret's. When they pulled up in front of her house, I was so shocked, I just kept driving. I circled around the block and killed the lights, then pulled up a few houses down from the Johnstons' just as Ret was taking the stairs two at a time and slipping into the back of the Mustang. I followed them as far as the Market Street Bridge before turning toward home. Whatever they were doing downtown without me—Dave, Matthias, and Ret—whatever adventure awaited them, it was an adventure made for three. *She's too good for the rest of us.* That might be Dave's truth, but I know the real reason I wasn't invited.

I'm so absorbed in my not-so-sweet trip down memory lane that I don't notice Abigail until she's standing right in front of me. Dark, curly hair and warm, amber skin. Dimples for days. I think she's Chinese and Latina, but I've never met her family. Falling out with Ret aside, I don't know much about Abigail at all.

"Cool piece," she says, her eyes wandering over my half-finished sculpture. "You're really talented."

I pop my earbuds out. I want to defend myself, tell her this disjointed thing is definitely not my best work, but it hits me that she's being sincere. "What are you doing here?" I ask instead.

As if Abigail weren't already oozing enough cuteness, today she's wearing cat ears, and I can see a striped tail pinned to her jeans. I want to tell her to fuck off, but it's impossible to be mean to Abigail Lin. It's the main reason I've been avoiding her.

"You're a hard one to track down."

I glance over to Mr. Michaels for backup, but his desk is empty. I didn't even see him leave the room.

"Maybe I don't want to be tracked down," I manage in an almost cold voice.

"Right." She tilts her head to one side, studying me. "I promise I'll be quick."

I put the metal triangle—the one I've been holding for at least five minutes—down on the worktable and pull out a stool.

Abigail is five foot one at most, and I'd rather not feel like a giant in her presence.

"I know we don't really know each other, but I thought you might want someone to talk to."

I press my lips together. Once upon a time, Ret made Abigail's life hell. I get why she thinks I'd want to talk to her now, but she's wrong.

"No, thanks," I say. Abigail thinks Ret left me too. But she's wrong again.

She smiles, undeterred. She's sugar and spice and everything nice. She's not what I need.

"I know what Ret did to you," I say when she's still standing there a minute later, showing no signs of leaving. "But it's not the same."

"What Ret did to me?" she asks. She sounds genuinely curious.

"Back in eighth grade. When she cut you out over break."

"Is that what she told you?" she asks. "I always wondered where that story got started."

My mouth falls slightly open, and Abigail laughs.

"No one walks away from Ret, right?" she says. "But I did. Not the other way around."

"But that day in the locker room," I say. "We all saw you."

Abigail frowns, remembering. "It was a tough time. My mom and I moved into a motel when we left my dad over Christmas. One of those cheap places out on the highway. He kept calling my phone, trying to use me to get to her."

"Did he . . ." I start to ask, but I'm not even sure what I'm asking. Did he hit her? Did he come after you? It's none of my business, but why is she telling me this?

"He's not a good guy," she says when my words trail off. "But my mom was an inspiration. She stood up to him, and she got me out. After that, I didn't need anyone else pushing me around."

"So you walked away from Ret."

Abigail nods.

That day in the locker room hadn't been about Ret at all. Until Ret had taken the story, twisted it into something she controlled. How she'd dropped Abigail cold. How Abigail couldn't hack it without her. I wonder if Ret even knew her parents were getting divorced.

"Why are you telling me all this?" I ask.

Abigail takes a minute before she speaks, chooses her words carefully. "I think you know what it's like to be the star of a story that you didn't write."

"But everyone else believes," I say softly.

Mr. Michaels comes back in the room, and I glance up at the clock. Lunch is almost over.

"Anyway," Abigail says, "if you ever want to talk."

And then she's gone, cat ears and cat tail and fractured fairy tales disappearing with her out into the hallway. She thinks she knows things. About Ret. About me. But she doesn't know what I still have, the long afternoons down by the river, the story that isn't over.

11

SEPTEMBER, JUNIOR YEAR
(THEN)

I drummed the tips of my fingers against the steering wheel while I waited for Ret. It was two weeks into junior year, but it still felt like summer, hot, bright, slow. I hated being trapped inside school, but I hated being late even more. I checked the time on my phone and kept drumming until Ret finally skipped out of her house in a Yeah Yeah Yeahs T-shirt, a tiny corduroy skirt, and a pair of ridiculously tall snakeskin heels she'd nabbed from the remainder bin at Hot Topic.

"Your mom's going to freak when she sees you in that."

"What? It's corduroy, it's preppy. Besides, you know Veronica. She'd say something gross about harnessing my self-expression." Ret slid into the passenger's seat, and I backed out of the drive.

"Anyway, she's not going to see me. I have jeans in my bag."

I shook my head but kept my mouth shut as Ret leaned forward to refresh her lip gloss in the visor mirror. After a minute, she said, "We should talk about your behavior, Ellory May. With Matty? It's textbook enabling."

I lifted my eyes from the road to glance at her. She pressed her lips together, sealing some secret in and daring me to turn the key.

Enabling. Matthias hadn't pulled anything like abandoning me in front of Sally's again, but his phone habits left something to be desired, and the string of nighttime errands had carried on from summer into fall. When I asked, he mumbled something about Cordelia. I couldn't imagine what he was getting for his kid sister so late at night, but he didn't explain, and something in his eyes warned me not to press. I'd only met her twice so far—a special screening of *Finding Nemo* in August and a pool day last Saturday—but she seemed like a pretty normal kid. Not someone in need of secret missions.

"Do tell," I said after a beat, keeping my voice casual, but taking her bait.

"His concert habit. You're enabling it with caffeine?"

"Oh. Right." So that's all she'd meant. I leaned back in my seat and kept driving.

We were headed to the Susquehanna Roasting Company, better known as simply the Roaster, for pre–Pine Brook coffee. On Thursday mornings, Ret's mom had a team meeting at her real estate office downtown, so I left early to get Ret before school. The bus was for freshmen, athletes, and losers. The bus was not for us.

I liked Thursdays. About once a month, Ret and I would ditch, but it was too early in the year for that now. Teachers were still forming their impressions. You had to be on your best behavior for the first month at least. On time, awake, homework done, hand raised.

Matthias was not winning at that game. Already, he was slipping into his sophomore year habits, falling asleep in class, doing his homework but forgetting to bring it to school. Sometimes, I let him copy mine. I figured I had a whole year of Comparative Religions notes to make up for.

Coffee helped too. Maybe Ret was right, maybe I was enabling his concert habit, but whatever. No sixteen-year-old should have as much on his plate as Matthias did. If staying out late, listening to music in dark, sweaty clubs helped him escape his shitty home life for a few hours each week, fine. The longer we'd been together, the clearer it had become how vital music was to him. I regretted my earlier claim that I didn't want anything to do with his music stuff. After three months together, I was curious. I wanted him to take me along.

I turned on the radio and flipped through the stations. As always, there was nothing good. Ret waited a minute for me to open up about the caffeine or concerts or whatever, but when it was clear I wasn't going to humor her, she launched into a detailed description of yesterday's after school hookup with Jonathan Gaines. (Pants off, underwear on, everyone satisfied.)

"God, Ret, it's too early to think about sex. No hookup details before coffee."

"Oh, please." I could feel her rolling her eyes at me through her sunglasses. "I have to tell you what he said when we were messing around. He was babbling like a baby; it was amazing."

"I thought you were breaking up with Jonathan," I teased. "Like two weeks ago."

"Yeah, well. He's not totally boring in bed, so maybe I'll let him stick around for a while. Did I tell you he wants to go to homecoming? You know I hate a school dance, but I found this lacy red minidress? He's going to die dead."

I let Ret chatter on. She was so not breaking up with Jonathan Gaines. And whatever she wanted me to believe, this was not just about sex. I was a virgin, and so was Ret, but she had hooked up with a few different guys. To Ret, it wasn't anxiety-making or embarrassing, not like the emotional stuff, which turned hard core Ret into a quivering blob of sky dome Jell-O. She wanted to talk about sex all the time. Until now, I'd been a willing audience, as if by soaking up her experience I might gain some of my own.

But things felt different now that I had a boyfriend. I gripped the wheel as Ret debated the pros and cons of ordering a corset from ModCloth. "Not like a real one to shrink your waist. Just for fun, you know? I think it'll work under my homecoming dress, but I hate not trying things on."

I nodded and bit at my lower lip. Every time Ret started talking about sex, I could feel my stomach clench up. She couldn't understand why I wouldn't open up to her, believed fervently that the idea that sex was some private, taboo thing was an outdated notion left over from our parents' generation. She said we shouldn't let archaic social mores hold us back.

Matthias and I had messed around a little, but it never went very far before I pulled the plug. It's like I was waiting for something inside me to click. Something that would guide me, tell me exactly what to do, make me feel less inexperienced, less naive. I kept waiting for that click, our lips meshed together, my body pressed against him, his hands running up and down my shirt, my jeans. When the click didn't happen it's like I'd zoom out of the moment, collapse into myself, pull back. Matthias never pressed, just backed off, kissed my forehead, buried his face in my hair.

Ret always pressed. She clearly assumed Matthias and I had done more than we had, but when Ret pushed me to spill, I held my tongue. She got her way about most things—*don't you trust me, Ellory?*—but on this I held firm. When there was something worth sharing, she'd be the first to hear it. In the meantime, the last thing I needed was every fumbling step of my Journey Toward Womanhood to be socially critiqued by Ret Johnston.

We pulled into the lot at the Roaster. All of the regular spots were full, so I grabbed one of the spaces up front reserved for environmentally friendly vehicles or expectant mothers.

Ret threw me some serious side eye. "Something you're not telling me?"

"Yeah, the Subaru is expecting a litter of kittens. Come on, we're going to be in here five minutes. I probably would have gotten a normal spot if you hadn't made me wait." I bumped my hip against Ret's, nudging her toward the door.

Inside, the smell of freshly brewed coffee and vanilla bean brioche was intoxicating. We got iced vanilla lattes and croissants (chocolate for Ret, plain for me), and for Matthias, I got a large drip coffee, dark roast, with four sugars and no milk. *Enabling.*

We piled back into the car, and Ret proceeded to spend the entire ride to Pine Brook on her phone.

"Who are you texting?"

"Jenni, who else? She's pissed. I don't know what the big deal is, it's just coffee."

Our Thursday morning Roaster runs had always been a Ret & Ellory tradition. Bex squeezed in an hour of dance before school, and Ret had never invited Jenni, so I hadn't either.

"I told her you needed a private consult on the art of the blow job."

I threw Ret a glare from the driver's seat as we turned onto the street that ran down to the high school. She could have told Jenni anything, but why make up something tame when she could go for my weak spot?

"Oh, come on," Ret said, mistaking my look for concern. "A little white lie won't kill her. Jenni needs to lighten up, and it always falls to me to steer her in the right direction. It's exhausting."

We pulled into the student lot with exactly eleven minutes to spare before the bell. It was barely enough time to walk with Ret as she teetered across the unevenly paved lot in her giant heels, but I gritted my teeth and matched my pace to hers. Chicks before dicks. When we got to the front door, the last bus was pulling up, and the kids who didn't have cars or rides to school were streaming through the three sets of double doors that formed the main entrance to Pine Brook High.

Jenni was standing to the side, one leg bent at the knee, the sole of her boot propped back against the redbrick wall. She plucked her gold aviators away from her eyes and smiled thinly at us.

"Cutting it close, ladies."

Ret leaned in to give her a big hug, as if she hadn't seen her in ages, as if they hadn't just spent the last ten minutes texting back and forth about my supposed tutorial in R-rated activities. Suddenly, Jenni had Ret's full focus.

"Honey." Ret's voice was a purr. She tucked a red strand of hair behind Jenni's ear. "I need your advice."

I shifted the coffee tray from one hand to the other. Ret seemed to have forgotten I was there, but I hadn't been let go, either. Jenni glanced at me and poked the side of her tongue into her cheek, and they both giggled.

"Well, go on, you still have six minutes." Ret waved me toward the door.

"Sex minutes?" Jenni asked, but I was already shoving my way through the bottleneck of freshmen and into the first-floor hallway. I bounded up the stairs two at a time, carefully balancing the coffee, watching out for teachers who might flag me for running.

Matthias was already at his desk in homeroom, using his backpack as a pillow. His not quite blond, not quite brown hair fanned out against the bag. Today was a flopped down day—no time for styling when you can barely drag yourself out of bed. He'd been out at a show until early this morning. I'd dozed in and out of sleep until his text came through at 4:13, letting me know he was home. His parents didn't seem to care, but I did.

"Special delivery." I waved the cardboard cup under his nose, the smell of strong black coffee seeping out through the little cutout in the lid.

"Hey, sunshine." He opened his eyes and raised his head to grin up at me. Deep creases from the bag cut across his cheeks, and he looked unshowered as well as unstyled. He was imperfect and beautiful and mine. His hair smelled like cigarettes. It didn't matter that Matthias didn't smoke, or that technically smoking wasn't allowed in most venues—the smell always clung to him after a show.

"You should take me with you," I said. "Next time."

He accepted the coffee and took a long swallow. "To a show?" He sounded surprised.

"I want to see what all the fuss is about."

He frowned, then took another swig of coffee. "I don't know. You'd have to break curfew. I don't think it would really be your thing."

"Please." I could hear my voice slip dangerously close to a whine. "Let me decide what's my thing." Maybe he was right, maybe I'd hate it. But I wanted to know exactly what I was enabling. I wanted him to invite me in.

The first bell rang, signaling that I had exactly one minute to make it to the third floor. I had Mr. Samuels for homeroom, and he did not mess around with punctuality.

"I'll think about it," Matthias said.

I started backing away from his desk, toward the door. I wanted to stay, wanted to breathe in his smell a little longer, wanted him to promise to take me with him next time.

"Promise?" I asked.

"Promise." Matthias raised his coffee as if in salute as I turned toward the door and slipped back into the hall. All around me, lockers were slamming and everyone else who'd waited until the last possible minute was rushing toward open classroom doors. As soon as I was outside, I sprinted toward the stairwell. I had twenty seconds to make it to homeroom, thirty if you counted to the end of the second bell. If I ran, I could just make it.

NOVEMBER, SENIOR YEAR
(NOW)

Saturday yawns out before me with no plans, no obligations, no expectations. I have an English paper due on Monday, but it's already written. It'll take an hour to edit, tops. My math homework is done, and I'm actually caught up in Spanish. This is what happens when you have no Friday night plans to speak of. When your only structured activities are weekly therapy sessions and the metal shop.

I push back the comforter and reach for the big navy sweatshirt crumpled at the foot of the bed. Shrugging it over my head, I stumble across the room to the air vent, push down the little lever, and let the heat blow full blast.

Down the hall, Mom and Dad have long finished breakfast,

but there's still fruit on the counter and a half-full bag of bagels. I pick out a whole-wheat everything and rummage in the fridge for the cream cheese while Bruiser weaves in and out around my ankles.

"There's lox on the top shelf!" Mom's voice rings out from the family room. "We saved some for you."

As I fill up the coffeepot and plug in the toaster, I try to visualize the weekend in thirty-minute blocks. Breakfast with *Jane Eyre* keeping me company at the dining room table. Thirty minutes. Shower and put on real clothes. Thirty minutes. Fiddle around with my college apps. Two thirty-minute blocks. Then the day goes blank.

While the coffee brews, I peek my head into the family room. Mom is sitting on the sofa, a blanket pulled over her legs and a mug in her hands. She's totally absorbed in an advance reader's copy for the new Ruth Ware thriller. I can see her librarian wheels turning—how many copies to order for the branch she manages, how many in hardcover, how many ebooks.

Dad is at the long table by the windows, his desk, his domain. I can't see for sure from where I'm standing in the doorway, but it's safe to say he has the science sections of at least three major papers spread out in front of him. Peter Holland is basically a professional science geek. He's covered the science and tech beat for the local paper for the past decade, a job he calls "barely work," which is not to say he isn't always working. He was at the office late last night, so this is the first time I've seen him since before school on Friday.

He looks up and spots me in the doorway. "How was the end of your week, sugar?"

Splendid. Just super-duper. This is a variation on Dad's favorite question—*how was your day?* It's like someone—probably Dr.
Marsha—told him that frequent check-ins are important to the
ongoing assessment of my mental health, but he never quite got
past pleasantries. I want Dad to stop asking how my day was so
I can stop lying to his face. But I know it's not his fault; he just
wants me to be happy. I smile and try to give him what he wants.

"It was fine. I put in some more work on that new sculpture
project, the one with the carburetor? I have some ideas for where
it might go." Lie. I've been messing around with that thing for
weeks, and I have zero ideas for where it might go. It's November,
and I still can't make myself focus. I'm losing my touch.

"That's great, sweetie."

Don't ask anything hard, Dad. Don't dig. Don't press.

The coffee hisses, and I duck back into the kitchen. When I'm
settled and two pages into my book, Mom comes into the dining room and sits across from me. Crap. Emma Holland is not
content with pleasantries. She's going to ask me what I'm doing
today and look at me with that Worried Mom Face when I don't
come up with a good enough answer.

"What's on the agenda for today, baby?" she asks, reaching out
to pat my hand. Her smile is a tight line of concern. It makes me
squirm in my seat, and I can feel my insides crackle and pop like
Rice Krispies, but I can't really blame her. I've looked like misery
warmed over for months. If I were her, I'd look at me exactly the
same way.

"I'm going to put in some work on my college apps. And there's
some stuff I've been wanting to check out on Netflix."

Mom's smile crumples.

"Ellory May, I'm starting to regret letting you sign up for that. Don't you want to make plans with Bex? Go out to the mall?"

Right. The mall or the movies or all those other places I've been going with Bex when I've really been down at the river. What Mom doesn't know won't hurt her.

"Sure," I say. "I'll probably call Bex this afternoon." I smile wide and take a big bite of bagel. "This is delicious," I say through a full mouth.

Mom shakes her head and pushes herself up from the table.

"Try to get outside at least once today. Promise?"

"Promise." And I mean it. It hits me that there is somewhere I need to go.

Mom stands in the doorway between the dining room and kitchen and looks at me for a long moment. She wants to say something else, I can tell. Something deep and meaningful. Something only a mom could say to make the world right.

Then she retreats back to her thriller, leaving me to my own devices. It's not her fault for coming up empty. It would take more than mom-powers to make things right again.

Two hours later, I'm stashing the Subaru in its usual spot on a side street near my house and walking down to the river, two vanilla lattes in hand. Scrambling down the bank is a little precarious, but I manage to arrive safely at the bottom, lattes unscathed. Then I walk along the bank toward the hollow Ret likes, the spot where the grass now bears a permanent impression of her back. The river water smells dirtier than usual today, a mix of old fish and mud.

"Fancy meeting you here on a weekend," she says.

She's gotten started without me. Her grin is watery and warm, and she's waving her favorite flask in greeting, the print of a pink cat face getting dull in the spots where her fingers have worn away the paint.

"Figured you could use some company." I keep my voice light. "No fun drinking alone."

Ret accepts one of the lattes and lifts the lid, then pours in a stream of amber liquid from her flask. I've brought my own nips of Bacardi, liberated from the back of the pantry where they've been gathering dust. I empty one into my cup without comment.

I blow across the surface, and the steam swirls up into my face, the rich smell of coffee and the sweet bite of the booze dragging me back to last March. I'd stayed late in the metal shop, even later than normal, so when I emerged into the student lot, it was already getting dark. The Subaru was parked toward the back, where the pavement runs up against a thin strip of woods. It's hardly a forest, just a densely planted thicket of trees about twenty feet deep, separating the school property from the residential area behind it. As I got close to my car, I could hear them. Voices in the woods. *Come on, man. Plant was the seminal front man of the seventies. I don't know how you can make that claim— What, are you fighting for Mercury again? Shit, Freddie Mercury does not even—*

Boys, really? A new voice. Ret's voice. Cutting through the banter, cutting sharp and deep into my heart.

I walked past the Subaru and straight into the woods. They were camped out a few feet in, backs pressed against trees, safe-for-school paper coffee cups raised to their lips. Unmistakable even through the half-light: Matthias, Dave, the Smurf, and Ret, holding her own with the guys, holding up a flask, holding a party without me.

"Ellory." Matthias saw me first, scrambled to his feet. "What are you doing here?"

As if I needed an excuse. I jutted my chin toward the lot. "You're practically tailgating on my bumper."

Ret looked up at me through a haze of whiskey and caffeine. "The more the merrier. Come join the fun!" She leaned toward Dave, but misjudged the distance between them, and collapsed giggling into his lap, liquid sloshing out of her cup and into the pine needles. "Oops!"

I let my eyes wash over the two of them. Jonathan was nowhere in sight. Of course not. They were obviously drunk and asking to get caught. Their coffee cups weren't fooling anyone. But whatever, let them get caught. No one had asked me to hang. *Matthias* hadn't asked me. Ret's invitation rang hollow in my ears, too little too late.

I stood there with a scowl on my face, the perfect girlfriend mask I'd perfected in recent weeks cracking to expose the depths of my hurt. Why was he shutting me out?

The next thing I knew, Matthias's arm was around my shoulders, leading me through the trees, back toward the parking lot. "This isn't your scene," he murmured in my ear. "Let me drive you home."

I shook his arm off. "You're drunk," I snapped. "I can drive myself."

I waited for him to apologize. I waited for him to explain. I waited for him to offer to leave the others behind and come with me—his girlfriend. Not because he wanted me out of there. Because he wanted *me*.

Then I stopped waiting and got in the car. He was right. This wasn't my scene.

"Ellory? Ellory May?" Ret is waving her coffee cup under my nose, luring me back to the present.

"I have to ask you something," I say.

She leans back into the bank and takes a sip. "Thought I lost you there for a sec."

There are so many questions I want to ask about last spring, but we made a promise. *No wallowing in the past.* But even more than that, I need to ask about Abigail. It's the whole reason I came here today. I rationalize that eighth grade is hardly the past we meant; it's basically ancient history. *Ret's* history that's slamming right up against my present.

I drain half my coffee in two swallows and lean back into the bank, my shoulder brushing up against hers. The booze rushes through my insides, warm and tingling.

"So hit me," she says.

"It's about Abigail."

Ret doesn't say anything. Her eyes sharpen, and she unscrews the cap on her flask. Instead of topping up her cup, she lifts it straight to her lips and tilts back her head. It's a warning to keep my mouth shut, but I don't care. Old Ellory would have fallen in line, played my part. But I'm not that girl anymore.

"What really happened between you two, that winter break?"

"Jesus, Ellory. We were practically babies. Who even remembers?"

"She came to talk to me," I say. "The other week in shop."

Ret's head snaps toward me. "What did she say?"

I shrug. "You tell me. What happened over break, Ret?" Even

as the words slip out of my mouth, I know she's not going to say.

She scowls and puts her drink down so she can pick at her nails. "Nothing happened. I didn't do anything, *she* stopped talking to *me*, no reason. She tricks everyone into thinking she's all sweetness and pie, but she's a stone cold bitch, Ellory. I don't want you talking to her."

I take another swallow and practically choke.

"You don't get to tell me who to hang out with. I have no friends because of you. You get that, right?"

Ret takes my hand, pries my gloved fingers apart, slips hers between mine. "You have no friends because of *you*, Ellory. And anyway, you have me. Abigail will poison you against me. Do you want to lose me all over again?"

That's it. Coming here this afternoon was a mistake. Her words are lies and truth all tangled up together, and it's too much. What am I even doing, crawling back to Ret, letting her slip beneath my skin, letting her make me feel like hell all over again?

I extract my fingers from hers and lurch onto my hands and knees, the booze suddenly sour in my stomach. I crawl toward the river, and the smell hits me hard, fish and mud, and then my own vomit, pouring out of my stomach into the water and weeds. When I'm done, I drag my coat sleeve across my mouth. My eyes are stinging.

I don't look at Ret, don't give her the satisfaction. I pull myself to my feet and start walking toward the break in the guardrail.

"Two roads diverged in a wood," she calls out behind me. It's her idea of an apology, a do-over, but I leave her hanging. I keep walking.

OCTOBER, JUNIOR YEAR
(THEN)

I parked the Subaru outside Matthias's house and waited. He had made it apologetically but firmly clear that I was not allowed inside the Cole's "sad museum of neglect." The house looked like it had the potential to be nice, with a little TLC. It was a two-story, for one thing, half siding and half stone. But the paint was cracked and flaking, and the roof tile was peeling up in large flaps. The small front yard was brown in some spots and overgrown in others. I didn't care about any of that, but Matthias held firm.

Then, just when I was starting to think he'd forgotten, he opened an even better door. Two tickets to a show: My Name Is Molly, Friday night at the Crow. As he jogged across the lawn and slid into the Subaru, I glanced up to the second floor, where a window had just snapped from black to yellow light.

"Is that your parents' room?"

He leaned across me to check. I wondered if they wanted to get a look at me as much as I wanted to get a look at them. Before he could answer, a small hand pulled the lacy curtain aside, and Cordelia's face appeared in the window. I watched as he pulled out his phone and started to type.

> Go back to bed, C. I'll be home before you wake up.

> Pumpkin pancakes for breakfast, promise.

In a minute, the window went dark again, and I pulled the car into a three-point turn and headed toward the bridge.

"It's not like she's alone." I glanced over at his frown reflected in the window glass. "Your parents *are* home."

"I know, I know," he agreed. "I still feel bad."

I got it. I worried about Matthias, and Matthias worried about Cordelia. "We should take her out again soon, the two of us. I want her to actually get to know me."

"We'll go to a movie or something next week. She can take a while to warm up to people." *But I'm not just people. I'm your girlfriend.*

I nodded. "It's a date."

He plugged his phone into the MP3 port and started searching for the right track. "This is from FlipFest last August. Consider this the preshow."

I leaned back into the seat and let the music fill up the car. I'd never been to a club before, unless you counted waiting for Matthias outside Sally's Pub, which I didn't. They were all eighteen plus if not twenty-one plus, and I didn't have a fake ID. But Matthias knew the guys who worked the door and said not to worry. Tonight, he'd given them a heads-up about me. Tonight, I was going inside. I was finally going to find out where and how my boyfriend spent so much of his life while I was watching *Center Stage* at Jenni's for the fourteenth time.

Once Matthias had warmed up to the idea, he'd given me a sweet and meticulously detailed rundown on the selection process for tonight's after-hours excursion:

1. There were exactly four venues worth going to downtown, and Crowbar—known as the Crow to its regulars—was at the top of that list. (Sally's was apparently number four out of four.)
2. The Crow was still pretty shitty. But the broken neon fixtures and plastic palm trees were part of its charm.
3. My Name Is Molly was an indie band from Philly that was "worth checking out" now, before they got signed and inevitably sold out to the corporate machine.
4. The lead singer was a dude, not named Molly. The band did have a girl drummer, which was cool, and she was also not named Molly.
5. Matthias thought Molly might be a reference to MDMA, but there was nothing on the blogosphere to definitively support the drug hypothesis.

6. Matthias had recently seen them at FlipFest, so while
    he would still need to take a few pictures for his site,
    he could mostly hang back with me and chill since
    he wasn't doing a full-on review.

Matthias usually "borrowed" his dad's truck when he went to shows, which was easy since Ricky Cole was always passed out on the den couch by nine. It was a short drive across the river from the West Shore, and since the CAT buses never ran when you needed them, and certainly never at night, short-term auto theft was practically mandatory. Tonight, however, I had the Subaru since I'd driven it earlier to Ret's, where I was supposedly staying. It wasn't a total lie. We *had* hung out after school. And sometime before it got light, I would drop Matthias off at home and then ease the car into Ret's drive, slip in through the back door, and burrow into her bed smelling like nighttime and somebody else's cigarettes.

Now, Matthias beside me in the passenger's seat and a bootleg recording pumping through the speakers, I rolled down the driver's side window to let the night air rush in as we drove across the bridge that spanned the Susquehanna. Below us, the river sparkled dark and choppy and mysterious in a way it never did during the day. Driving across the bridge always felt like a kind of alchemy, like I was crossing from the known into the unknown, and I might transform in the process. Even though we were just going to the East Shore, just going to the same strip of bars and restaurants downtown, I still felt a tingle across my skin. Fit to Be Thai'ed, Cordelia, the Crow. One by one, Matthias was opening the windows into his life, allowing me to peer through. He reached across the seat and rested his hand on the bare skin just above my knee.

"Is that a new skirt?" he asked.

Earlier, getting ready at Ret's, I had let her dress me up. I liked long dresses that didn't draw attention to my awkward, coltish legs. But Ret insisted that my usual "hippie shit" had no place at a rock show, so I slipped on her denim skirt and black tank top, and I let her sling a studded belt low across my hips. She finished off the look with a thick coat of Three Alarm Fire gloss and thin stripes of black eyeliner. *You look amazing, Ellory. Matty is going to go wild.*

I could feel his eyes flicker across my legs. I felt like I was wearing a Ret costume, but I also felt good, an edgier version of myself. Like a bit of Ret's confidence had come woven into the fabric of her clothing.

"It's Ret's," I said. "I borrowed it for tonight. You like it?"

He shrugged, lifting his hand from my knee. "Sure. I always like what you wear."

I didn't know if that meant *I kind of hate it, but I'm too polite to say it to your face* or *I wish you'd dress like this all the time.* I wasn't sure how to ask, and then the moment was gone, retreating into the distance with the bridge and the churn of the river.

I turned onto Second and pulled the Subaru into an open spot a little ways down from the Crow. I cut the ignition and sat still for a moment, just taking it in. Across the street, two older couples were leaving an Italian restaurant hand in hand. A few places had set out heat lamps, and their patios were filled with late night diners and groups lingering over glasses of wine. Sally's was doing a good business; I could hear the husky voices of older men shouting along to live music inside, and a cluster of guys in their twenties was standing around out front, smoking. Down the sidewalk, a shoulder-slumped man with a long, gray beard sat collecting change in a cup.

A group of college girls in tight jeans, tight tops, and stilettos that they obviously weren't used to wearing stumbled past us on the sidewalk. One girl tripped, shrieking, and caught herself against the hood of my car with a two-palmed thud. For a moment, her bright blond hair flashed across the windshield. The Subaru was parked, motionless, but I gasped, as if we had crashed, certain for one heart-thudding second that something had gone horribly, irrevocably wrong. Matthias grabbed my hand.

"Sorry!" the girl half shrieked, half laughed as her friends pulled her up, away from us, onward down the street toward whatever establishment would honor their fake IDs.

"I almost had a heart attack." I turned toward Matthias, red heat flooding my cheeks.

"Freshmen. Friday night. You get used to it." He gave my hand a squeeze, then let it go, turning to unclasp his seat belt and open the car door. "In two years, that'll be you."

Two years. College. "That will never be me."

There was no way I was staying in central PA, drinking my way through four years at Dickinson or Penn State. The only place I wanted to go was Portland, all the way across the country in the rainy, coffee-soaked, flannel-wrapped Pacific Northwest. I'd never been, but there was something about the mythology of the place, its indie bookstores and hipster doughnuts and the ever-present rain clouds fleecing the sky. Or at least that's how I imagined it would be. Every time I thought about college, I pictured myself on Portland State's grassy campus in the middle of downtown, drinking coffee and reading a book about late nineteenth-century metalworking against a soundtrack of nineties classics. Nirvana. Silverchair. Soundgarden.

"You *are* going to college, aren't you?" Matthias was out of the car now, his arms resting on the roof, peering down at me through the open passenger's side door. I grabbed my bag from the backseat and joined him outside. *Beep beep.* Locked.

"Of course I'm going to college. Just not here. Not in a halter top and stilettos. I think there's a ban on attire that basic in Portland."

"Oregon?"

"I'm thinking Portland State." I tried to make it sound casual, dropping my keys into my bag as he swung around the back of the car to meet me. I could feel my heart thudding against my chest. I could see us in Portland, together. Matthias, sprawled out on the grass, his head resting in my lap while I read my book, the latest release from a not-yet-discovered West Coast indie band pulsing through his earbuds. He would love it, I was sure.

Now that the image was there, it was impossible to unsee us in Portland. But in that moment, walking across Second Street, I wanted to take back any mention of college. I wanted it too bad— the city, the two of us together there.

"Portland's cool," he said, lacing his fingers between mine, leading me down the sidewalk toward the Crow. And then the conversation was over. I guess he wasn't ready to talk about college either, even though he'd brought it up. I let out a slow stream of breath. We hadn't even stepped inside the Crow yet.

There were probably a few crucial steps separating our first rock show from my college lawn fantasies.

At the door, Matthias leaned in to shake hands with the bouncer, a stone-faced guy with a full sleeve of tattoos, a big gut, and a flashlight for checking IDs.

"Hey, Frank."

"Didn't know I'd be seeing you tonight, Matty. I don't think Rob's around." His voice was warm, unexpected. I stood next to my boyfriend, trying not to shift back and forth on my feet, trying to look cool. Older. Hadn't Matthias said he'd given them a heads-up about me? I let my eyes wander up and down Frank's sleeve. The focal point was a sacred heart pierced by a nasty-looking dagger. Blood poured down the sides. I couldn't tear my eyes away.

"Nah, we're here for the show. Frank, this is Ellory. The girl I was telling you about." His words were easygoing, but there was something tight underneath. I stuck out my hand, and Frank clasped it.

"Ah." He nodded briskly. "Welcome to Crowbar." Some tacit understanding had passed between them, and I was on the out-side. Probably because the understanding had to do with me. "Tickets?"

Matthias opened his wallet and pulled out two folded sheets of paper. I waited while Frank stamped both our hands with something that looked like Bugs Bunny smoking a carrot, or maybe a blunt. Then, Matthias touched my shoulder, ushering me through the door and into the club.

Inside, the room was packed with people waiting for drinks, mostly college kids and twenty-somethings with shaggy hair and black jeans. Red and green string lights flickered above the bar, illuminating signs for Pabst Blue Ribbon and Jim Beam. I looked away, around the rest of the room. A few tables were jammed against the opposite wall, and a sign for the restroom flickered at the far end. I didn't see a stage or any evidence of a band.

"Music's downstairs." Matthias took my hand and steered me away from the bar, through a door to the left.

"Who's Rob?"

"What? No one."

I paused ahead of Matthias on the stairs, and he almost walked into me. I turned to look up at him.

"Seriously, no one. Just a friend of Frank's. Sometimes we all get a drink together after the show. But tonight—" He paused to lean down and kiss the top of my head. His lips were a soft press of heat against my scalp. "—I am here with you."

I knew he was lying to me. But I'd waited long enough to get here. I wasn't about to ruin it before the music even started. I tried to push Frank and Rob out of my mind. As I continued down the stairs, I could feel Matthias's eyes following me, fixed on my long legs in Ret's ridiculously short skirt and my yellow hair flying out against her black top. Suddenly, I longed for the comfort of my own clothes. With the back of my hand, I rubbed at my lips until the red gloss smudged away.

I pushed open the double doors that led into the room at the bottom of the stairs. The band on stage was putting away their equipment, and some song I didn't recognize was blasting through the speakers from the DJ booth.

"Perfect timing."

"What?" I screamed at Matthias against the music.

He leaned down to cup his hand over my ear. "I said perfect timing. That's the second opener packing up. Here." He reached into his pocket and produced two sets of ear plugs. Then he brushed back my hair, and I tilted my head to one side. His hand was cool and dry against my ear, my hair, my neck. With the little pieces of foam in place, the din in the room was suddenly muffled, softened around the edges. Matthias leaned forward and spoke directly into my ear. "My Name Is Molly's going on next. Better, right?"

"Better." Strangely, I could hear him more clearly now.

"Be right back." He ducked toward the small bar in the back of the room.

I dug my phone out of my bag and checked Hot Vampires, our current group chat. I scrolled through the night's messages, which started with an APB from Jenni to come over for scary movies and ginger spice martinis at eight. The rest of the texts were for my benefit.

BEX LANDRY
You're missing some classic slash and
spurt action over here, Ellory.

RET JOHNSTON
Boo Ellory, leaving us all alone.

JENNI RANDALL
It's scaaary!

RET JOHNSTON
Not as scary as Ellory's foray into crime.

JENNI RANDALL
It starts with sneaking out. Where
does it end?

BEX LANDRY
Corrupted by Rock and Roll: The
Ellory Holland Story.

RET JOHNSTON
Will we ever see the West Shore's
good girl gone bad again? Dun dun
duuun…

Jesus. It was only like the third Friday I'd spent with Matthias since we got together. Just a few hours ago, Ret had been dressing me up for tonight, squealing over how good I looked. Now they were all giving me shit for ditching them.

ELLORY HOLLAND
Sorry, ladies. Necessary
anthropological deep-dive.

I pressed send, but I guess the universe didn't want me to defend myself. I only had one bar down here, and the message wouldn't go through.

I shut off my phone and looked around. There were the plastic palm trees on either side of the stage, just like Matthias had described, lit up with more string lights. The room was full enough to look busy, but it wasn't packed like it had been upstairs.

I dropped my useless phone back into my bag and hooked my thumbs around the top of Ret's belt, feeling its strangeness and weight around my hips.

We weren't the only underage people here. I glanced at the faces around me, careful to not get caught staring. I didn't recognize anyone, but there were two girls standing together, with spiky hair and nose piercings, who didn't look older than fourteen, and the place was scattered with pimply high school guys. I guess the bouncer had a few friends. But there were college kids here too, and couples and groups of guys in their twenties and thirties. The floor was sticky, and the air smelled a little like beer and a little like disinfectant.

In a minute, Matthias returned from the bar with a couple of sodas. He handed one to me, then reached into his pocket and brought out a silver flask.

"I only buy soda here." He poured a long stream of something brown into his cup. "The price for keeping up my good reputation with the bouncers."

"I thought you said you go drinking with Frank."

"Sure, but not here. Not under his roof."

Matthias's East Shore world was like an onion. The kitchen, Sally's, the Crow. The errands for Cordelia I still didn't understand. Every time I thought I saw something clearly, he'd peel back another layer. But just a little. Not far enough that I could really get a good view.

He tilted the flask toward me, offering.

"No thanks. I have to get us home later, remember?"

He nodded and slipped it back into his pocket. We were there at the Crow, just like I'd wanted, but everything felt off. There were West Shore secrets—his parents, his house—and East Shore secrets. Most days, I thought Matthias saw me. But sometimes, I didn't know what he saw. Sheltered. Baby. If you added up all the things he wouldn't show me . . . I wasn't sure I saw him, either.

I sipped my whiskeyless soda and kept my thoughts to myself. Matthias brushed his lips against my shoulder blade just as My Name Is Molly strolled onto stage, and the crowd started clapping and shouting. When the music started, Matthias tossed our cups into the trash and stood behind me, wrapping his arms around me, folding me back into his chest. I let myself sink into him until I was buzzing with the energy of the crowd and the band and the drummer, who had a bright pink streak in her hair and the most beautiful arms I'd ever seen, long and lean and strong. And Matthias. His heat. His breath soft and sticky-sweet in my hair. His hands squeezing my arms, my waist, holding me to him, holding me close.

I could feel the music pinging something inside me, something alive and new and partly belonging to him, partly belonging to me. I went to the Crow because I wanted in on my boyfriend's secrets, but I didn't feel on the inside of anything other than the music. Maybe that was the only thing that mattered. I didn't want to think about secrets anymore. I wanted to be there, with him and the music and the heat of the club. I let myself get lost in it.

Five songs into the set, he took out his phone and snapped a few pictures. Then he pressed his lips to my ear. "Gotta run to the bathroom. You'll be okay for a sec?"

I nodded.

"Be right back." He kissed my hair right where it covered the top of my ear, and a shiver shot through me. I turned around to watch him go. He walked toward the bathrooms in the back, then swerved right and ducked up the stairs. I was alone.

I crossed my arms tightly against my chest. Suddenly I was back at Dave Franklin's party, standing in the middle of the living room floor, lying about looking for the bathroom.

"You probably want to skip the one down here," he'd said. "There is another, shall we say, more hygienic option on the second floor."

Except this time, he was the one lying. I tried to listen to the band. Maybe he wasn't lying. Maybe the bathrooms upstairs were cleaner here too. Anyway it's not like he needed my permission. I stared straight ahead and focused on the drummer until I couldn't see anything else, the beads of sweat collecting along her forehead, her lips pressed into a neon knot, her arms slicing wild streaks through the air again and again and again. A few minutes later, Matthias was back, his arms locked tightly around mine like he'd never been gone at all.

NOVEMBER, SENIOR YEAR

(NOW)

She's in front of me before I even realize she's in the hallway, long limbs and ever-so-slightly out-turned feet blocking my path to fourth period. Bex.

It's not as if I've made it through eleven weeks of school without ever seeing her or Jenni, but my routes are solid. They've been mostly avoidable, and it's not like they've come looking for me. Not after I blew Bex off the day before school started. And not that Jenni would ever come looking. I shove my hands in my hoodie pockets, and my fingers close around the folded triangle of notepaper I plucked from the bottom of my locker earlier today.

"I've been trying to catch you all week," she says, but her body says otherwise. Her fingers twist her backpack straps around her hands, and she looks poised to run. "Ellory?"

"Hey," I mutter, forcing my chin up to face her. Directly behind her shoulder is the open door to math class, safe passage to an hour of blissful boredom. All around us, students are walking toward open doors. When they near Bex and me, they give us a wide berth, a tide of bodies parting like we're the island and they're the stream.

All I want to do is follow them toward class, slip into my seat a minute early, unfold this week's note beneath my desk. Bex has lunch now. She should be headed up two more floors to the sky dome, not that I have her schedule memorized or anything.

"Listen." Her voice is determined, but I can see a russet flush rising in her deep brown cheeks. She wraps and unwraps the black straps around her hands. She doesn't want to be talking to me either. "We're going to see my grandparents in Montreal over the break, so we're hosting a kind of pre-Thanksgiving at my house on Sunday. It'll be mostly dance team, a few of my parents' friends. It would be nice if you came."

I don't know what to say. I can feel my eyebrows arching toward the ceiling.

Bex lets the straps fall to her sides and shoves her hands in her pockets. I know that trick; your fingers can't fidget if they're tucked away. "My mom asked about you," she says. She drops her voice to a stage whisper. "I told her you didn't need any handouts, but she thinks I'm not making an effort."

"It's not—" I start to say. *Personal. About you. Good enough.*

"Forget it," she whisper-hisses. "You haven't been around all semester. I got the message. But I said I would ask, and I asked."

So she doesn't actually want me there. She's just humoring her mother. It stings for a second, even though I have no right to feel hurt, but then I realize this is better. It would be worse if she actually cared.

"I can't this Sunday. We're getting the house ready for the aunties."

Bex withdraws her hands from her pockets and returns to twisting her backpack straps. "Fine then. If you change your mind, dinner's at four. I assume you still know where I live."

At the end of the hallway, the door to the girls' bathroom swings open, and I watch Ret walk out into the hall. I haven't been back to the river since I left her there last weekend. She pauses midstep when she sees me talking to Bex. Her mouth hangs slightly open in a very un-Ret-like manner. For weeks, she's kept her promise. *If you see me in the halls, you ignore me.* But I dug up Abigail on Saturday, and then I left her hanging. I wouldn't blame her for thinking our deal is off.

For a minute I think she's going to come over here, get in my face again like she did last spring, but then she walks coolly to the water fountain and takes a long drink.

"Ellory?" Bex turns to look behind her shoulder, following my dazed stare down the hall toward Ret.

"Tell your parents thanks anyway," I say.

The second bell rings, and classroom doors start to close.

I push past Bex and hurry down the hall. Ms. Elkins is standing in the doorway, her hand on the knob, waiting. But when I get to the door, she holds out her arm to stop me.

"Why don't you stay after class, Ellory?" she asks, her voice low and soothing. "I'd like to take a few minutes, check in."

I'm pretty sure this has nothing to do with math. I watch her eyes follow Bex as she disappears into the stairwell and the door swings closed. I want to say *no, thank you*, but something tells me this is an invitation I'm not allowed to decline. I nod, and she lets me into the room.

As I slide into my seat and dig my book out of my bag, I try to forget the note of concern in her voice. Had she been eavesdropping on my conversation in the hall? No matter what my math teacher thinks, I know what I'm doing. I do have to help my mom get the house ready for the descent of her two sisters and their families this weekend. It's not like I could go to Bex's thing anyway, even if she actually wanted me there, even if I wanted to go.

"A little housekeeping before we get started," Ms. Elkins is saying from the front of the room. "Your chapter five exam is on Wednesday. Don't leave the entire review packet to the night before."

Don't worry, Ms. Elkins. I'm already halfway through. Gold star for Ellory. I open up my text and smooth down my homework on my desk, then I tune her out. I reach into my pocket and carefully unfold the little triangle in my lap. I tell myself I can stop reading the notes any time, that they contain more questions than answers, that I should probably do myself a favor and set them on fire. Not that I haven't gotten myself in enough trouble that way before.

But I can't help it. I have to know what they say, even if they don't say much of anything. I start to read. *I know how it sounds—a cop out, a cliché—but I couldn't stop things. So I fucked it all up. Beyond repair. On purpose.*

On purpose? My fingers gravitate to the black band around my wrist. It's tight, but I twist until I'm sliding it around and around my skin. Then I refold the note and silently slip it back into my hoodie pocket. I think about all the things I'm not telling Dr. Marsha. The notes. Abigail. Ret. Drinking myself sick. She'd be so disappointed in me. I'm disappointed in myself, but I can't help it. How am I supposed to live in the present if I can't even understand the past? If I told her, she could help me solve it, but I'm not ready to let her. I have to work this out on my own. But from where I'm sitting—November, senior year, Ms. Elkins reviewing inverse trigonometric functions on the board—trying to put last April in crystal clear focus is like trying to check your makeup in a fun house mirror. Except a lot less funny.

It hits me that this is exactly how I used to see Matthias's world. An onion, endless layers. You know you're going to end up with stinging eyes and tears streaming down your face. But you grit your teeth. You keep peeling the layers back.

15

"On Monday I have gymnastics at Holy Trinity. Mommy says they have a real gym with the beam and the uneven bars and the vault because it's privately funded by the pope. On Wednesdays and Fridays I have soccer after school, and then sometimes we have games on Saturdays, but if we don't we have weekend practice. Then on Tuesdays and Thursdays I have ballet with Madame Simpson at Little Miss Dance Studio."

I took Cordelia's outstretched hand and held it high while she spun around. Her life sounded exhausting.

"Madame *Simpson*?" I asked. "That doesn't sound very French."

Cordelia gave me a puzzled look. We were on the lower tier of the Crestview Mall, my first return excursion for anything but new gym shoes since June. It was our fourth time hanging out, and I still felt like we were in the "getting to know you" stage. And even though Matthias wouldn't say it directly, Cordelia's approval clearly mattered.

"She's not." He reached down to tug his sister's long, messy ponytail. "I think Madame Simpson is Greek. But like in a bleached blond, fourth generation, *Real Housewives* kind of way."

"Madame Simpson says that in ballet all the girls call the teacher 'Madame' and the teacher calls the girls 'Mademoiselle.' I'm Mademoiselle Cordelia." Her eyes were eager, her face the epitome of nine-year-old seriousness.

I laughed. "I think Madame Simpson is pulling your leg, but that's pretty cute."

Her lips turned instantly into a scowl. Wrong move. "I am not cute," she insisted. "I am graceful and ripped."

She bent her arms into a display of wiry kid muscles before spinning off in a series of twirls and leaps while Matthias and I hung back by the cell phone kiosk.

"She's good, huh?" he asked.

"Yeah, she is." She was no Bex, but I had to admit, the kid had promise.

"She's seriously smart too. It hasn't dawned on her yet what complete deadbeats her parents are."

"You make her life normal." I reached over and slipped my hand into his hand, but he wasn't looking at me. For a moment, Matthias was somewhere else entirely.

Then, he kissed the top of my head, which he could barely do without lifting up onto his tiptoes. His lips felt like paper against my hair. Light, fluttering. Something jolted in my stomach, something deep and demanding and powerful. I leaned against his chest, sinking into the slightly sweaty smell of his T-shirt and the press of my cheek into his neck.

"Ew!" Cordelia was back, breathless and grinning. "You guys are all mushy. Can we get ice cream?"

I tugged on the strap of my bag and gathered my long, fine hair over one shoulder, as if by making a few small adjustments, I could snap my brain back in line.

"Sure thing, Cordelia-bean," Matthias replied. "Carvel or Baskin-Robbins?"

Cordelia steered us toward the food court, then broke away. She had skipped ten steps ahead when my phone chimed. Ret.

You guys still at Crestview?

                                                    Yeah. Food court.

Stay there, I'm on break.

"Ret's on her way," I said to Matthias. "You mind?"

"Course not. She can hang."

Cordelia was waving us toward Carvel. I ran toward her, leaving Matthias to catch up, and grabbed her hand. She beamed up at me and took long, purposeful steps, matching her pace to my long gait.

"Hey, losers." Ret paused to give Matthias a half hug, then strolled up to Cordelia and me. "Who's the squirt?"

"I'm Cordelia." She clutched my hand tighter, and there was a hint of defiance in her voice. "Who're you?"

"Oh, yeah, Matty's little sis. I'm Ret. I go to school with Ellory and your brother."

"Your earrings are cool." Her gaze was fixed on the little pink skulls dangling from Ret's ears.

"Thanks, squirt." Ret leaned down to study Cordelia's bare ears. "Yours pierced yet?"

She shook her head, no.

"Tell you what. When you get your ears pierced, tell Matty here to let me know. I'll get you a matching pair, any color you want. We have it all at Hot Topic."

"You," Matthias said, "are trouble." He turned to his sister, who was still beaming up at Ret. "No pierced ears until you're twelve, got it?"

"Yeah, I know." She scuffed the toe of her shoe against the floor. It was amazing. Ret had been here all of three minutes, and already she had Cordelia wrapped around her finger. A pang of jealousy knifed through my chest, but I swallowed it back. Ret was just being Ret. Ushering disciples to her altar was what she did best.

"Ooh, new subjects, three o'clock!" Ret grabbed my shoulders and spun me around to face the Chinese buffet. The Coles turned with me to look.

Ret pretended to adjust a nonexistent pair of glasses. "Dr. Holland, observe Human Subjects X and Y at the window table by Panda Express. Would you say we're at orange or full-on red alert?"

Bad Parents was one of our favorite games. You could play almost anywhere, but the mall was always a prime spot for discord.

"Good question, Dr. Johnston." I pursed my lips and scribbled into an imaginary notepad. Ret and I liked to pretend we were ecologists in the field, researching human behavior. "Subject X has affixed monkey backpack leash to Subject Y in an apparent effort at containment. Subject X is presenting total iPhone dependence while Subject Y rolls around in what appears to have once been pork fried rice on the food court floor."

Ret turned to Matthias, inviting him to play. "Dr. Cole?"

He considered. "I'd say we're at yellow headed toward orange. I've seen worse."

"A generous classification from Dr. Cole," I said.

Ret rested her chin between her thumb and forefinger and leaned forward, totally absorbed. "Critical update: Subject X has put down the phone. Will she notice Subject Y's transformation into a Floor Monster?"

"Nope, she's going for the lipstick refresh." I shook my head and pretended to update my notebook.

"Definite bump to orange." Matthias reached down to give his sister's shoulder a squeeze. "C'mon, C. Carvel time."

I took Cordelia's hand, and she led me up to the counter.

"You know what you want?" I asked.

She turned around and looked at Ret. "What kind do you like?"

"Cake mix, all the way. In a cone, rainbow sprinkles."

"Can I try the cake mix kind?" Cordelia asked, and the kid behind the counter handed her a little plastic spoon.

I glanced back toward the Panda Express, where the mom had her kid propped up on a table. She was furiously brushing him off, and whatever she was saying, he was clearly in trouble. Poor tyke.

"You want kids?" Ret asked. She and Matthias were standing right behind us.

"Definitely. You don't know my parents, but they'd be perfect for your game. I have this running list of everything I would do better."

"Yeah, my parents are the worst. My mom still thinks she's twenty-five, and my dad's basically just a check in the mail."

"He's not around?" Matthias asked.

"Kansas, since I was ten."

"Cordelia's almost ten. Ours are both around, in the technical sense, but they may as well be in Kansas. *You* want kids?"

"If I make it to my thirties, maybe," Ret replied.

"Are you ready to order?" The kid behind the counter was talking to me. Cordelia was already holding a towering cone covered with rainbow sprinkles. I didn't know Matthias wanted kids. I'd never asked. He'd never asked me either. I guessed it was easier to have that conversation with Ret.

"Chocolate," I said, answering the easy question.

Matthias got mint chip, but Ret declined, looking mournfully at her phone. "Time to get back to the poser-punks." She walked backward for a couple steps, blowing us all kisses, then spun on her heel and took off. I watched two sets of Cole eyes follow her until she was out of sight.

"She's pretty," Cordelia said through a mouthful of sprinkles.

My boyfriend's lips parted into a slow smile as he reached down to tug his sister's ponytail. "Not as pretty as you, Cordelia-bean," he said. Then he leaned over to kiss my cheek and reached into his pocket to pay for our sugar boost. "My treat."

NOVEMBER, SENIOR YEAR
(NOW)

The Holland family turkey is carved at two. I stay at the table just long enough to convince the aunties and their respective families that everything's just great. Rock solid grades. Artistic portfolio complete, courtesy of art camp. (No thanks to wherever my brain has been these past three months, but they don't need to know that.) College apps ready to go. Nothing to see here.

So no one objects when I slip away to drive downtown. It's hard to argue with volunteer work on Thanksgiving. My mom was positively glowing when I told her I'd made plans to put in a shift at Capital Harvest with "a few new friends from school." It's not a complete lie. I am going to the food kitchen, and I am looking forward to a couple hours of helping others. But I'm only meeting one person from school, and calling Abigail a friend is a bit of a stretch. I'm not in the market for new friends, but I can't get Ret's words out of my ears. *I don't want you talking to her. Abigail will poison you against me.*

Ret doesn't get to call the shots. Not anymore. So three weeks after she found me in the shop on Halloween, I tracked Abigail down in the sky dome yesterday at lunch. She and her mom were supposed to volunteer together this afternoon, but some sort of deadline came up at work. I said I'd take her mom's spot.

As I drive across the Market Street Bridge, I let my thoughts wander back to last Thanksgiving. I spent hours curled up on the couch with Auntie Darla, peppering her with questions about her job as assistant curator of East Asian art at the Philadelphia Museum of Art, until my cousin Zach ran his Thomas the Tank Engine through my mom's chocolate pie. I can barely picture the girl who tossed Zach up in the air until he squealed while Auntie Pauline scrubbed brown streaks off the carpet. The girl who slipped away after dark to gather at Jenni's for a holiday debrief and late night screening of *The Ice Storm*. The memories make my heart pulse with something like nostalgia mixed with bitter bile.

I find a spot down the block from Capital Harvest and shift the Subaru into park. Then I close my eyes and picture my former friends' faces. It's something Dr. Marsha taught me. A technique for forgiveness, for letting go. You visualize an event or person or place on a giant balloon, and you let yourself feel all those feelings you can't get rid of. The ones that hold you back, that burn so deep a pit of anger and hurt ignites beneath your skin. And when the wind kicks up, you set the balloon free. The bad memories float away along with the pain.

I made a list for Dr. Marsha. People, dates, words, rooms. We did the visualizations together, but the one balloon I was never able to release was the one holding my own face. I pretended that it worked. That I had let it go. But every time the wind kicked up, the cord yanked fast around my hands, binding me to the pain, dragging me up along with it into the storm.

I open my eyes and let the East Shore register around me. Capital Harvest is on a side street made up of boxy concrete buildings, mostly warehouses and mini-storage units. The sign out front is friendly, an engraved wooden plaque hanging from an iron post. It looks more like the doorway to a cheery tavern than a food kitchen, which I guess is the point. I walk inside to find a big room with a bunch of long tables and a serving counter up front. The place is warm and filled with people, and it smells intensely like gravy. I find the woman with a clipboard, checking in volunteers. Her name tag reads PEG, one of those old-fashioned nicknames you never hear anymore. I tell her I'm Mary Pérez, Abigail's mom's name, and she doesn't blink at my blond hair or fair skin. She hands me an apron and points me toward a bussing cart.

"You put empty plates in here, keep the silverware separate. And scrape trash into this bag. Only clear a place after the guest has gotten up. Kitchen's through that door when your bins are full."

"Got it." I take the cart and start wheeling down the first row of tables. It's toward the end of their dinner service, so there's a lot of bussing to do. I fill up my bins, taking care not to disturb the men and women silently chewing their turkey and potatoes, the families grinning over coffee and slices of pie. I know I should be thinking something meaningful here about how lucky I am to have a warm house to go back to filled with family and leftovers. I know I should be thanking a higher power—God or Joan of Arc or Frida Kahlo—for the many blessings in my life. I reach for an empty plate, and my insides crunch as I bend over the table. I can picture the ash flaking off the cavern inside, collecting at the pit of my stomach.

It's Thanksgiving. I'm well fed and warm and bussing plates at a food kitchen, and all I can do is feel sorry for the girl I've become. It makes me hate myself even more.

I need to find Abigail.

It doesn't take long until my bins are full, so I wheel the cart back toward the kitchen. When I push through the door, Abigail is carrying a giant tray of mashed potatoes that looks heavier than she is to the back end of the service counter. She slots it into an open rack, then sees me by the sink.

"Help me with these?" I ask.

Abigail walks over and grabs a stack of plates. "Service is almost over," she says. "I think that was the last batch of potatoes."

Another busser, a middle-aged guy with tiny glasses slipping down his nose, wheels his cart into the kitchen.

"Unload these, and I'll go out for another round?" he asks. We agree, and he grabs an empty cart.

For a minute, we make conversation about the holidays as we rinse plates and load them into a big commercial dishwasher. She and her mom have been volunteering here for years. This year they signed up for the last shift of the day because her mom needed to work this morning, and then the morning became the whole day. Abigail shrugs, forever positive. Her mom really loves her job at an advocacy nonprofit for gender-based violence prevention, and all the food Abigail cooked will still be good late tonight. After all, leftovers are the best part of Thanksgiving.

I tell her about the aunties, about the chocolate pie and pumpkin bread pudding I'll be returning to when the shift is over. Then, when the small talk evaporates in the air between us and there's still a second heaping cart to unload, Abigail pauses to look at me.

"I know you didn't come here for the community service points."

She's right. Except for the metal shop and a few artistic awards, the activities section of my college apps is pathetically bare. No amount of scrambling now would make up for my lack of initiative over the last three years. I could blame Ret, her blatant disdain for extracurriculars, but the choice was all mine. I devoted the first three years of high school to her, to Jenni and Bex, and eventually to Matthias. *Two roads diverged in a yellow wood . . .*

"I wanted to know," I start, but then I don't know how to finish. I want to know what really happened between Abigail and Ret over break, what Ret wouldn't tell me. I want to know how she closed the chapter on Ret so neatly, went on to move through high school completely unscathed. Captain of the Rockette dance line for the Pine Brook Marching Band, surrounded by friends, perpetually cheerful and bright. Perhaps the real question is how she and her mom moved past her father, how she didn't let the pain he caused define her. As I tie off the first bag of trash and look around for somewhere to put it, it hits me that maybe I've answered my own question—Abigail doesn't let pain define her. Or maybe Ret never had the hold over Abigail that she has over me.

"I just wanted to ask," I start again, but then falter. When I still can't finish, Abigail speaks up.

"You wanted to ask something about Ret?" she prompts.

I find the row of garbage bins lined up behind a counter and toss the bag inside. The busser with the tiny glasses returns with another full cart and drops it off with us, exchanging it for the cart we've emptied. We have a pretty good system going.

"I'm not sure what," I admit when Abigail and I are alone again at the sink. "I think I just want to understand what happened, and how you moved past everything."

She chews on the corner of her lip, considering. "Before Ret, my life was one giant push to be perfect. Perfect grades, perfect weight, perfect attendance, perfect volunteer record." She laughs, seeing the look on my face. "If you think that's how I am now, you should have known me in middle school. I was obsessed. If I could be perfect, maybe my parents would stop fighting. It was ridiculous; it didn't even make sense. But I was thirteen, what can I say?"

"And Ret fit into that how?"

"She didn't. That was the whole point. I was so stressed out, and Ret was like an escape route, daring me to break the rules, let go. She was almost like a drug."

"Until she wasn't?"

"Until being friends with Ret was just another way of trying to be perfect. Her rules, her plans, her dares. It wasn't freedom; it was just a different cage. When we got back to school, she was on a rampage about this Philly trip I'd missed." She launches into a classic Ret story: how Ret had devised a weekend escape plan for herself, Jenni, and Abigail, gotten bus tickets and everything, but at the last minute Abigail couldn't go and the whole thing fell apart. "I felt bad about ditching out, but honestly it wasn't my biggest problem that week. When school started back up, I was going to explain everything, about moving into the motel, how my mom turned off my phone when my dad wouldn't stop calling. But Ret just went off about how I'd ruined her entire break. She was all about what *I'd* done to *her*, how I'd let her down. She didn't want to hear my side; she just wanted an apology."

"Did you ever tell her?" I ask.

"I guess I figured she'd hear about my dad eventually. Or not. I know it sounds horrible for me to say this now, but I didn't need negative people in my life. Moving on wasn't so hard. I didn't miss her."

We work on our bins silently. Grab, rinse, load. Grab, rinse, load. The dishwasher is almost full. I realize that's the difference between Abigail and me—moving on wasn't hard for her. Life without Ret wasn't something that filled her insides with ash. This afternoon has been nice, but in the end, Abigail doesn't get what I'm going through at all.

After a moment, she speaks up again. "I don't know how to say this exactly, but I've seen you down by the river."

My head snaps up. "You were spying?"

"Not on purpose. Sometimes I jog that way. I saw you a few weeks ago, going down the bank at that place where the guardrail's broken."

"You followed me?" I wonder if she heard us talking. What she's seen. I think about the empty bottles and coffee cups

Ret and I haven't exactly been meticulous about cleaning up. I should bring a trash bag down there soon. Save the planet. Clear away the evidence.

Abigail tucks a wayward curl behind her ear and looks at me with big, kind eyes. "Not exactly. If you lean over the rail right before the river bends, you can see down to that hollow in the bank. Sometimes when I'm jogging I stop and check, just to see if you're there. I'm sorry."

Heat floods to my cheeks. I put down the plate I'm holding and wipe my hands on my apron. *She knows.* I should be mad at her for spying, but her face is so open, so filled with concern. Mostly I just feel embarrassed. She's practically a stranger, and she's seen me at my weakest. Naked, exposed.

"It's not what you think," I start to say. Me going back to Ret. Even though that's exactly what it is. "I mean, it's over now." And in that moment, I know it's true. I've felt it for days, ever since I left her there that Saturday. I'll go back to pick up the bottles, do my part. But I'm not going back to her.

"I'm not judging," Abigail insists. "I'm not here to tell you to get over it or move on, or anything like that."

"But that's what you did, right?"

"That was different. I would never compare—"

"I know."

A man and a woman wearing thick rubber gloves come over to run the dishwasher and set about scrubbing the remaining dishes by hand. Abigail is sent off to collect trash bags, and someone directs me toward a vacuum. When I push through the door into the main room, I'm surprised to find it nearly empty. Dinner is over.

While I vacuum under the tables, I consider my options. Abigail is sweet, but I would never fit in with her crowd of Rockettes and Leadership Council kids. This isn't about trading Ret for someone new. This is about letting Ret go. About starting to figure out what comes next.

I finish my chore and check in with Peg. She tells me I can go, wishes me a happy Thanksgiving. I find Abigail in the kitchen before heading out.

"Thanks for letting me take your mom's spot today."

"Of course," she says brightly. "If you ever want to volunteer again, just let me know."

"Thanks," I say, knowing I won't take her up on it. Not that she's not perfectly nice. Not that I didn't actually enjoy myself today. It would probably be good for me—not to mention the world—to give back a little more. But if I learned anything today, it's that Abigail doesn't hold any magic solutions. I need to focus on figuring things out for myself. What letting go of the past actually looks like.

I say goodbye to Abigail and get back in my car. On the drive home, I picture the rest of my senior year. It's not even half over; there's a little more than six months to go. I've made it this far on my own, but not really. I may have kept Ret a secret, but she was still there, still mine. Without her, I'll be totally alone. I grip the wheel until my knuckles go white and wonder if I'll really go through with it. When I can't think about Ret anymore, I let my thoughts drift to pumpkin bread pudding. Chocolate pie.

17

"*Step Up, Center Stage, Stomp the Yard*, or *Honey*?" Bex was sitting cross-legged on the braided rug in Jenni's TV room, holding court, holding up four DVDs from her massive collection of all things choreographed dance sequence.

"Shouldn't we add *Magic Mike* to that list?" I asked. Three heads turned to stare at me. "What, not refined enough for our tastes?"

"It's just we watched that last week," Bex said.

"Which you might know if you ever turned up for movie night anymore," Jenni added, looking up at me from the floor. She looked genuinely kind of hurt. "I made pumpkin chai margaritas last Friday."

"Pumpkin *chai-mai*!" Bex practically sang, clutching Jenni's wrist, and both girls collapsed into a fit of giggles on the TV room rug. *I miss a couple Fridays, and they already have new in-jokes?*

Ret didn't say anything, just shifted her weight on the couch so her legs pressed sharply into mine. Then she twisted around on the cushions and leaned down to run her fingers through Jenni's hair.

I winced. I'd missed two movie nights out of the last four, but I couldn't help it that Friday was the only time I could feasibly sneak out to go to shows with Matthias. When I received a repeat invitation, I wasn't about to turn it down. Last week we'd seen Golden Jackal, a new band from Pittsburgh that I thought was kind of meh, but Matthias couldn't stop talking about their guitarist. Anyway.

"I brought crack-snakes?" I offered, pulling a giant bag of our favorite sugar-coated gummy worms out of my overnight bag.

Bex's eyes lit up. She snatched it from my hand and tore into the plastic. "And all is forgiven. Anyway, I'd be down for watching the sequel if we can find it online."

By eight, we'd settled on an all-Channing Tatum double feature of *Step Up* followed by *Magic Mike XXL*. I reached across Ret and plucked a slice of aged gouda from the plate on the end table. Jenni had put together one of her characteristically classy appetizer selections. Tonight it was fall vegetable crudités and creamy watercress dip, poached shrimp crostini, and a cheese plate from the international market at Wegmans.

"Pass one of those shrimp thingies?"

I picked up the plate and handed it to Ret. She held a tiny toast up to the light.

"Did you know flamingos turn pink from eating shrimp? Thank Maude that doesn't happen to us. I would turn shit-green from all the kale Veronica's been force-feeding me this week. She's on some kick."

Bex narrowed her eyes at Ret and me. "Shh, ladies. Channing and his crew are about to get busted trashing the school. This is critical stuff."

Ret's eyebrows shot up, but before she could say anything, Bex folded forward into a remarkable display of flexibility, blocking Ret out. Somehow, from her position parallel to the floor, her eyes were still fixed on the screen.

Ret's mouth hung open for a second, then she popped the shrimp toast onto her tongue and leaned back into the couch. Point Bex; only she had the power to leave Ret speechless.

I checked my phone, but there were no new messages. Matthias was still working at the restaurant, but he'd be heading over to Sally's soon. I wasn't sure what bands he was seeing tonight, just that I hadn't been invited. Which was totally fine; I owed tonight to the girls. But he'd promised to text me pictures from the show.

Jenni glanced at me glancing at my phone. "How's Matty?" she whispered.

"Just checking the weather," I whispered back. "It's freezing in here."

I turned off my screen and dug around for a Henley in my bag. Jenni's house was big and drafty, and even in the little TV room, it was still below optimal sleepover temperature for November. I found my shirt and pulled it on over Ret's Nirvana tee, which I'd had on loan since freshman year and she was probably never getting back.

"Ellory Ellory Ellory." Ret tugged on my sleeve and stage whispered under her breath, all melodrama and spark.

I raised my eyebrows, angling to avoid another shushing from Bex.

"Major S-O-S. Kitchen?"

Jenni's eyes flickered over us. I'd barely managed to leverage myself back into my friends' good graces. The last thing I needed was to set Jenni off by monopolizing Ret.

"I'm sorry," I mouthed. I gestured for her to come with us, secretly hoping she'd decline. Jenni looked like she was about to push herself up from the floor, but then she shrugged and popped a purple carrot into her mouth. The bright TV light flickered across her face.

I could still feel her eyes as I grabbed Ret's hand and pulled her out of the TV room. I shrugged them off. We stumbled through the hall and into the kitchen before Jenni could change her mind. Before Bex could call us out for talking through the first Jenna Dewan-Channing Tatum senior showcase rehearsal. Before I could think too much about what it meant to be Ret's favorite.

The kitchen counters were a total mess of cheese wrappers and vegetable peels. I pulled out a chair from the table and sat down. Ret brushed off a section of counter and perched on the edge.

"So spill. We're missing the male pirouette action."

"Sorry, private debriefing necessary. Jonathan invited me over for Thanksgiving."

"Okay, and . . . ?"

"And?" Ret looked at me like I was bat-shit. "That's like a major holiday. With his whole freaking family."

"So don't go. Say you're doing dinner with your mom. Which you probably are anyway?"

"I already told him how we do Thanksgiving at regular dinnertime in the Johnston household. His Thanksgiving starts at one."

"So say you have to help cook."

"Ellory May, he knows I do not cook."

"Margaret, Jesus. All I'm saying is make something up if you don't want to go. You're resourceful. Be resourceful!"

Ret slid down from the counter and pulled out a chair, then hid her face in her arms at the table.

"You are *so* lucky you don't have to deal with Matty's family. You do realize you're getting a total pass in the boyfriend-parent department."

Did Ret even hear herself? I would have killed to snag an invite inside the Cole's home on a regular day, let alone Thanksgiving. I slid my phone out of my pocket and clicked it on. No new messages. "I guess that's one way to look at it."

Ret lifted her head slightly, just enough to stare up at me through a curtain of tousled hair. I put my phone away before she could see. "Trust me, Ellory. This is the end of the world."

When there were cracks in Ret's facade, it was my job to patch her back up again. Under the thick layer of theatrics, she actually seemed to care about Jonathan. And she was definitely going to mess it up if I didn't nudge her in the right direction. I brushed a piece of hair behind her ear.

"Let's make a list." I went over to the fridge and took the magnetic notepad off the door. "We'll start with the bad stuff, since that is clearly where your brain is. Cons of going to Thanksgiving at Jonathan Gaines's house. Go."

"For starters, his family is going to think I'm a freak. What am I going to say when they ask what the hell their son sees in me?"

"They are not going to ask you that. They're going to be way too stuck-up and polite to ask probing questions. Just leave the black eyeliner and snakeskin stilettos at home, and you'll be good to go. Next?"

"I'd have to tell my mom where I'm disappearing for several hours in the middle of the day. She knows I avoid your house with all the aunties like the plague."

"Hey, watch it with the aunties. Tell her the truth, what's the big deal?"

"The big deal is then I'd have to tell her about Jonathan."

I could feel my eyebrows arch up. "You mean tell her how serious things are, or tell her that he exists at all?"

"The second one."

"Ret, you've been going out since summer. You went to homecoming together!"

"My mom isn't one to 'take an interest.' You know how she is."

It wasn't really true. Veronica Johnston would have gone ape-shit over every single Jonathan Gaines detail. But Ret liked to punish her mom for not noticing things. She liked to keep secrets.

I let Ret's misdiagnosis slide. "This doesn't have to be such a big deal. Look, pros. First off, Jonathan is totally head-over-heels for you. He wouldn't have asked otherwise. Second, you get an inside look at an all-American Thanksgiving. I bet they'll even recite the Pledge of Allegiance or say a prayer about the football game. Third, major girlfriend points with his mom and dad."

"I'll think about it." Somewhere between the beginning and

end of my pros list, Ret had pulled herself back together. All the drama was gone from her face like it had never even been there. She was cool and untouchable. Above it all. She'd go or she wouldn't, who cared?

I could hear Bex and Jenni from the TV room, shrieking as the music pitched up through the speakers.

Ret would go. She cared. She'd tell me about it later, like it was just a good story, like it was no big deal. I watched her spin the black band on her wrist around and around. *You are the sun, and I am the moon.*

"We're missing the critical influence of hip-hop on the contemporary moment in modern ballet," I said, nonchalant, matching her beat for beat. Ret smiled.

We slid back into the TV room, collecting sideways glances from the other girls. I sank into the couch cushions and checked my phone again. Maybe the show hadn't started yet. Maybe he'd let his battery die.

Ret kicked her legs up on the back of the couch and scarfed some goopy Italian cheese. "This is beyond amazing," she whispered to Jenni. "You should be, like, what do you call a cheese specialist?"

"A cheese monger?" Jenni asked, grinning.

"The cheesiest mongress," Ret agreed.

Jenni's face glowed in the blue TV light. Bex passed me the gummy worms, Channing and Jenna fell in love, and I wrapped myself in a giant knit blanket and nestled back into the couch beside Ret. I told myself everything was fine. With Matthias, with my friends. I told myself the universe was thrumming along in perfect equilibrium.

DECEMBER, SENIOR YEAR
(NOW)

This morning, school is a blur because my college applications are in. Thanksgiving is over, and only three weeks of Pine Brook stretch between me and winter recess. Submitting my apps gives me a new kind of hope. I'm moving forward. In a few months, I'll be moving far, far away. I can picture the notifications popping up on the admissions systems at my five schools. *New application from Ellory May Holland. Ping.* I picture the campuses coming to life this morning, the admissions staff arriving to work, getting their coffees, turning on their computers. *There's only one that really matters,* I want to tell them. *Skip down to Holland. Read that one first.*

My good mood lasts until math, when a note lands on my desk

in the middle of quadratic equations. I look around, but no one catches my eye. I know I shouldn't let my curiosity get the better of me, but I can't help it. I unfold the paper. It's a poor excuse for a pen sketch of an overgrown toddler, evidently supposed to be me, throwing a temper tantrum and screaming bloody murder. An adult, apparently Principal Keegan, stands over Toddler Ellory and wags his finger. The speech bubble extending from his mouth reads *Ellory Holland, you can serve your suspension IN HELL!*

My insides crunch and buckle. I crumple up the paper and shove it into my bag. Across the room, Tina Papadakis and Courtney Drummond erupt into a fit of barely disguised giggles. Ms. Elkins calmly asks them to stay after class, then resumes her overview of graphing for real roots, and everywhere around me, fingers fly across calculator buttons.

I try to shake it off, but the day is ruined. It's been weeks since anyone has bodychecked me in the halls or shouted my name across the parking lot. I let my guard down, and now I'm paying for it.

At lunch, I skip the metal shop and head toward the empty green room behind the theater. I need to be alone; even the minimally intrusive company of Mr. Michaels seems like too much today. I sit on the worn couch, the only piece of actually green furniture in the small changing room, and bite into my sandwich. I want to go back to my college admission fantasies, but the green room presses on the edge of my memories, drags me back to sophomore year. Jenni and Bex were auditioning for the musical that winter, and that's when we discovered the large and windowless storage room that held Pine Brook's collection of costumes from decades of plays. We spent huge swaths of January afternoons trying on wigs and petticoats, sending snaps to each other, each picture wilder than the next.

I can clearly see Bex on the day she uncovered a jaw-dropping white mink coat. She's right there in front of me, emerging like a movie star from the costume closet and spinning around for us in front of the brightly lit makeup mirrors, the white fur almost glowing against her deep brown skin. Her voice is crisp and bright in my ears: "Pine Brook is letting this go to waste. This little mink would find a much better home at Chez Bex."

"You can't just take that," I said, waiting for Ret to back me up. "That coat belongs to the school. They're going to notice a missing floor-length mink."

We all looked to Ret to decide. It's funny-not-funny in a bitter, acid burn kind of way. How we turned our heads like a sea of lemmings. How we trotted behind her, prepared to cliff-dive in her wake.

Ret was flipping through an old issue of *Rolling Stone*, her head on the armrest and boots kicked up across the back of the pea-green couch. She rested the magazine across her stomach and propped herself up to get a better view.

"I'm not condoning you wearing that dead animal," she said, crinkling up her nose. "But I could give a shit if it hangs at the back of Pine Brook's closet or yours."

Ret's attention returned to *Rolling Stone*, and the conversation was over. It seemed like a victory for Bex, but really, Ret had won. No matter what Bex decided, it had Ret's blessing. Where's the fun in that? In the end, Bex tucked the mink in the back of the closet and said maybe she'd come back for it later, when it wasn't spitting sheets of snow and ice from the sky. She never cared about that coat, not really. But later? When there were real choices to be made, real loyalties tested? Bex was no different from Jenni. Insert GIF here of cute little lemmings plummeting down to the ocean floor.

I crumple up the bag and the rest of my sandwich and toss it in the garbage. I thought the green room was empty when I came here, but I was wrong. It's chock full of memories, just like every other room in this place. I push through the doors that lead out onto the stage and walk across the dark floor.

All afternoon, I try to pull my shit back together. In AP English, we're studying Faulkner yet again. I take out my book, but I can't focus. Not with Ret sitting across from me, staring down at the desk like there's something really interesting carved into the wood. It's been four weeks since I left her down at the river, and nothing's resolved. She's kept her promise, kept her distance. But I can't just leave this space between us like a gaping wound.

Her hair brushes down past her shoulders and ends in deep, violet tips. She's wearing her Nirvana T-shirt, the one I finally returned last spring. She's wearing it for me; she knows that I'll notice. Out of nowhere, she looks up and blows me a kiss.

She is being cruel or sincere.

With Ret, it's always been impossible to tell.

I need to face her. Soon. I chew the tip of my pen and look away.

After school, Abigail's waiting at my locker. Thanksgiving was nice and all, but does she think we're friends now? I walk up to her, still feeling pissy after the day's downward spiral, not really in the mood for a pick-me-up.

"I was wondering," she says, stepping away from my locker to let me open it. No "hi," no pleasantries. She just dives right in like this was a conversation we started a while ago and need to finish up. "Do you ever think about why Ret picked each of us?"

I stop dialing my locker combination midspin. "What do you mean?"

"You know. Why she picked us as friends. You and me, Jenni and Bex."

I shrug and start dialing again. Why does anyone become friends? "Common interests, I guess. She and Jenni were friends since grade school."

"Sure, but think about it," Abigail presses. "What did any of us really have in common with her? Or with each other for that matter?"

She's right. We're all pretty different when you break it down. Abigail fits in much better with her Rockettes and Leadership Council friends. Bex with the dance team girls. I don't know who Jenni's been hanging out with this year, but I think she might be dating this kid Elliot, who looks kind of like the oldest Hanson brother, back when they were a thing. Hair scraping his shoulders, long brown leather jacket a permanent fixture on his skinny frame.

"I don't know, we were all a little on the fringe of things. She thought we were interesting."

Abigail's lips turn down at the corners and she reaches up to pull her curls into a bouncy ponytail. "Nuh-huh. Guess again."

I empty out my backpack and exchange the contents for the

books I'll need tonight, then zip my bag shut. This is annoying. Our heart-to-heart on Thanksgiving was great, but I'm in no mood to play games.

"Why don't you just tell me if you have it all figured out?" I snap.

Abigail flinches.

"Sorry, I didn't mean it like that. I just have to get going." I close my locker door and sling my bag across my shoulder.

"She chose us because we listened to her, Ellory. We hung on her every word. Ret didn't pick us because we were special snowflakes. She wanted followers, not friends."

I shake my head. No way. What does Abigail know? She stopped being Ret's friend four years ago. Maybe that's why Ret picked *her*—unflagging niceness; big, trusting eyes—but that's Abigail. That's not me.

"You're wrong," I say. Sure, Ret thrived on playing follow-the-leader, everyone knows that. And sure, we all let ourselves be led. But that's not *why* we were friends. That's just how things shook out. I make a move down the hall toward the stairs, and Abigail falls in step beside me.

"I know people think I'm naive," she says. "I'm small, I'm a Rockette, I get it. But I'm not, okay? I know I can't fix anything for you."

"Then why are you here?" I ask, still walking. All this proves is that I was right on Thanksgiving—Abigail doesn't hold the answers. "I mean, we had our talk, so thanks. But why do you care so much?"

"Because I get what it's like to feel totally alone," she says. "And I get what Ret did to people. What she's still doing to you."

I stop at the door to the stairs and turn to look right at her. What could Abigail possibly know about Ret and me?

"Thanks, but I don't need any more of your help," I say. Then I push through the doors into the stairwell and leave Abigail standing there. I'm not trying to be mean, but I'm not anyone's charity case either.

I speed through my work in the metal shop and hurry outside to the student lot. Then I throw the Subaru into drive and head downtown. I don't have a plan, don't have anywhere to be, I just need to go, to move, to be anywhere but here, stewing.

Driving across the bridge, the radio blasting and the water flashing with the last of the already fading sun, I feel antsy, on edge. Crossing the river used to feel more transformative. Now I need something more to transform me. As I drive, I can't get Abigail's words out of my head. *Ret didn't pick us because we were special snowflakes. She wanted followers, not friends.* I don't want it to be true, but I can't shake the nagging suspicion that Abigail's right, that she might have some answers after all.

I drive past the restaurants and bars, further into the East Shore. The streets darken, the sidewalks are bare. I keep driving, aimless. When I turn down a narrow side street, I realize I'm back on the block with Capital Harvest—a reminder of the promise I made to myself on Thanksgiving. That I'd give Ret up, for real this time.

I pull over and shift the car into park. I may have left Abigail behind in the hallway, but the echo of her voice is right here, all around me. *She chose us because we listened to her, Ellory. We hung on her every word.* No. Ret chose me because she could see inside me, right down to the core. I was her favorite, her secret-keeper, Sleeping Beauty to her Snow White, Serena to her Blair.

Even as I think the words, they don't quite ring true. Damn Abigail and her unsolicited soul searching. I try again. Why did Ret pick me? What did she see that day in ninth-grade English when she looked inside my eyes all the way to my heart?

A blank canvas, begging to be filled up.

I swallow. Deep down in my stomach, *crackle, pop*. I *was* her favorite. The most eager, the most naive, a girl thirsty for every drop of truth about who I was, what made me tick. I thought Bex and Jenni were the lemmings, but the biggest lemming was me. And Ret could see it. *She saw me*. And then I let her tell me who to be.

NOVEMBER, JUNIOR YEAR

(THEN)

The bed of Ricky Cole's truck was cushioned with heavy wool blankets and the old linens that live in the back of the closet for guests. Thanksgiving and its collection of aunties and their families had come and gone, so I had taken advantage of all the second-string bedding at my disposal.

Then I had commandeered Ricky's truck—which Matthias was legitimately borrowing for the evening—and turned its bed into a kind of homage to camping, complete with sleeping bags, an abundance of pillows, Jenni's homemade trail mix, and a big cooler stuffed with soda and three kinds of dip.

Matthias rolled over onto his back. "Toss me a pillow?"

I reached behind me and grabbed one. "Incoming."

He tucked it behind his head and propped his feet up onto my legs, which were crisscrossed on top of the Hello Kitty sheet from my third-grade bedroom. An unsupervised camping trip was out of the question, but City Island wasn't a bad substitute. Right in the middle of the Susquehanna, between the East and West Shores, City Island was home to minor league baseball (go Senators!), water golf, horse-drawn carriage rides, and paddleboat tours in the summer, and a whole lot of nothing during the off-season. Especially by late November. You could pull up right to the shore of the river in the empty stadium lot and pretend you were in the wilderness. Almost. The air smelled like damp leaves and river water with a dash of hay and horse. I leaned back on my elbows and breathed in deep.

The sky was perfectly clear in that prefrost, last gasp of fall kind of way. Head tilted up, I drank in the infinite spray of little lights. "You can really see all the stars tonight."

"I wish we could just stay here. All night." Matthias ran his fingers through my hair. His touch was slow and easy, like we really did have the whole night, and then all the nights after this one.

I glanced over at the sleeping bags, which I had brought along mostly for the ambience. Maybe Ricky and Rebecca wouldn't notice if Matthias didn't come home, but there was no way my parents would have gone for a night spent under the stars, even if it was my boyfriend's birthday. Probably especially because it was my boyfriend's birthday. I tucked my chin into my scarf and waved a gloved hand up at the sky. "There's Orion. I can always find his belt."

Matthias followed the line of my glove. It was only six, but the night was closing in earlier and earlier each day. "Doesn't looking at the stars make you feel like a little kid?" he asked.

"What do you mean?"

"You know how you used to think that wherever you were in the world, you'd see the same stars? Like I could be here and you could be in China, and we'd see the same exact sky at night?"

I tilted my head back toward Orion and chewed on my lower lip. I'd never been to China, but we had taken a couple family vacations when I was a kid—the Grand Canyon, Disney. Had I ever looked up at the night sky from Arizona or Florida? Had I paid any attention?

I guess I was quiet too long, because Matthias shifted, sitting up, peering down into my face. "You do know that we see different stars in different hemispheres, right?"

I shook my head. With anyone else, I'd be embarrassed, but with Matthias, I felt safe. When we were together, all the insecurities that piled up when we were apart just crumbled into dust. Sometimes I wondered if I'd really felt them at all.

"It's pretty cool, actually. It's how sailing ships used the stars to navigate the seas. So for example, in Australia they can see a constellation called the Southern Cross, but we can't see it here. And we can only see the Big Dipper in the northern hemisphere." Matthias may have been a terrible student, but when something sparked his interest, he soaked up facts like a sponge. Music. Cordelia. And I guess stars.

"What about Orion?"

"I think you can see him everywhere. He's close to the celestial equator."

"Then he can be ours. Clearly we should lay claim to some stars on your birthday, and I want to be able to see them everywhere."

He pulled me toward him. His hair tickled my skin as he pressed his lips against my lips. "I love you, Ellory Holland."

I pulled back just far enough to open my eyes and look directly into his. His lashes were so long, it was hardly fair.

"I love you too." The words felt easy. By now, we'd said them a hundred times. A thousand. I was locked in his gaze, the little flecks of green glinting in his eyes. Matthias was shining down on me, but I was the one who glowed.

I looked out across the river to a cluster of East Shore lights. I was used to seeing downtown from the West Shore, driving toward the Market Street Bridge. Tonight, from our vantage point on City Island, everything was even closer, like we were looking at the lights on zoom. The city was small, but the river made it special at night. In the dark, you could almost believe there was something thrumming beneath the surface.

"I almost didn't let Ret drag me to that party," I said.

"What party?"

"I was just thinking back to last June. We owe our happily ever after to Dave Franklin, for hosting that classic celebration of adolescent debauchery, and to Ret Johnston, for making me drive her there."

"To Ret." He lifted his can of root beer up toward the sky, as if he were clinking glasses with Orion.

"And Dave," I said, snuggling into his neck.

I could feel his body tense up against mine. He tipped his head back and downed the remaining root beer in one gulp, then tossed the can toward the front of the truck bed. Little drops of soda sprayed across Hello Kitty.

"Sorry, I'll wash that," he mumbled. He ran his fingers through his hair, loosening the effect of whatever product had been holding the strands in place. A few pieces flopped down across his forehead.

"What did I say?"

"Nothing, it's not you. Dave's been kind of a dick lately, that's all. Let's talk about something else." He reached into his pocket and pulled out the silver flask he always carried to shows, then took a long swallow. By this time, he'd stopped offering to pass it my way. Someone had to be the designated driver. I tried not to think about the nights I wasn't with him, how he got home.

"What's going on with Dave?" I reached over and put my hand on his. Even through my glove, I could feel how cold his fingers were, how tightly they gripped the steel. He flinched, just slightly, but didn't pull away.

"Meeting you there—really meeting you—that was the best thing about my whole summer."

"Okay."

"When I'm with you, I don't have to think about Dave."

"I don't get it—you guys are friends," I said.

Matthias let go of my hand and raised the flask to his lips again. With each question I asked, he took another deep swallow, but I couldn't stop. I couldn't handle one more secret.

"Did something happen? You can tell me."

He wiped his sleeve roughly against his mouth and tossed the flask down in the truck bed. Then he reached out, cupping my cheekbones in both his hands, and pulled my face toward him. He pressed his lips hard against mine, like he was trying to seal them shut. It didn't feel warm or thrilling. It felt harsh and raw, like anger. I pulled back, gasping.

"You can't just kiss me like that." My lips were stinging, my voice rising. "We're supposed to be on the same side here. Why won't you tell me what's going on?"

"Fuck, Ellory. Why do we have to tell each other every single thing?"

Everything that happened next was a rush of movement and sound. Matthias was standing up, jumping out of the truck bed, and then I was following him, three steps behind. A minute later he was in the cab of the truck, the keys in the ignition, and I was standing outside, banging on the door.

"What are you doing?" I screamed. "You can't just leave."

"Get in," he shouted at me through the window glass.

"Don't be an asshole! You just drank like five shots of whiskey."

He slammed his fist into the steering wheel, and the horn squealed loud and sharp. I jumped back from the truck.

"Fine, don't get in," he yelled.

"What, are you just going to leave me here?" I shouted back. Hot tears spilled down my cheeks, and I swiped at my nose with my glove. Matthias didn't say anything, just slammed his fist into the horn again.

Who was this person? Ten minutes ago, we'd been eating trail mix and claiming stars. Now my boyfriend was screaming at me from the driver's seat of his dad's truck in some sort of whiskey-fueled rage. I'd seen him drink before, plenty of times. But he'd never been like this.

"Please don't," I said, trying to keep my voice under control. "Just let me drive." I took a small step back toward the truck, then another. He turned to look at me through the glass. I must have looked pathetic, creeping toward the truck like a mouse, snot and tears streaming down my face.

It was like a string inside Matthias snapped. He slouched back into the seat, dropping his hands from the wheel. His head slumped forward. A minute later, the driver's side door swung slowly open, and he climbed out.

"I'm so sorry." He collapsed against me, wrapping his body around mine in a head-to-toe hug. "I'm so, so sorry."

I didn't say anything. I let him hug me for an eternity that was probably only a minute, then I slipped into the driver's seat before he could change his mind. Matthias climbed in the other side.

"Are you okay?" he asked.

"I don't know." I took the key out of the ignition and slipped it into my pocket. I wanted a tissue, but my bag was still in the back so I swiped at my face with my glove again.

"You know how there are things about yourself that you wish would just go away? And if you don't talk about them, you can at least pretend they don't exist?" he asked.

I didn't know. I wanted to share everything with him.

When I didn't answer, he continued. "There's stuff I didn't want to tell you because . . . you're so good, Ellory. So perfect. *We're* so good. I didn't want to mess that up."

"And whatever that was, that didn't just mess things up?"

"Fuck, I know." He slammed his head back into the headrest and tilted his eyes toward the ceiling.

There were so many secrets swirling between us. *His* secrets. He had them all, and I had none.

Finally, he spoke up again. "My dad doesn't just drink. He does other stuff too, coke mostly."

"I'm sorry." I wasn't sure what else to say.

"Dave's his dealer."

"What?"

"Yeah."

We sat in silence for a moment, the words dissipating into the November dark. I'd always thought Dave and Matthias were kind of an odd match. They dressed the same, with a tousled kind of indie disregard, but Dave was wild parties and family money and a revolving fan club of freshmen girls. His life was everything Matthias's wasn't.

Matthias kept staring up at the truck ceiling, refusing to meet my eye. "Ricky installed some sound equipment in the Franklins' house a couple years ago. He thinks it's hilarious, like they're really friends. He'll tell me he's going to meet up with 'our friend Dave.' He's totally obvious about it. It's sad, you know? To Dave, he's just another fucked up old dude who used to be in a band once."

"So why do you hang out with him at all? You have the Smurf. You have *me*. Screw Dave Franklin."

"It's complicated, Ellory. Dave and I go way back, before the whole Ricky thing. Before he was dealing. There are other reasons too."

I raised my eyebrows. I didn't say anything, and finally he had to tilt his head away from the ceiling. To look at me.

"Other reasons?"

"For one, Dave knows exactly how messed up my dad is, and someday he's going to let it slip. Someday, he's going to tell the wrong person, and the whole school will be talking about how my dad and Dave bump coke together on the weekends. It's in my best interest to stay good with Dave. Keep an eye on him. In a few years, Cordelia's going to be at Pine Brook. And I'm not going to be there to protect her. The less dirt people have on the Coles, the better."

"Okay, I get that. And two?"

Matthias stared at me blankly. He was totally calm now, but I could still see the whiskey ruddy in his cheeks, hear it thick in his voice. I pressed anyway.

"You said there were reasons. Multiple."

"Maybe another time."

So this was all I was going to get tonight. I felt a little afraid of the boy sitting next to me in the truck, but mostly I felt afraid *for* him. I wanted to unzip my skin and let him curl up inside. I wanted to punch Dave Franklin, never mind that I'd never punched anyone in my entire life. Most of all, I wanted to lock up Ricky Cole until he dried out and apologized for being such a colossal screwup. Instead, I took off my glove and placed my hand on top of Matthias's hand, lacing my fingers through his.

He leaned his head against my shoulder. "How are your hands so warm?" he asked.

"Gloves. All the kids are wearing them."

I could feel him smile against my collarbone. "I'll have to get a pair of those." He was silent for a minute. "When I'm with you, I want to forget about Dave and my dad and everything else. You're my escape."

"I want more than that," I said. "I want you to make it up to me."

He lifted his head from my shoulder to look me in the eye. "Anything."

"You have to trust me," I said. "You can escape into a cave, right? You can hide. But you can also shout your secrets there. I can hold them." I could feel my heart pulsing in my throat. I needed something good to come out of this disaster of a night. I needed things to be different from now on.

"Okay, cave girl," he said finally, whispering into my neck. "I'll try to be better. I'll try to shout a few more secrets your way."

I tilted my head down and found his lips, and we were kissing again, softly this time, carefully, as if we didn't want to break each other, as if there was only so much this night could hold, and we had reached its limit. He'd promised to try. I had asked him to trust me, so that meant I had to do the same. I let myself sink into the softness of his skin.

DECEMBER, SENIOR YEAR
(NOW)

It takes me most of December to get up the nerve, but on Friday afternoon—the last day before winter break—I make sure every-thing's clean and in its place in the metal shop, and then I zip my coat up tight and head down to the river. This time, I drive all the way there and park across the street from the gap in the guardrail. There will be no spiked vanilla lattes today, no swilling amaretto from the bottle. Besides, it's too cold to be out here long, too cold to walk home after.

As I cross the street, I wonder if the bite in the air will have pushed Ret inside, to a new spot where I'll never find her. But when I get to the bottom of the bank and shove through the grass, she's there, wrapped in a big flannel blanket, looking toasty warm with her earbuds tucked beneath a red wool hat and her flask nestled in her lap. She looks surprised to see me. Considering it's been well over a month, I can't blame her.

"Look what the cat dragged in." She doesn't move, just peers up at me from beneath her snow hat. Her voice is thick with whiskey or sweet liqueur or whatever she has in there today, but there's a sharp edge to her words. This is going to be barrels of fun.

But it's also what I need. I can't take devoted, cajoling Ret today, her honey-toned flattery. I need her to be mean.

"We need to talk," I say.

She pats the grass next to her, but I don't take the bait. If she wants to be even close to eye level for this, she's going to have to stand.

She doesn't move. "Go on."

"I'm not coming down here anymore," I say. "I can't."

Ret turns her head away from me and unscrews the cap on her flask. Typical.

"You came here to tell me that you're not coming here anymore." Her voice is flat. "That's classic. You know over the past six weeks, I kind of figured that out."

"Then why are you still here?" I ask. "It's thirty-six degrees. We're officially on winter break. Why are you getting buzzed down by the river, waiting for me?"

Her head jerks toward me. "You think I'm waiting for you?"

I know she is. Once Ret sets her mind to something, she doesn't give up. There are plenty other places she could go to hang out. But she told me the river.

I remind myself I came here for a reason, that I'm not a quitter either. I need us to talk about the things we swore we wouldn't. *No wallowing in the past.* But this isn't wallowing. I need her to take some of this blame away from me, so I can find some way—any way—forward without her. Because there's no Ret & Ellory anymore. We've both been fooling ourselves for months.

"I want you to admit you screwed up," I say, ignoring her question. "I need to hear you say it."

Ret sucks in a sharp breath. "Jesus, Ellory. Which time?"

"Last spring. All of it." I hear the coldness in my voice. Ret never apologized because I never gave her a chance. But now I need to hear the words that could wash away some of this regret. Just a little bit. For the party I skipped, the flames that turned to spluttering smoke, the fight I couldn't walk away from. The parts of the story that only we remember.

She stands up slowly, the flannel blanket falling down around her ankles. She's not even wearing a coat, just jeans and a long, striped sweater.

"Aren't you freezing?" I ask.

She slides up her sleeves, as if to make a point. "Not exactly one of my worries."

For a moment, we stare at each other, eyes flashing. I'm towering over her—even her chunky black boots are no match for my genes—but we both know she holds all the power. Even now.

"Everything was for you," she says finally. "I told you, I only wanted what was best. So if that means it was all my fault, fine."

It's not a real apology. Or maybe it is, it's just not anything better than what I got last spring. The same words, recycled eight months later like they'll mean something different now. But what did I expect? A different Ret? I should have known this is all she has to give. I glance down at her bare arms where the sweater is shoved up around her elbows.

"Where's your bracelet?" I ask. I've been wanting to say it for months. Now's my chance, because after today, I'm not coming back.

She looks puzzled, like for a moment she doesn't know what I'm talking about. Then her eyes soften, and I put the pieces together before the words are out of her mouth. "Veronica," she says. "You know my mom, always borrowing my things."

"Oh." *My mom still thinks she's twenty-five.* I picture Ms. Johnston in Ret's bedroom, lifting the bracelet off the dresser, sliding it onto her wrist. I've seen her wearing it on her way out of United Methodist. The band had looked so different on her wrist, I hadn't made the connection until now.

Suddenly, I'm not mad at Ret anymore. For her half apology. For all the things she should be apologizing for. And for the first time in a long time, I'm not mad at myself either. The sadness is still there, for all the things we used to be to each other, for all the things we'll never be again. The sadness will probably never leave. And I'll never get the apology I'm looking for, the one that would set me free.

But I'm ready to move on.

"You should probably find a new spot," I say. "It's only going to get colder. Or stay here, but don't do it on my account."

Ret sniffs, then snatches the blanket from the ground and wraps it around her shoulders. "It's always for you, Ellory May," she says, refusing to make this easy.

Deep down, I know Abigail was right: Ret needs me to trust her, follow her, to believe her implicitly. But that's only half of the story. The other half is this—Ret loved me. She still loves me. Both halves are right here in front of me, complicated and messy and neither less true than the other.

I never asked for easy. I walk away.

When I scramble up the side of the bank toward the road, I know Ret won't follow. I remind myself that I need to come back here with a trash bag some day over break. Something tells me Ret won't be doing any cleanup. Something tells me she won't be coming back here either. But she'll still be around.

As I walk across the street toward the car, my stomach floods with an intense mix of relief and panic. I have to find a way to live through the rest of senior year without Ret. I hop onto the hood of the Subaru and bend over at the waist, waiting for the fluttering, sticky swamp to settle into its usual crackle, my blackened insides crunching together. But there's nothing. No crackle. No crumbling ash.

Just regular old queasiness, which rumbles through my gut, then subsides.

The air is sharp and cold against my skin. My very soft, warm skin, wrapped around my squishy, pink insides. I take a deep breath, gulping in the icy air, letting it sting my lungs all the way down to my stomach. No cracking. No ash. It's gone.

Oh my god.

I was sitting in the Pine Brook auditorium, Ret to my left and Bex and Jenni to my right. We were to be talked at for the next hour on How to Jump-Start Our College Application Process. Every member of the junior class was either already slumped down in their chairs or still shuffling in through the doors at the back.

"You know they scheduled this now so we'd feel like apathetic slackers over winter break." Ret blew a big Margarita Burst bubble and smacked her gum back between her lips. She was asking to get caught, but the authority figures were too busy poking at a laptop on stage while some frazzled-looking A/V Club kid tried to make them stop helping.

"No way." Jenni leaned across Bex and me to look Ret in the

eye. "There's a *Hell's Kitchen* marathon on Sunday, and no school-sponsored guilt trip is interrupting my one-on-one time with Gordon."

"I can't believe you watch that show," Ret said. That was all it took to send Jenni slouching back in her chair. Ret holding the controls, pushing the buttons. Every. Single. Time. My shoulders tensed, and I tried to make myself relax.

"Get over it." I thought Bex was talking to Jenni at first, but then she squeezed Jenni's hand. She turned toward Ret, a smile tugging at the corners of her lips, a challenge. "You know you wouldn't kick Gordon Ramsay out of bed."

"Gordon Ramsay is old," Ret pushed back. Gordon Ramsay *was* old. Super old, and married. But this wasn't about him, it was about taking sides, like always. And I just couldn't. Ever since the fight in the truck, I'd been on edge. For the past three weeks, even the regular back-and-forth between my friends that was more banter than bicker made my jaw clench. Their voices volleyed in my ears, transforming into the sound of his shouts, his fist against the truck horn, my own choking sobs.

"Just stop," I burst out. Everyone shut up and stared at me. "Who cares, right? Why does everything have to be a *thing*?"

"Jesus, Ellory. Sensitive much?" Ret asked.

Everyone was quiet for a minute. "Sorry," I said. "Can we just talk about something else?" I let my hair fall forward over my eyes and hoped no one noticed the hot patches spreading across my cheeks. What was wrong with me? It was just talk, just some ridiculous TV show. I felt like a freak. Like a baby.

A minute later, something whirred through the sound system, and a giant image of Principal Keegan's chow-boxer mix chewing a squeaky duck floated across the projection screen. *Sorry*, I mouthed again toward Ret, and she made a swishing motion with her hand, releasing my outburst into the air, gone.

"I guess we're in business," Principal Keegan quipped into the microphone. I tried to focus, but it was hard to take seriously a man whose hair was flying up in yellow wisps like he'd just stuck his thumb in a socket. I drew in a deep breath and tried to get it together. *Be normal, Ellory. Grow up.*

The A/V kid scurried over to the laptop to bring up the PowerPoint. Soon, Principal Keegan's voice filled the auditorium with an itinerary for mapping out the next twelve months until college applications would be due. I let myself zone out.

I would be going to Portland State; I had my plan. The more important itinerary wasn't about college; it was much more personal. And immediate. In the days since Matthias's birthday, everything between us had been careful, timid. We were suspended on the blade of a knife, afraid to make any sudden movements. The fight was with me all the time, casting a shadow across everything, even things that had nothing to do with him. We needed to get past it, and fast.

"Which is why I cannot stress enough the importance of a well-maintained database." Principal Keegan was gesturing behind him with the PowerPoint clicker at something titled "Your College Application Action Plan." It was a dizzying grid of Reach, Target, and Safety Schools organized by every date and application component imaginable.

"It doesn't have to be anything fancy," he chuckled. It was impossible to tell if this example was supposed to be *too fancy* or *just right* on the scale of college acceptance to obsession. "Just a simple Excel or Google Sheet will do. What's important is having a system. It's not enough to simply organize all the elements. You have to stay on top of your deadlines and mark off the steps as you go. That's how you keep things *manageable* and *attainable*. That's how you reach your goals."

I craned my neck and shoulders around in my chair and combed through the sea of Pine Brook juniors. My eyes found the Smurf, who gave me a little salute from the back row. No sign of Matthias or Dave, which wasn't much of a surprise. This was exactly the kind of thing they'd skip. We hadn't talked about Dave since the fight, but they'd been sitting together in the sky dome and hanging out like everything was normal. Guys could just do that. Go on like everything was normal.

I spun back around and buried my face in my notebook. From my quick survey of the auditorium, I ventured that nearly half the juniors were asleep or trying to be. A solid quarter were furiously scribbling notes and nodding cheerfully, as if organizing their college applications was the greatest opportunity that Pine Brook had ever handed them. The remaining quarter—the really smart ones—were doodling idly in their neat spiral notebooks, looking every bit the attentive pupils from stage while secretly daydreaming about whatever boozy or directionless plans their winter breaks held in store.

I envied them. I wanted to want nothing more than boozy and directionless. That was my problem. I was too serious, I wanted too much. Why couldn't I just ease up, be happy? My fingers found the black band on my wrist, spun it around and around.

A minute later, Jenni passed a note to Bex, signaling her to read and pass it on. Bex unfolded the paper and handed it to me. *Twenty-six more minutes until Keegan reveals the secret to getting into Harvard. Then, viewing of* The O. C. *Chrismukkah episode at my place.* I smiled in her direction and passed the note to Ret. Maybe normal was that easy. The four of us—Ret, Jenni, Bex, and me. Always the same.

A few minutes before the bell rang, Ret pressed another note into my hand. This one was intricately folded into a perfect square and had *FYEO* written across the top in curvy, intricate script—"For Your Eyes Only." Ret hadn't just written this note in assembly; she'd clearly been carrying it around, waiting to give it to me. I let my eyes flicker across Bex and Jenni. They were focused on the screen. Then I unfolded the paper slowly, careful not to make any sound. In tiny handwriting I had to bend over to read, Ret had written: *I had sex with Jonathan. Twice!*

My head shot up. Ret was grinning.

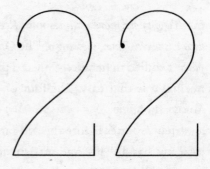

New year, New Ellory. I can almost hear the power ballads pulsing behind me as I push through the school doors on Monday morning, the first day back, first day of spring semester. Nothing can touch me today. There's no crackling inside as I receive my ball of clay to begin the pottery unit in Studio Art. No falling flakes of ash in Spanish or math. I left them down by the river, left them with Ret.

I ride the high until lunch, when it hits me I didn't pack one this morning. Head in the clouds, out of the game. So instead of walking down to the shop with my usual brown bag, I wait in the bathroom until the bell signaling the start of fifth period rings, and then I take the stairs up to the sky dome. I tell myself the fourth period lunch crowd will be gone, the coast will be clear. I tell myself I'll grab a bagel, be down in the shop in no time.

Obviously, I am wrong.

When Jenni turns the corner into the eighth-floor hallway, I freeze. I want to disappear, but there's nowhere to go. It's just me and Jenni, her satchel bag swinging loosely from one shoulder, walking straight toward me. No one else in the entire hall, the entire world.

You know how they say that time stops in moments of extreme joy or fear or despair? It doesn't. It keeps barreling forward, and there's literally nothing you can do about it. No pause, no rewind, nowhere to run.

She doesn't see me at first. Her eyes are cast down, deep in thought, maybe about whatever or whoever has made her late to fifth period, has set her down in this particular hallway on a collision course with her past. When she looks up, she's so close she's practically on top of me. I take a step back.

Jenni's pace slows almost imperceptibly for just one step. One tiny falter. Then she raises her chin and shakes her head, slow and deliberate, her hair flashing around her shoulders and down her back in a bright red wave. She looks straight into my eyes and lifts one hand to her forehead. At first I'm not sure what she's doing, but then it hits me: With four little taps of her fingers—forehead, chest, shoulder, shoulder—Jenni is making the sign of the cross. I guess her time in Tennessee last summer had a lasting effect. Is she blessing me? No, she's crossing *herself*—this is a warding away, a protection. Jenni doesn't just hate me. She's actually afraid of me.

I take another step back, stumbling into a wall of lockers.

Jenni laughs. Just one short *ha* like a gunshot echoing in the empty hall. *Ha ha ha.* I'm wrong again. She's not scared, she's putting on a show. She's *thriving* on seeing me this way. Trapped. Alone. I'm the one radiating fear, my rabbit heart beating wild inside my chest.

Then she picks up the pace and breezes past, staring straight ahead as if I'm not even here.

Maybe I'm not.

I can hear the sharp thud of her platforms retreat down the hall, then turn the corner. Gone. She didn't touch me, but my body reverberates with the impact, as if I've been slapped. Until now, I've been doing such a good job of avoiding Jenni. It's been easy, really; she doesn't want to see me any more than I want to see her. My mind shoots back to her single text from the summer: *I'm praying for you.* Are you really, Jenni? Or are you just praying for yourself?

Jenni's pious performance is a wake-up call—leaving Ret behind won't be enough. *Fallout, fall from grace, fall guy, fall apart.* There are other chapters to close; the past is everywhere. Did I really think it would be so easy to walk away?

I'm shaking all over. I sink down to the floor, my back sliding against the metal until I'm sitting on the cold tile of the eighth-floor hallway, head tilted against a locker door, heart thudding. My fingers gravitate automatically to my wrist, but they close around bare skin. I want the comfort of the band to twist, but it's been in a box in my room since the start of winter break. I can feel my breath coming faster and faster, the blood beating in my ears. I would take the crunching again any day. The hollow emptiness. Anything but this.

"Are you okay, Miss Holland?"

My back stiffens and my head bangs sharply against the locker door.

"I'm fine." I'm not. I rub the back of my head and stare up at Mr. Samuels, my homeroom teacher, trying not to visibly shake. He doesn't look happy to find me out in the hall when I should clearly be somewhere else.

"In that case, shouldn't you be in lunch?"

"I just got dizzy. I think I forgot to eat breakfast." I push myself up from the lockers, willing my legs to stop shaking. "I'm fine now."

Mr. Samuels twists his mouth to one side and eyes me. He clocks in about two inches below my forehead, but he looks deadly serious staring up into my face. "If you're not feeling well, I strongly suggest you head down to the nurse. Otherwise, it's been several minutes since the second bell. You need to be inside." He glances down the hall toward the sky dome.

"Right," I mumble, starting back down the hall. Right foot, left foot. I can do this. "See you tomorrow in homeroom."

He nods, and I can feel his eyes on my back until I push through the door and it swings shut.

The sky dome is filled with people, but everyone's wrapped up in their own drama, sharing stories from winter break. No one notices me walk in, no one cares. I take in a deep, shaky breath. There are a couple of empty tables on the far side of the cafeteria, and sitting here with a book sounds better than going back out into the halls, walking all the way across the school to the art wing. I get in the line, which is short, since I'm late. I start to reach for a bagel, then change my mind. A bagel would sit like a rock in my stomach. I go for the hummus and carrot sticks instead and grab a lemonade from the soda-less bin of cold drinks by the cashier.

When I sink into a chair at a vacant table, I'm not sure I even want the hummus, but I force myself to eat. When I'm done, I shove my tray aside and fold my arms across the table. The back of my head is still throbbing a little where I hit it against the locker, and I rest my forehead across my arms. I feel like I could sleep for a week. With my eyes closed, I imagine the impossible— time moving in reverse, back to the moment where everything started to unravel. Was it last spring, watching Ret get into the back of Dave's car, watching them drive away? Or January, that dismal day with Matthias at the Roaster? Or before that, the fight in the truck, the night at the Crow, a thousand sleepovers at Jenni's, Dave Franklin's living room? Or further, Comparative Religions, freshman English, Abigail sobbing in the locker room, back and back and back. Before Pine Brook. Before any of us ever met.

I can't make it stop. My eyes fly open, and I force my head up. I could go on avoiding Jenni and everyone else forever. But it's not working. I don't want to spend the rest of the year sneaking through the halls, avoiding everyone, avoiding anything that could drag me back to junior year. I'm not going to go around begging for forgiveness, begging them to take me back. But I can't just leave Pine Brook filled with ghosts. When I came back this year, I knew I was going to have to face them eventually. Didn't I? Isn't that why I refused to transfer, why I made myself return? Walking away from Ret felt like an ending, but it was just the beginning. Moving forward means facing each and every one of them. If I can figure out how.

DECEMBER, JUNIOR YEAR
(THEN)

By 5:45 on Christmas Eve, my parents were at a holiday party across town, two shots of celebratory schnapps had been consumed, and I'd fired off a text to Ho-Ho-Holidays letting everyone know I'd be going dark for the night. For once, no one gave me any shit. At six, Matthias arrived on my doorstep bearing a foil-wrapped plate. He looked freshly scrubbed, and he smelled amazing, like apricots and vanilla. It was only the second time we'd been alone—really alone—since the fight.

I let him inside and kissed him, breathing him in.

"Rebecca baked," he explained, handing over the cookies. "Exactly once a year, she comes down from her office and gets inspired to do parental things like drag the tree up from the basement and bake cookies with Cordelia. It's almost heartwarming."

"I don't know whether that's sweet or sad."

"Mostly sad. Lures Cordelia into a false sense of assurance that she's going to have a real mom for at least two months following Christmas every year. I stopped believing in the magical Mom Claus around her age. We'll see how long it takes C to become hard and bitter."

He followed me into the kitchen, where I placed the cookies on the counter next to several tins of my mom's own holiday baked goods and the bottle of peppermint schnapps.

"You start the party without me?"

"I was feeling a little festive with the elder Hollands out." No careful, meek Ellory tonight. No dancing around. I picked up the bottle. "Join me?"

Matthias tipped back two shots and I had a third, and then I took his hand and led him into the family room. I was warm and soft around the edges. The carpet was squishy beneath my feet. My shirt was silky against my skin. We floated over to the couch.

I clicked on the TV and flipped through the channels until *It's a Wonderful Life* came up on the screen. Matthias plopped down on the couch and pulled me gingerly after him, onto his lap.

"I won't break," I said.

He started to say something back, but I leaned in and pressed my mouth against his. His lips were smooth and his skin was hot and everything was spinning just a little. His hands moved lightly across my stomach, across the green fabric of my shirt. I drew in my breath.

"Too much?" he asked.

I shook my head. "Not enough."

He hesitated for just a second, then a light seemed to turn on in his eyes. He yanked his sweater over his head, pulling his arms roughly out of the sleeves. I reached for the buttons on his shirt. When his chest was bare, I pressed my face against his skin and breathed in the smell of bar soap mixed with flour and vanilla.

He gathered up my shirt at the hem and pulled it off. For a second, I felt the shock of cold air against my skin. Then I leaned back into the couch and pulled him with me, on top of me. His breathing was hot and ragged in my ear, and I felt instantly warmer. I thought about those first times we were together, how I would wait for something inside me to click, how eventually I'd pull back when the click never came. I was a different person now. The fight had changed something inside me. I couldn't have all of Matthias, but I could have this. This was mine, and mine alone.

His lips found my mouth, my ear, my hair. He reached for the clasp of my bra. It was violet and lace. His fingers fumbled with it for a minute, and then I felt the fabric relax, the straps ease down my shoulders. *Click*. His lips moved across my shoulder, my neck. My heart was beating firm and loud inside my chest. I could feel it sending blood through every vein, pulsing beneath my skin. His hands were everywhere—on my stomach, my sides, my back. They felt good, necessary. *Click click click*.

The movie was playing in the background. The couch was soft and deep. I let my hands drift across the sides of his face, detecting just a trace of roughness along his jaw and chin. His hands moved from my hair, down to my breasts, down further to the button on my jeans. I slipped them off. When he moved the thin cotton of my underwear aside and slid his fingers between my legs, I drew in a shallow breath. I closed my eyes and sank into the rhythm of his fingertips, which moved in light, steady circles against me.

My eyes took a minute to focus on the little digital numbers on the DVR. We were curled up on the couch, and I didn't want to move, but something told me it was getting late. The spell of the fight had been broken. We hadn't had sex—not tonight, not yet—but I couldn't imagine the drowsy, warm, tangled-up closeness that happened after could be any better than this. I made a mental note to ask Ret as the numbers came into focus.

"It's after ten. How did that happen?"

Matthias stirred and kissed my shoulder, then reached for his jeans, which were crumpled in a heap on the floor. "I should go soon. I have to get downtown."

"You're going to a show?"

For a moment, he didn't answer. Then he said, "But before I go, I have something for you. Wait here."

He pushed up off the couch and disappeared into the hall. I sat up, a little cold and still not quite awake. I retrieved my underwear from the floor and slipped them back on, then I clasped my bra behind my back. Being naked with Matthias felt amazing, daring, far outside the risk-free zone we'd been occupying for days. But it was undeniably weird sitting alone without any clothes on, in my family room, with *It's a Wonderful Life* on TV. When Matthias came back, he was still shirtless, his hair all over the place, beautiful. He was carrying a small wrapped box in his hand.

"Where did that come from?"

"Coat pocket." He grinned.

"Wait a sec." I grabbed my shirt and slipped it back over my head. "I have something for you too." I ran down the hall and lifted a rectangular package from its place on my dresser.

Back in the family room, Matthias was sitting on the couch fully clothed. His hair was, to a certain extent, back in order. I held out the box to him, and he took it.

"You first," he said. "Sorry it's not the best wrapping job."

The paper was a little crooked, but it didn't matter. I tore the tape; inside was a small white box with a gold seal. I opened the lid. The ring was silver and across the top were three interlocking stars: one silver, one bronze, and one gold.

"Orion's belt." I smiled up at him. "It's beautiful."

"If it's not the right size, we can have it adjusted. The guy at the shop said it's no big deal."

I slid it on. "It's perfect." Then I held my breath as he untied the curly ribbon and tore open the paper on his box. His face split into a wide grin as he held up a pair of brown leather gloves, the insides lined with black cashmere.

"Try them on."

He slipped them onto his hands and held them up in the air, wiggling his fingers. "Perfect."

"No more cold hands."

"I love them. And now I really do have to go." He kissed my forehead. "I'm not going to a show, just some quick errands. And I still have gifts to wrap."

"I love you." We said it together.

After he was gone, off to ensure his little sister would have a Christmas morning filled with gifts, I sat on the couch twisting the ring on my finger. I wanted more nights like tonight. But tomorrow was Christmas, and then we'd pack up the car to head to Fox Mountain for the Hollands' annual week of downhill skiing and family fun. It used to be my favorite week of the year. Now, all I wanted was to spend the days curled up with Matthias.

I told myself I could wait.

I told myself there would be so many more nights like this.

I sat there, watching the television while *It's a Wonderful Life* finished and started over again from the beginning, spinning Orion's belt around and around on my finger, waiting for my parents to come home, late and tipsy and giggling. I sat there and mapped everything out—how I'd get home next week, and how we'd go back to school, and how spring would become summer would become senior year, and everything was ahead of us, shining, just waiting for us to get there.

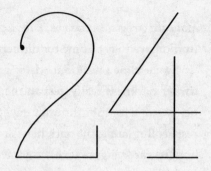

JANUARY, SENIOR YEAR
(NOW)

Mr. Michaels raises his eyebrows as I start disassembling the project I've been working on for weeks. I started it before break, but now it feels off. A torso twisted thin enough to snap, a long, angular neck, and a blank, moon-shaped face.

"I'm just not connecting with it anymore," I explain, popping one earbud out. The girl in the sculpture wears her pain in each sharp angle. Touch her, and she'll hurt you right back.

After Mr. Michaels heads home, I stay late working. I feel inspired for the first time in months, since school started, really. I want to start something brand new, something big and round and brightly enameled—something . . . happy? A thought tickles my brain, something cheesy, something I'd never say out loud.

Make the girl you want to be in the world. I blast Rihanna and work until I have to get home for dinner.

By the time I walk outside, it's pitch black. Usually, the deep winter darkness really gets to me, tugging at my insides like a heavy stone for months until daylight savings time comes to the rescue. But lately, the dark has felt like a challenge. Can't see the way forward? Figure it out anyway. The giddy high of returning to school after break is gone, replaced by pure, unfiltered determination. I can't make out the path ahead, can't make sense of what I need to do quite yet. But before graduation, I will face every piece of my past. I will find my way.

The Subaru is almost the last car left in the student lot. As I walk across the pavement, the sparsely scattered yellow lights on metal poles don't do a whole lot to break up the dark. But the light is enough that, as I get closer to my car, I can see a figure leaning against the hood.

I freeze, fifteen feet away. It's too dark to make out a face, but I would know that silhouette anywhere.

"Ellory?"

And there goes the universe, throwing my darkness metaphor right back in my face.

"I'm sorry for commandeering your car. I just want to talk." The figure straightens up, moving away from the hood. His hands are shoved inside deep coat pockets, but his shoulders are straight. Perfect posture.

I try to speak, but the words are stuck somewhere down in my throat. I take a step back, breathing quick. This is not what I need right now. This is not okay. I mumble something, but it doesn't come out in sentence form.

"What?" he asks, stepping toward me.

I clear my throat, plant my feet. "I said, it's not a good time."

"I'm sorry." He hangs back. He can see how rattled I am, and I hate it. I don't want him to see me shaken up. I don't want him to see me at all.

"Look, can I get by?" I force the words out without a quaver. It's more of a demand than a question. I shove my hand into my bag, and my fingers close around the keys.

Matthias steps aside, clearing my path to the driver's side door. He takes his hands out of his pockets, raising them in front of his chest. He's wearing my gloves, the ones I got him last Christmas. Like they don't remind him of me every time he slips them on. Like they're just things to keep his hands warm. His body is in retreat mode, but his voice presses against me, full force. I don't want to hear anything that comes out of his mouth, not one single word, but I can't shut it out.

"I didn't mean to upset you, honest." He takes two more steps back. "It's just I never see you in school, ever. It's like you don't even go to Pine Brook anymore. I left you some notes. . . . I don't know if you read them?"

I don't say anything. Of course I read them. They're in a box in my room, one for each week of the semester. He knows perfectly well that I know where his locker is. That I could have responded if I'd wanted to.

When I still don't say anything, he continues. "I was at school late, making up a French test. I had the flu last week. . . . Anyway, it doesn't matter, the point is I was there late, and then I came out here and saw your car. I wanted to see you. I knew you had to leave the shop eventually, so I waited."

I make a beeline for the car door. There's a reason we never see each other in school. There's a meticulously orchestrated schedule motivated by a strong desire for self-preservation. There's a reason I've never acknowledged the notes. See above, regarding self-preservation. I've made it to January with a blissful lack of hallway run-ins and zero words exchanged. Until now. I had been aiming to maintain that record until I figured out what to say. My words, on my terms. But this is an ambush.

I open the door and stand behind it like it's a shield. Matthias stays where he is, a good five feet away. His hands are back in his pockets. He has a wool hat shoved down over his head, and the ends of his hair spill out around the rim. Even with the hat on, I can tell it's longer than I've ever seen it. His face looks thinner, like he's lost too much weight.

Not that I care. Not that I have any reason to give one fuck if Matthias has been losing weight, or losing sleep, or losing his mind. My hand moves automatically to touch my ring finger, something I haven't done in months. The bare skin throbs, a dull ache where three little stars used to be.

"The notes have to stop," I say from behind my door shield. I feel less vulnerable here, protected. Strong enough to shut this conversation down. "I get that you have things to say, but I really don't." I make my voice mean. I slide into the car and put the key in the ignition. Before I can close the door, Matthias is right outside, crouched down in the path of the open door. If I try to close it now, I'll hit him.

"Okay, I'll stop. I'm sorry. I just have one question, then I'm gone. Promise." His eyes are wide, pleading. Jesus.

I don't say anything, and he takes my silence for permission to go on.

"Did you get your application in? To Portland State?" Of all the burning things Matthias Cole might have to say, he's using his one question to ask about college?

"Yes . . ." I don't even try to keep the skepticism out of my voice. Why the hell does he care? "Portland State and four other schools with art programs." I raise my eyebrows, silently asking if he's satisfied.

"Good, that's great. I'm really happy for you, Ellory. You'll get in, to Portland or wherever you want to go. I'm just really happy to hear that." He's rambling. He straightens up, backing out of range of the car door. I stare at him for a moment, not sure what to make of any of this.

What I do know is that I am complicit, and he is complicit too. He should want to forget me as much as I want to erase him from this parking lot, from my past, from my life.

"Thanks," I finally manage, and then I close the door and start up the car. If I still cared, I would ask how he was getting home. If I still cared, I would offer him a ride for his trouble. But I'm so far past the point of ever giving Matthias a ride ever again. I throw the car into drive and pull forward, turning toward the exit, toward home, away from Pine Brook and Matthias Cole.

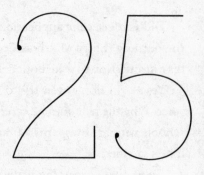

Matthias propped his boot up on an empty chair, and a big gray clump of slush dripped onto the Roaster floor. It was too cold and wet to do anything outside, so we were camped out at a table between the art deco fan lamp and the hall leading back to the bathrooms.

"It felt like you were gone for five years."

"If *you* felt like it was five years, imagine how last week felt for me. No you, no Ret, no real-life adolescent contact. Just me, my parents, and miles and miles of snowbound slopes."

He grinned and shook the hair out of his eyes. "One sec."

"How's Cordelia?" I didn't even need to ask who he was texting. It could have been Dave or the Smurf, but it was pretty much always Cordelia.

"Fine, bored. None of her activities start up again until next week." He clicked off his screen and set his phone face down on the table, giving me his full attention. My group chat was filled with new messages from this morning—*Was I back? Was I stranded on the slopes? Had I run off with a yeti?* But I hadn't responded yet. Matthias was the only person I wanted to see.

God, I had missed him. The runaway brown-blond strands. The way his face broke so easily into a wide, open smile. Every warm inch of his skin, covered now by an armor of winter layers.

"So what did I miss around here?"

"What is there ever to miss?" He shrugged. "I ran into Ret at the mall."

"Yeah?"

"More like Cordelia dragged me into Hot Topic. Ret was busy. We didn't stay long. She said they're promoting her next month."

"She didn't tell me that." Ret had told Matthias, but not me. I filed away that bit of information to think about later.

"She didn't seem too excited about it. You know Ret. Anyway, tell me about Fox Mountain. I bet you perfected your downhill game."

"Not much to tell. It's not like kicking ass on the slopes is going to do me much good in Portland." I took a long swallow of my vanilla latte and popped the lid back on the cup.

"Portland, huh? That's still the plan?" He swirled a spoon through his Midnight Runner—a big mug of dark roast spiked with a shot of espresso, no milk, no sugar.

"Sure is." I took another sip, never taking my eyes off Matthias. He seemed to be considering something thoughtfully, his eyes fixed on the mug in front of him. It had been ages since I had first mentioned Portland, and he still remembered.

"So why Portland, anyway? Is it the city, or did your parents go to school there or something?"

I hadn't really been planning to have the Portland Talk today—the one that involved big words like *College* and *Future*—but suddenly it felt right. We'd been together for seven months. We loved each other. If I wanted Matthias to be open with me, I needed to be open with him.

"It's like six parts the college, four parts the city. There's this art professor I want to study with; he does really progressive work with copper and stone. I've been stalking their website for months. And the city just seems perfect. The bookstores and the coffee shops and the art scene. There's this donut shop that's supposed to be out of this world."

"Sounds awesome." I tried to get a handle on his tone. I wanted him to be excited about this, about the idea of us there, but his face gave nothing away.

I chose my next words carefully. "College might be the only time in our lives when we get to just pick a place and move there. And Portland feels right. The water, the bridges, the river dividing the city in two . . . It's like here, but bigger and better and far away."

"Sounds like a really great town." Still totally neutral, totally flat.

Screw careful. I dove in headfirst. "Let's not go to Penn State, okay? Let's promise right now not to be those people. Who wants to get stuck in State College? People *go* to Portland. Like on purpose." Then I pulled out my ace. "There's a big music scene—you'd have so much to write about." Once I started, I couldn't stop. He'd love it—he had to see. "Think about where your website could go. All the shows, and not just local bands. Musicians come through Portland all the time. You'd be in the epicenter of indie cool."

He was silent for a moment, staring intently at his coffee. When he spoke, his words shot straight down into the mug. "Portland State sounds really great for you. Especially the copper and stone guy. It's not like there are a lot of opportunities for art here. I think you should go for it, definitely."

There was no hint of *we* in his words, not even a whisper. My face crumpled.

"I think it's great," he said quickly, "that you have it all figured out and stuff. I think it's awesome, Ellory. I really do."

"But you don't?" I felt like he was patting me on the head. Good girl, very smart. It felt awful. "Have it all figured out?"

"Not really." He picked up a sugar packet and began turning it over and over. "I guess I'm not like you."

My eyes were fixed on the packet, the white blur weaving faster and faster through his fingers.

I tore my eyes away and looked him straight in the eye. "Maybe it's really easy." My voice threatened to shake, but I forced it to stay steady. This was probably the single most important thing I'd ever say to Matthias. More important than a thousand *I-love-you*s. I needed him to hear me. "Maybe all we have to do is decide to be together. Maybe there's nothing else to figure out."

Suddenly the air between us was filled with a spray of white powder. It was on my hands, my face, all over my hair.

"Shit, I'm sorry." He reached across the table with a napkin to dab at my face. The ruptured sugar packet lay between us on the table.

"It's okay," I sputtered.

"Listen." He ran his fingers through his hair. He was looking at the table, the fan lamp, the out-of-order sign on the bathroom door. Anywhere except at me. "I'm just not ready to talk about college. I might not be ready for a long time. Maybe not ever. I know it's not fair, but I just can't."

My stomach twisted. But he'd brought it up. He'd asked about Portland. Had he been setting me up on purpose?

"What do you mean *can't*?" The words came out in a stranger's voice, high and thin.

"I'm sorry."

"So that's it?" My heart was pounding so loud, so fast, it was going to tear out of my chest.

He was silent.

"Is it money? Because they have financial aid. Or we could go somewhere else. It doesn't have to be Portland. There are so many options."

Matthias pushed back from the table, his chair scraping loud against the Roaster floor. "Can we go?"

"Go where?" I looked outside. The Subaru was covered in a fresh coat of snow. Everything was wet and cold and gray.

"I just need to get home, okay?" He followed my gaze out through the big glass window. "Give me your keys. I'll go brush off the car." He slipped on his gloves and held out his hand, and I fished around in my bag. This didn't make sense. Not at all.

"Cordelia's been cooped up in the house all afternoon," he said. An offering, a cover.

I didn't say anything back. He paused for a moment, my keys in his hand, caught halfway between me and the door.

I made myself speak before he could disappear outside. "Please don't shut me out. You promised to let me be your cave. Remember?" The words that had sounded so romantic, so beautiful in the cab of Ricky Cole's pickup truck sounded suddenly childish. Ridiculous.

"I told you we were messed up. All of the Coles. I told you I wouldn't be mad if you wanted out. I'm not hiding anything—you knew from our very first date." His voice was cold.

I stared at him, speechless.

"I'm trying really hard, Ellory. But I guess I can't be perfect all the time."

A minute later he was outside, popping the trunk, grabbing the snow brush.

I shrugged on my coat, not bothering to button it up. The snow outside was heavy and wet, the deep, ugly snow of mid-winter. Matthias had finished cleaning off the car and was climbing inside to start up the engine.

Every molecule inside my body was screaming *no*, screaming *why*. But there was nothing left to say. Nothing that wouldn't just make this worse. He scooted over to the passenger's seat, and I sat down behind the wheel and nudged the Subaru into reverse.

We sat in silence the whole way to his house. This was somehow worse than the screaming fight we'd had on his birthday. Lots of couples went to different colleges; I got that. They stayed together, or they broke up. I wasn't expecting a magic eight ball. But if we couldn't even talk about it—if the future was suddenly taboo—what the hell was the point?

I ignored the tears slipping down my face as I drove. I stared straight ahead. I refused to look at Matthias in the seat next to me. I refused to lift my hand from the steering wheel to wipe my cheeks. I kept my eyes on the road, which blurred, then came back into focus. I drove like that all the way to his house, and when he leaned over to kiss me, I turned away. Somehow, hiding the tearstains felt like a small victory.

For a moment, he froze, suspended midlean toward the driver's seat. I could feel his body stiffen next to me. Then, the unclasping of the seat belt, the release of the door handle as it swung out into the cold.

"I'll see you in school." This time, his words came out in the voice of a stranger.

"Yeah," I said into the driver's side window, not turning around. I couldn't look at him. I didn't know who I'd see. "See you in school."

All day, my stomach flutters. I told myself starting with Bex would be easy, but that was a lie because nothing about this is easy. I sit in eighth period and stare down at my list: five little names. *Bex, Jenni, Jonathan, Matthias, Ret.* Dr. Marsha had me write them down in our last session. She thinks if I have a physical list, something that looks official, I won't lose my nerve. I'm glad one of us feels confident about this. I don't even have a real plan; just five names and four months until graduation.

I read through my list for the twentieth time, and Principal Keegan's voice echoes in my ears. *Manageable, attainable.* Start with number one, and worry about the rest later. When the bell rings, I'm the first out of the classroom and into the fifth-floor stairwell, heading all the way down to the first floor and through the diagonal hallway to the art wing. On the way, I spot Abigail and two other girls in maroon and gold Rockette uniforms, heading in the opposite direction. I wasn't exactly nice to her before winter break, when I told her I didn't need her help. But really, she helped me more than she could possibly know. She gave me permission to see all of Ret—the complicated, messy, hard to see parts. Without Abigail, I might not have walked away from her in December. I might not have had the guts to make my list, either.

"Hey, Abigail." She stops in her tracks. One of the other girls grips her arm just above the elbow, but Abigail murmurs something under her breath, and her friends keep walking. The elbow-gripper turns around to gawk at us over her shoulder, then quickly whips back around when I catch her staring.

"Hey," Abigail says when we're alone. She smiles, because she's Abigail, but keeps her distance. I can tell she's not super happy to see me, and I don't blame her after last time.

"I just wanted to say thank you, for what you said before break. It actually meant a lot."

"Oh." Her face lights up. "I'm really happy to hear that."

"So anyway, thank you. You were right. And I'm sorry I was kind of a bitch."

"It's okay." She tugs at the end of her short uniform skirt, and there's not really anything left to say. I smile, one quick flash of gratitude. I have business to take care of, and I have to get to the green room before Bex does.

"See you around." I give her a little wave, and Abigail turns to catch up with her friends.

When I duck through the door to the theater, the place is empty. No rehearsal on Fridays. I walk stage left, through the door that opens into the green room, and throw my bag on the couch. I sink into the worn cushions for a minute, but I can't sit still, so I get back up and walk over to the costume closet and back. Finally I settle for perching on the counter in front of the makeup mirrors, my feet tapping the back of one of the chairs. I can do this. I *have* to do this.

Outside the theater, I can hear a group of voices singing "Luck Be a Lady" at the top of their lungs, and for a moment I think I'm wrong about rehearsal, and they're about to come in here, but then the voices pass by the theater and fade down the hallway, out the back entrance, and into the parking lot. Then, there's silence.

Maybe she won't show up.

Maybe she's ignoring my text, even though I know she got it.

Maybe she doesn't want to do this any more than I do.

But then I hear the soft scuffle of feet walking across the stage, and Bex pushes through the door to the green room and stops in the middle of the floor. For a moment, we just stare at each other.

I push myself up from the makeup counter and walk over to the couch, gesturing weakly toward the cushions. "Want to sit?" This is so awkward.

I sit at one end of the couch and Bex sits at the other like we're on some sort of formal first date, our bags a protective barrier between us. Now that we're here, my mouth feels dry, and nothing I've rehearsed feels right anymore. How do I explain that walking away from Bex wasn't personal, that cutting her out was so much bigger than either of us? That I have to be alone—really alone—to find my way forward. Somehow, I don't think *it's not you, it's me* is going to cut it.

I let my eyes wander across her face, try to focus on the memory of Bex twirling and twirling in the mink, the fur like snow against her shoulders sophomore year. Ret's legs kicked up on the back of the couch, the *Rolling Stone* slipping from her fingers as she passed judgment on the almost purloined coat. But after a minute, the room gets hot, time moving us forward, dragging us through junior year. The memory shifts. There are flames licking up my cheeks, smoke in my lungs, the squeal of tires in my ears. Time wants to drag me down, and I can't go back there again. It's not her fault; she was on the periphery of it all. But I can't be with her without remembering. *This* is why I had to walk away.

I squeeze my hands into fists and press my fingernails into my palms until the pain snaps me back to the present. One conversation, then this will be over. I cut straight to the point, my second apology of the afternoon. "I've been really shitty to you," I say. "I'm sorry."

Bex's mouth drops open. I don't know what she was expecting me to say, but it definitely wasn't this.

"I just wanted you to know that I noticed. Calling me before school started. Inviting me over at Thanksgiving. It meant something."

Bex shifts uncomfortably on the couch. "Are you trying to make up or something?" she asks.

"I just wanted to explain. The reasons we can't be friends, they don't have anything to do with you, okay?"

"I get it," Bex says sharply. "I always got it."

"Oh." This conversation was supposed to make us both feel better, like something was finally resolved between us. But maybe I'm the only one who needs the resolution.

"It's okay." Bex gives me a tiny smile. "It's nice to hear anyway."

A small knot releases in my chest. "We never had much without Ret," I say. "You and Jenni and me."

"I guess not." Bex is silent for a moment, then she asks, "Do you ever talk to her?"

"Ret?" Not since December. Not since I left her down by the river.

Bex nods.

"Not anymore." I thought I was the only one to fall back under Ret's spell. "Do you?"

"All summer." Bex's words are full of breath, like it's a relief to tell me, like this is something she needs to unburden. "Every single night."

We're both quiet for a minute, lost in our own web of memories.

"Anyway, it ended when school started back up," Bex says. "I just needed to tell someone, I guess."

She's waiting for me to open up to her, to confess that she's not the only one who's been cheating. Who couldn't leave the past in the past, who couldn't so easily forget Ret the siren, the charmer, the bellwether, and replace her with Ret the betrayer. Who couldn't so easily forgive her, either.

I can't say it.

"Thanks for understanding," I say instead. "How I've been this year, it was never about you. I guess you knew that already, but I just needed to say it."

"Thank you." She stands and picks up her bag from the couch. "Take care, Ellory." Then she's gone, her back disappearing through the green room door. There's a huge swell of sadness rising in my chest, and I don't know why. This is what I wanted. To say I'm sorry, then move on. But it still hurts.

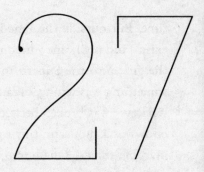

27

JANUARY, JUNIOR YEAR
(THEN)

After Matthias took the future off the table, the days were filled with pleasantries and *how was the French quiz?* And *did you see what's on the menu in the sky dome today?* For two weeks, I was the model girlfriend. The *perfect* girlfriend. I kept it light. I didn't fuss and I didn't push and a perma-smile lit up my tear-free face.

And we didn't make plans.

At all. Not just future plans. We didn't hang out after school, and we didn't see each other on weekends. During the week, we held hands in the hallways and we stopped by each other's tables in the sky dome at lunch. Just like normal. Just like always.

Between the hours of eight to three, we were Ellory & Matthias. Matthias & Ellory. All smiles, all small talk, all the time. But outside the Pine Brook walls, it was like we didn't exist. I did my homework and I hung out with Ret and I piled the girls into the Subaru to go thrifting and no one asked if something was wrong, because what could possibly be wrong? Whatever was broken between us was on the inside. My entire body was a thousand tiny robin's eggs, stitched together with invisible thread. One bump, one push, one too hard shake of my hand, and everything was going to shatter.

Inexplicably, Pine Brook went on around us. The classes, the winter break war stories, the relentless January gray that settled in my stomach like a stone. By the third week back, I couldn't take the niceness anymore. The stubborn avoidance of anything real. On Tuesday at the end of lunch, as everyone was packing up bags and beginning to filter through the doors, I touched Matthias on the shoulder and motioned him aside.

"Meet me down in the shop after eighth?"

The hesitation before he spoke was palpable. For a moment, we were standing there in the sky dome, only the palest scraps of January light filtering through the dirty glass above our heads, and I thought he was going to say no. Maybe this period of self-enforced politeness within the bounds of eight to three would go on forever.

Maybe we would never break up and we would never get back to normal. How long could we go on like this, suspended, hovering?

But then he said yes, he'd meet me. It was the only thing I'd asked of him in over two weeks.

While I waited for him to show up, I went through my routine: sweep beneath the machines, wipe down the worktables and stools, check the supply shelves, update the inventory list. I grabbed Mr. Michaels's list of materials for the next day and started to pull supplies for his classes:

- *¼-inch-round bar stock*
- *stainless steel filler rod*
- *⅛-inch-diameter rivets*
- *rivet washers*
- *bin of sheet metal scraps*
  15 students x 3 periods, 13 students x 2 periods

When I had finished and Matthias still hadn't arrived, I walked over to the bin in the back that held my own stuff. Recently, I'd been bringing in scrap from around the city and working on large, abstract sculptures. I wasn't sure where they were going yet, but I was interested in combining different types of metals, bending sharp objects into curved shapes that could look almost delicate, soft. I liked finding the unexpected in something hard and cold.

At a quarter to four, when I was starting to worry that he wasn't going to show, the shop door opened, and Matthias stood in the doorway.

"Blast from the past." He looked around. "I haven't been down here since freshman year."

"Welcome to my home away from home." My heart was fluttering. He looked like my boyfriend one minute and a stranger the next.

"I've thought about coming by before," he said. He was still standing in the doorway, looking in. "But I didn't want to interrupt." My thoughts skipped back to our first conversation at Dave Franklin's party. How I'd told him what I was working on. How he'd said, *You should show me sometime,* but he'd never come. Maybe it was my fault. Maybe he'd been waiting for an invitation. The door swung shut as he stepped into the shop and dropped his bag. "Anyway, sorry I'm late. The Smurf caught me after eighth. He wants my help painting their basement this weekend."

"Painting their basement?"

"They're converting it into a man cave for Mr. Murphy's birthday, installing a bar and everything. Could be fun when his parents are out of town."

It's not like he said it could be fun *for us* or *we should throw a party there,* but the mere hint that we might go there, together, in the future, was like a tiny, dangling scrap. Until this second, I hadn't realized how hungry I'd been.

My heart was starving.

"Could be fun, for sure." I kept my voice light. Perfect girl-friend voice.

I placed the rag and bottle of Fantastic back in the cleaning bin and walked over to him. Not some stranger. My boyfriend. In the past two and a half weeks, he'd touched me exactly nine times: four pecks on the cheek, three touches to the small of my back, one tuck of the hair behind my ear, and one brush of his hand against mine in the sky dome, which may have been acci-dental. I needed more than small talk.

Before I could overthink it, I reached up with both hands and pulled his face down to meet mine. I could hear his breath catch, surprised. His lips were still against mine for a moment, but then he leaned into the kiss, into me, and he brought his arms up around my back and pulled me close. It was everything I'd been missing, everything that had been hovering between us, untouched, both of us too afraid to reach out, to risk something.

In that moment, kissing Matthias felt like coming home to a warm house after being out all night in a storm. My whole body ached, but he was made of heat and light. We made our way to the shop floor, tangled up in each other, our breath coming in hot, fast waves. The floor was cold and hard, but I barely felt it. I felt his hands running along the length of my legs, my stomach, my neck. I felt my body collapse into him, come back alive.

When the January gray had become a deep, five o'clock dark, we shrugged on our coats and walked out to the student lot. I slipped my hand into his hand as we walked. Everything had changed and nothing had changed. Now that our bodies weren't pressed together anymore, now that we were two people walking out in the cold, the air between us felt empty, waiting. Waiting for me to say something.

"So are you going to help out this weekend? With the basement?"

"Guess so. I don't really have any other plans."

"We could go to that new Marvel movie on Sunday. Or Saturday. Whatever day you're not at the Smurf's."

"Maybe. Painting might take all weekend."

"Oh." Suddenly everything was crystal clear. The last hour was a deviation, a blip. Apparently, we still weren't making plans outside school. Nothing had changed.

We were standing in front of my car. Where the hell were my keys? I was so sick of this—the forced politeness, the perfect girlfriend act. Screw it.

The words came out in a rush. "I don't get it. A minute ago, you were probably going to help because you didn't have plans. But then you can't take two hours to go to a movie? Help me out here, Matthias. I don't know what's going on with us."

"Yeah," he said. "Me either."

I could feel my keys, jammed underneath my wallet at the bottom of my bag. I gave them a yank.

"If making out in the metal shop for an hour fulfills some sort of quota for the week, I guess we cashed in." I didn't even try to keep the bitterness out of my voice. I threw my bag into the back and slid into the driver's seat while he walked around the front of the car and opened the passenger's side door.

"I didn't mean it that way. I'm sorry." He slid in and reached for his seat belt. Inside the car, with both doors closed, I could feel the quiet press in around us. The lot was pretty much empty, and the houses across the street from Pine Brook were closed up tight. I turned the key in the ignition and let the heater kick on.

"Where do we go from here?" My words were half voice and half breath. I didn't want to fight, not again. I just wanted my boyfriend back. I let the car sit there in park for a moment. I wasn't ready to drive away just yet.

"I need to take things kind of slow right now. Maybe we should dial it back."

"What does that even mean? Are you breaking up with me?"

"No!" He whipped around in his seat and grabbed my hands. "That's not what I want. Is that what you want?"

When I turned toward him, this time I didn't try to hide the tears spilling down my cheeks. "Of course not," I choked out.

"I don't want to lose you, okay? I just need some space to

figure things out. Can you do that for me? Can we just go easy right now?"

I let my head fall back against the headrest and wiped at my face with my coat sleeve.

"I didn't mean to make you cry. I'm really sorry, Ellory. Things are just really intense at home right now. I need things to be a little less intense with us."

"I get it." I didn't. I wanted him to tell me *how* things were intense at home, wanted to scream, *open up, tell me!* Instead, I shifted the car into drive and pulled out of the lot. "Less intense, coming right up."

I could do it. I could do anything. Easy, breezy, beautiful Ellory Holland. The light side of the moon.

Matthias turned on some music, and I drove us along the dark West Shore streets toward his house while he chattered on about some band he was going to see tomorrow night after his shift at the restaurant and how the new dishwasher wanted to come, but he wasn't sure he wanted company. It wasn't even remotely suggested that I might be invited, and I didn't ask. I nodded and smiled in all the right places. When we pulled up in front of his house, I let him kiss me. I could do this because for some reason, this is what he needed right now. Fine. Easy.

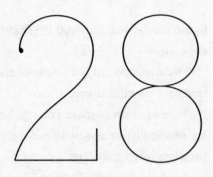

FEBRUARY, SENIOR YEAR
(NOW)

This next one feels like a cop-out, but as I go through my room and gather up what's left of her things, I have Dr. Marsha's voice in my ears, telling me they won't all be deep, cleansing heart-to-hearts. The point is to keep going. Sometimes there's only packing up what remains and moving on.

I fill up a tote bag with old issues of *Food & Wine*, three pairs of sunglasses I borrowed and never returned, a worn copy of *Go Ask Alice*, and a set of star-shaped cookie cutters. I picked tonight because it's the Senior Showcase, and pretty much the entire school will be there. Jenni will definitely be there, supporting oldest Hanson look-alike Elliot and his Christian rock band. As I walk outside, a few fat, wet flakes are starting to fall, and I'm grateful to sink into the Subaru's blasting heat while I wait for the windshield to defrost.

It's been almost a year since the last time I made the drive over to Jenni's, but I could still do it in my sleep. Maybe I'm a coward to make my last drive there this way, but Dr. Marsha's right. Jenni's not interested in forgiving or forgetting, and I have to accept that. I have to work with what I've got.

When I pull up to the house, the first thing I notice is how empty the front yard looks without us filling it up. I came here during the Showcase for a reason; still all I can see are our empty forms, transparent and hollow, bringing the lawn to life. Bex marking the steps to a new dance team combination. Jenni passing around curry cashews or a tray of lemon drop cookies. Ret and me hanging back, listless and lazy, taking it all in.

The way we used to be. The way we'll never be again.

I shake my head, and our bodies disappear. The lawn is brown and just starting to collect a thin layer of snow. I'm surprised to see two cars in the driveway. I guess her dad and stepmom are actually home. I don't really want to see them, but the storm is starting to kick up, and I'd rather not leave her things outside like a bad case of déjà vu.

I pop the trunk and grab the tote. It's weird to think that three years of friendship can be so easily contained, packed up, zippered shut. Jenni and I were never precious with one another, never tricked ourselves into believing we'd be anything without Ret at the conductor's stand, playing us off each other, note by note. But still. For three years, she was the Earth to my moon. For three years, we shared the sun's light.

On her porch, I ring the bell and wait to see who I'll get. I can hear the TV blasting inside, some little kid's show. I'm about to ring the bell again when I hear footsteps on the wooden stairs that connect the second floor to the entry hall. The door opens, and Jenni's stepmom is standing in front of me holding a stuffed frog. She looks a little harried.

"Ellory. What a . . . surprise." Her words are clipped, guarded. Like she's afraid of me. "Jenni's not here." She tilts her head to one side, probably trying to remember the last time she saw my face. Do I look different now? Troubled? Altered? I can only imagine what Jenni must have said about me at home. She gestures apologetically and starts to shut the door.

"Wait. Please." I smile big, going for my best impression of normal. "I know Jenni's at the Showcase. She just wanted me to drop off a few things." I slip the tote bag off my shoulder and hold it out, letting the small lie hover between us. "Would you see that she gets this?"

Jenni's stepmom sets the stuffed frog down on the hall table and slowly reaches for the bag. "I didn't realize you and Jenni were still . . ." Talking? Friends? Her face is clouded over in concern. It's clear she doesn't want me anywhere near her impressionable stepdaughter.

"These are some books of hers," I say. "Some sunglasses. I just wanted to give them back."

"I see." Her face softens for a second. "That's very responsible of you, Ellory. I'll put this in her room."

"Thanks, Mrs. Randall-Collins."

For a moment we stand there, just looking at each other. Unless I run into her at graduation, this is probably the last time Jenni's stepmom and I will ever speak. It's definitely the last time I'll ever drop by her house. I have so many memories here. Knowing that this will be the last time feels hard and strange in a way I hadn't quite expected.

"Well, it was nice seeing you, Ellory. We'll keep you in our prayers."

The sting in her words catches me off guard. It's like that thing some southerners say, *bless your heart*, when they mean anything but. I never knew anyone in Jenni's family to be religious; Jenni's summer with "the born-again Randalls" must have had a persuasive impact. It blows my mind that anyone's newfound devotion could have something to do with me.

"Thanks," I mumble. "It was nice seeing you too."

I turn and start back down the stairs. The wind is whipping icy ropes of snow against my cheeks, and the sky looks like it's about to black out completely. I slide behind the wheel and start the car. As I wait for the heat to kick in, my mind travels back to a day last March, winter dark and icy cold like this one. A day long before Jenni found God, the day she crossed the line with Ret.

Bex and I had pulled up outside Jenni's house, but we were still sitting in the car with the heat blasting, waiting for the wind to die down. Ret and Jenni were already inside; I'd picked Bex up from her dance studio before driving over.

"What's with Jenni?" I asked. "She was weird today, right?"

Bex played with a piece of hair and stared out the window into the swirling snow. "She didn't tell you? She asked Ret for her blessing, but Ret shot her down hard."

"Her blessing?"

Bex shrugged. "If Ret doesn't want Jonathan, I guess someone should have him."

I tried to think back. If Jenni had had any interest in Jonathan Gaines before, she'd done a good job hiding it. "They just broke up," I said. Not that we had a lot of ex-boyfriends in our small circle, but dating your friend's ex was a universal taboo. Everyone knew that. "What was she thinking?"

I knew Ret was right about this. Even if she had pushed Jonathan away. Even if she was scared. That didn't give Jenni the right to just move in. Bex pulled her snow cap down low over her ears, refusing to take the bait.

"Let's go in," she said. "They're waiting."

The heat kicks in, nudging me back into the present, and I angle the car into the road, turning it around in the cul-de-sac at the end of Jenni's street. In that moment, I had been so certain. It was uncomplicated, girl code. It's hard to imagine being so sure of anything anymore. As I drive, the world swirls into a dance of white and gray. The wipers do their best to keep the windshield clear, but it's a losing battle. I drive slow. As Jenni's house disappears into the background, I imagine her coming home after the Showcase, reading the note tucked inside the tote bag.

Jenni,

I'm returning your stuff because I don't want to owe you anything. So here we are, totally debt free, down to the very last magazine.

You know it was an accident. That's what everyone calls it, and as much as I hate that word, it's true. But those things I said—I didn't mean them, but I can't take them back. And I'm so sorry for that.

I take full responsibility for my actions last year. I've never tried to claim my innocence, and I won't start now. But, Jenni—we both know I wasn't the only one to blame. I live with it every single day, with or without you. Don't you get that I've punished myself more than you ever could? So you can keep on hating me, that's fine. But I'm done shouldering it all. I'm done letting you do that to me.

Take care,
Ellory

I pull into my driveway and step out of the car. As I walk up to the front door, I picture Jenni's face, her red hair bright against a black balloon. I hold the string tight in my hands until the wind picks up. It doesn't take long. The string bites into my flesh, and I gasp. Then I let go, let it carry her away. Goodbye, hard tile beneath my hands. Goodbye, scream trapped like a wild animal between my ears. Goodbye, hard flash of her eyes—an accusation, a blade cutting me in two.

Goodbye, Jenni.

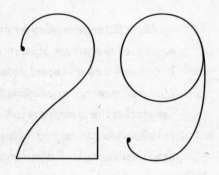

"How did you know Jonathan was the one?" I finally asked, dropping the paperback I'd been not-reading down beside me on Ret's bed. While she reorganized her vinyl collection by album title, I'd been skimming the same three paragraphs over and over. Something about two sisters driving cross-country. They were having an important conversation, but every time I got to the bottom of the page, I still had no idea what was going on.

"Huh?" Ret looked up from the floor, where she was surrounded by the A's. *Acid Tongue, Adore, Amnesiac, Automatic for the People*. She was humming something beneath her breath, harboring it like a secret.

"When you decided to sleep together. How did you know?" What I really wanted to ask about was what I'd seen the other day—Ret getting into the back of Dave's car and driving away. Driving downtown with the guys, without me. Without Jonathan, either. But asking would have meant admitting I was there, following Matthias, watching like some creepy stalker. So I asked about Jonathan instead.

"It just kind of happened, I don't know. I didn't decide in advance and wear my special panties or anything. The first time, we were fooling around at his place after school, and I just wanted to. It wasn't some huge deal." Ret blew a stream of breath straight up, fluttering through her bangs, which were streaked with Atomic Turquoise this week.

"So he's not the one?" I asked. *Come on, Ret. Take the bait.*

"Since you asked," Ret said, her voice almost a whisper, "I think things are winding down with Jonathan. The sex is fun and all, but I'm kind of into someone else."

"What!" I sat up straight, feigning surprise. "You did not tell me this."

Ret reached behind her, into her top dresser drawer, and pulled out a black flask decorated with a pair of crossbones and the face of a pink cat wearing an eye patch. She unscrewed the cap and took a sip.

"Not much to tell. I'm still with Jonathan, for now. You want?" She held the flask out toward me.

I took it from her and tipped it back. The warm liquid burned my mouth and throat. "What is this?"

"Whiskey." She grinned. "Veronica's finest."

I passed the flask back to Ret and sank into the mountain of black and silver pillows. "Must be something in the air."

She cocked her head to one side, waiting for me to continue. I had to give her something. A tidbit about Matthias in exchange for her secrets. *You are mine, and I am yours.*

"Things aren't so great with me and Matthias either. You can't say anything, swear."

Ret took another sip, then tossed the flask back inside the drawer. "Swear to Maude. But it's a little obvious."

"Did he say something?" *Was that the only time you've gone out with Matthias and Dave? Does Jonathan know?*

Ret looked me straight in the eyes. "Ellory May, you're my best friend. You've been moping around for weeks."

I ran my thumb against the edge of my book so the pages flipped out into a fan. Part of me wanted to tell Ret everything. About Portland, the eggshells, the special misery of *dialing it back*, a phrase I now loathed to my very core. As it turned out, *dialing it back* meant living in a perpetual state of ambiguous, unintense limbo that was killing me slowly from the inside. I wouldn't have wished it on my worst enemy.

"I really hate to see you so blue," Ret said.

The other part of me didn't want to talk about Matthias at all. Today marked the end of week six of perfect girlfriend Ellory. It was like he had removed his heart and stored it away in a tamper-proof vault. And I was expected to do the same until he was ready to be normal again, no questions asked.

"So tell me about mystery guy," I said, steering the conversation back on track.

"Mystery guy," Ret mused. "That's good. He definitely has a dangerous edge."

"What does that even mean?" I couldn't just admit that I knew. I played along, letting her make it a game.

Ret considered my question. "He has a dark side. He's the anti–Jonathan Gaines."

That was for sure. Did she know what a dick he really was? I studied her face closely. The delicate curve of her lip. The deep lapis blue of her eyes. She looked impossibly proud of herself.

"You are so not subtle," I laughed. "You've been crushing on him since before that party." I bit at the inside of my lip. Maybe she already knew Dave was dealing, but she didn't know about Matthias's dad. She was my best friend; she deserved to know the truth. But I couldn't betray his trust like that. The one big secret he had actually told me. "Look, I know he's all edgy or whatever, but that drug stuff is no joke. The bathtub full of coke, the contact high from licking Dave's walls? Those rumors come from somewhere."

"What are you, Miss Straight Edge all of a sudden?" Ret picked up a fresh stack of records. "You don't need to worry about me, Ellory May. I can handle myself. Besides, I never said it was Dave Franklin."

"Sure."

"Jonathan's a total peach, but he's just not the one. Onward and upward. And Ellory, this is just between us. I can't have Jonathan hearing that we're over, and I'm just not quite ready to break him yet."

At first, I thought she'd meant that she wasn't quite ready to break *up* with him. But Ret knew exactly what she was saying.

"So it's our secret, right?"

"Swear to Maude."

"Before I forget." Ret reached back into her dresser and pulled out a little red leather notebook. She didn't keep a real diary, but she always had a notebook going—ideas, quotes, lists, lyrics to songs she started writing and never finished. "Veronica's been snooping again. I left the others with Jenni, but I missed one. Hang on to it for now?"

I took the notebook and slipped it into my bag.

"I'll get it when the dust settles. A thorough snoop usually satisfies her motherly urges for a few months."

"Just pick it up whenever."

Ret reached toward me with a stack of records. "Now, are you going to help me alphabetize, or what?"

I took them and slid down off the bed. "Why are we doing this again?"

"Because sometimes, a girl needs to change things up. And the whole alpha by artist system is so passé."

For a moment, we sorted in silence.

"Two roads diverged in a wood, and I—"

Ret looked up, surprised. When she spoke, her words were dripping with intrigue. "I took the one deep into the darkest woods in the middle of the blackest night. And I never, ever returned."

Then she cracked a smile and put a record on the turntable, some old David Bowie track. If Ret wanted to trade in her totally devoted boyfriend for Dave Franklin, another deep, dark trophy to add to her collection, fine. Ret could make her choices, and I could make mine. And I chose Matthias. There were a thousand art schools, and college was still light-years away. In the meantime, I was not going to sit back and let us fade into oblivion. I was going to fight.

MARCH, SENIOR YEAR
(NOW)

I spend the next two weeks cleaning out my room. I haven't figured out what to do next, but at least this feels like doing *something*. Jenni's stuff is gone—what else can I get rid of? Old books from elementary school? Library donation box. Clothes I haven't worn since freshman year? Goodwill. Old magazines and hair clips and lanyards from summer camp? Trash, trash, trash. It feels great.

On Wednesday before school, I'm up early on a cleaning jag, going through the laundry basket of shoes I never wear anymore. I'm almost to the bottom of the basket when I see it: Under a pair of eight-hole, wine red Doc Martens is Ret's notebook. The red leather blends right in.

I sit cross-legged on my bed and flip through the pages. The paper feels illicit beneath my fingers. Like I shouldn't be allowed to have Ret's book, even though she *gave* it to me. Even though she never picked it up. *Separate the past from the present, Ellory. Move forward. Don't look back.* I know I shouldn't indulge my fixations, but I can't help it. I keep turning her pages. *Pine Brookians Most Likely to Peak in High School. The Authoritative, Annotated Guide to the Best Record Stores in PA.* We used to make these lists together. I stop on the last one we made, last winter, right before everything went to shit.

Hot Topic Customers Who Are Totally Secret Psychos
1. Blue goatee guy muttering under his breath in the CD aisle. Creepy AF.
2. Blond Penn State chick—third time this week. Not your scene, princess.
3. Maria Hidelman's dad. What the hell is he doing here!?!?!

Underneath item three, there's a sketch of Mr. Hidelman and his giant dad glasses. I remember drawing that while Ret tacked a new Velvet Underground poster to her wall.

I flip through the rest of the notebook. Mostly other silly lists, quotes from *The Outsiders* and *The Catcher in the Rye*, a whole page of dates logging every time Mr. Morris said *okalie-dokalie* during class junior year. (Twelve times in October—a record.)

The entries stop about a third of the way through. Part of me wants to keep the notebook, tuck it back beneath the Docs and forget about it until inspiration strikes. Another part of me wants to give it back to Ret, even though we haven't talked in months. Maybe I'll just toss it into the trash, pretend I never found it. But I can't stop flipping through. On the next to last page, after a section of blanks, I find what looks like lyrics to one of Ret's half-written songs. The words are upside down, as if she had made some weak attempt to keep the lyrics a secret. I flip the notebook over and start to read.

> *So many things*
> *I'll never say to you*
> *My touch is a drug*
> *And you're so clean*
> *So I can't touch you*
> *Not anymore*
> *Can't be around you*
> *Can't let you love me*
> *Anymore*
> *My words are drugs*
> *So I'll just be mean*
> *I won't say how*
> *You + me*
> *We're honey + poison*
> *Poison poison*
> *Gotta save you from*
> *My poison*

The page is dated last February, just over a year ago, the week Ret gave me the notebook to hold on to. That seems about right. Then it hits me—this is my next move. I tear out the page and shove it in my pocket and return the little red book to its former hiding spot beneath my boots. Then I grab a banana and last year's school directory from its spot on the kitchen counter. Dad gestures weakly at the boxes of cereal on the dining room table, but I'm in a hurry. I kiss him quickly and run out to the car.

I plug Jonathan Gaines's address into Google Maps. He lives less than five minutes away, but I've never been to his house before. When he and Ret were together, I always got the feeling that he wanted her to bring her friends around, let him into her life. But she never did. And now, it's been almost a year since I've seen Jonathan. Since my suspension last April. Since he transferred to Saint Anne's this fall.

I glance at the clock on the dash. Hopefully, I'm early enough to catch him before he leaves for school. I park in the driveway and ring the bell, steeling myself for one of his parents to come to the door, but Jonathan opens it, looking surprised. The pressed khakis and navy blazer suit him.

"Hey, Ellory. Did you want to come in?" He's only asking because it's the polite thing to say, but his smile looks genuine. I take a deep breath.

"That's okay," I say. "This will just take a sec."

I reach into my coat pocket and touch the slip of paper. Jonathan seems totally fine. Bright smile, fresh haircut. Giving him the song might do more damage than good. On the other hand, he deserves some kind of explanation, an everything-is-illuminated moment, even if I never get one. I hesitate.

"It's been a while," he says, watching me waver. He was always too kind to Ret. Now he's being too kind to me.

"How's Saint Anne's?" I ask, buying myself a minute to think.

"Fine." He runs a hand through his white-blond hair. "My parents wanted me to transfer. They thought it would be easier, a fresh start."

I nod.

"But you stayed?" he asks, even though he already knows the answer. The real question is *why*, but he's too polite to ask.

"I stayed."

He stares down at his shoes, and my mind is made up. I slip the paper out of my pocket and hand it to him.

"I came by because I found this in a notebook of Ret's from last winter. She really did love you. She thought she was trying to save you from herself."

I offer up a small smile, and after a minute, he smiles back. "Anyway," I say, "you should have it."

Before he can say anything, I'm spinning around, walking back to the car. None of us gets a happy ending. But I can give Jonathan Ret's song. Maybe make him feel a little bit better about what happened after she wrote it. At least there's that.

MARCH, JUNIOR YEAR
(THEN)

I grabbed Jenni before fourth, on our way into the sky dome.
"What's going on? Why wasn't Ret on the chat?"

In the middle of third, Jenni had started a new group chat
with just Bex and me, instructing us to come to her place right
after school. After a flurry of texts and a near-confiscation situ-
ation with my phone, I still had no idea what had prompted the
SOS.

Jenni looked around, her eyes lighting on the flood of bodies
starting to spill through the sky dome doors. "Not here, come on."

She took my hand and pulled me down the hall toward the
bathroom. The one by the sky dome used to be a smoker mag-
net because the vents lead straight up to the roof, but last year

the school wised up and moved Mrs. Krackow to the classroom directly across the hall. Mrs. Krackow had a reputation for sniffing out smokers and doling out punishment like candy, so now no one did anything in the top floor girls' room besides pee and check their makeup. It was usually empty.

The door swung shut behind us, and I slouched back against the wall with the hand dryers. "You're starting to scare me."

"Sorry, but everyone and their mom is in the sky dome right now. Ret wouldn't want an audience." Jenni adjusted the strap on her satchel bag against her shoulder and tucked a loose strand of hair back into her braid. "I don't know if you noticed that Ret's not in school today."

She delivered the news with a smug blend of satisfaction and concern. She knew something I didn't, one of Ret's secrets, and she was totally getting off on the power trip. Whatever. If something were really wrong with Ret, she would have told me.

"I never see her before lunch," I replied. "What's going on?" I kept my voice level. Hell if I was going to give Jenni the satisfaction of seeing me squirm.

"She called me last night. Jonathan dumped her."

"What?" I shot up, and my shoulder banged against one of the dryers. Every day for the last three weeks, I'd been waiting for Ret to waltz into school, announce that she and Jonathan were dunzo, and show off a collection of selfies with Dave. But every day, Jonathan and Ret were still together, and there had been no more mention of a pending breakup. I couldn't keep the surprise out of my voice. "*Jonathan* dumped *Ret*?"

But Ret had Jonathan on a string. He was hers for as long as she wanted.

"Over the phone. Last night. Ret says she doesn't care, but she wouldn't be taking a mental health day if she wasn't hurting. She's coming over after school, and we need a full showing of support."

Later that afternoon, when we were all assembled at Jenni's and fawning over Ret with soft blankets and pints of Cherry Garcia, I hung back. I called bullshit on this whole charade. Ret obviously wasn't broken up over this, but Jenni and Bex were too wrapped up in the showy melodrama of being a good friend to notice. The real question was how long Ret would allow it to go on. She wasn't brokenhearted. Ret got Jonathan to break up with her.

Of course she did.

A mug of hot tea and a serious amount of ice cream later, Ret finally spoke up. "This is very sweet and all, but it really isn't that big of a deal. I'm totally fine."

Bex got up from the floor at Ret's feet, where she'd been camped out on the braided rug, and sat down on the couch next to her. Ret flinched, just slightly, when Bex enclosed her hand in both of hers.

"You're just in shock. It's perfectly understandable. You've been together for almost nine months. It's going to take a while for this to really sink in." She glanced toward the kitchen, where Jenni was checking on something in the oven, and lowered her voice. "Remember when Jenni and Mark broke up?" She gave Ret a knowing stare that conjured up memories of endless prog rock playlists and a particularly grody band T-shirt that Jenni had refused to wash for two months. "Love is hell."

"I appreciate the concern. I really do." Ret extracted her hand from Bex's grasp. "But I basically asked him to dump me."

"What? You didn't tell me that." Jenni appeared in the doorway to the TV room, oven mitts on both her hands.

I sank down onto the arm of the couch and leaned my head back against the wall. Called it. Jenni thought she had the jump on me, but I was the keeper of Ret's secrets. I felt a little bad for Jenni, but that was just the way of things.

"He wanted, like, a white picket fence and three kids and a dog and stuff. I told him it wasn't my style and he could tag along for the Ret Show if he wanted, but I didn't think he wanted. I had to lay it out for him like five times. I guess he finally got it."

Jenni looked pale. I couldn't tell if she was more upset about Ret's blanket rejection of all things hearth and home, which she so dearly loved, or not having early access to the contours of Ret's heart.

I felt a little ill myself. All I wanted was for Matthias to make us a priority again. I was willing to compromise; Portland had been my dream, I should never have expected it to be his. And now the city I used to crave had become a sore spot I was afraid to touch. I'd mention other schools casually, how this one had a beautiful campus or that one had a brand new sculpture studio. I took Principal Keegan's advice and made a Google Sheet of the top studio arts programs all over the country, then left it poking out of my bag when I knew Matthias would see. All I needed him to do was meet me halfway, give me some sign that he saw what I was doing. Offering a compromise, waiting for him to take it. So far, my efforts had gone unanswered.

But for Ret, it was all a game. She had intentionally sabotaged things with Jonathan, and it wasn't because she didn't care; I was absolutely sure of it. She cared too much. All at once,

I totally got it. Ret wasn't bored. She was happy, and it scared the shit out of her.

"The truth is," Ret was saying, "I should have dumped him ages ago. We were a ridiculous match from the start. I don't know why I let it go on as long as I did."

"Maybe you actually liked him more than you thought." My voice was gentle but clear. I was not letting Ret off the hook that easy.

Ret was the sun and I was the moon, and I could see straight through her.

I got it now—why Ret called Jenni last night, not me. She needed someone whose motherly instinct was going to kick in, who was going to sympathize with her manufactured drama. I knew too much. I knew about Dave.

"Interesting theory." Ret threw me a look I couldn't quite place. "But there was no point. I was never going to marry Jonathan Gaines. We were not going to have a white wedding and a Hawaiian honeymoon and live happily ever after. Eventually, he was going to figure that out on his own. I just sped up the inevitable, that's all. End of story. Who wants to order sushi?" She pulled the pirate-cat flask out of her bag and passed it around.

Bex continued to fuss over Ret, but Jenni retreated to the kitchen. Her father and stepmother would be coming home from work soon, the baby in tow. Their evenings were entirely dictated by Jenni's little sister—her feedings, her bath, her bedtime. Sometimes Mr. Randall would poke his head into the TV room, but our paths rarely crossed. I got the impression it wasn't much different for Jenni when we weren't around. I didn't know much about her mother, just that she'd left when

Jenni was little, that she lived somewhere outside Vancouver and rarely called.

Everyone knew that Jenni was into cooking, fashion, and playing hostess; they were just the things Jenni liked. But maybe there was more to it than that. Three kids and a white picket fence might be Ret's worst nightmare, but one girl's trash is another's treasure.

After the sushi order was in and Jenni had rejoined us in the TV room, Ret insisted that we put a moratorium on breakup talk and find some junk TV on streaming.

"This is not going to be an all-night pity party," Ret decreed from her place of power on the couch. "We will eat small food with chopsticks, we will watch *The Real Housewives of Wherever*, and we will feel no shame about clowning on their terrible, absurdly rich, faux-dramatic lives. Let this reality television shit-show serve as a reminder that life could always be so much worse."

And so that's how it was, because Ret declared it so.

Everyone watched *The Real Housewives*, but I watched Ret. She laughed the loudest at Housewife One's brush with credit card debt and Housewife Three's bad collagen job. During the commercial break, she threw me a little smile and placed her finger across her lips as if to say, *Shh. You're the only one who knows the truth.*

I smiled back and shoveled a salmon avocado roll into my mouth. I knew more than Ret realized. I knew the real reason she'd forced Jonathan's hand. She'd never admit it, not even to me, but too much happiness scared her. It meant having something to lose. And now when she went public with Dave, she wouldn't look like the bad guy. Ret was a mastermind. And I was the chosen one, the sole secret-keeper in her own drama, *The Real Teenagers of the West Shore*.

For maybe the first time ever, I felt sorry for Ret. I was fighting for what I had with Matthias because he was worth fighting for. She'd had something good with Jonathan, but she'd pushed it away. And for what? A challenge, another bad boy. I'd never say it to Ret's face, but it was all kind of boring and predictable and sad.

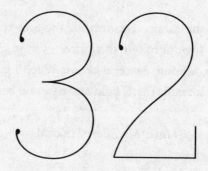

APRIL, SENIOR YEAR
(NOW)

Today is Friday, the notification deadline. So far, I've racked up two rejections, two acceptances, and radio silence from the only school I really care about. I check my phone between each period. Nothing. In the parking lot, starting up the Subaru. Nothing. It's four thirty, which means it's only one thirty in Portland. I toss my phone back in my bag and try to be patient.

At home, I run down the hall to my room and throw my laptop open. Maybe checking my email on a different device will change my luck. Bruiser follows me into my room and finds the sunny spot on my bed. He stretches out and yawns as if this isn't the single most important moment of senior year. Okay, Bruiser. Let's try this your way. I close my eyes and picture a bubbling mountain stream while my browser opens and my email loads. I count to ten, then fifteen for good measure. Gurgling water. A calming, peaceful breeze. When I pry open my eyes, the email is actually there, bold and new and begging to be read.

> *Dear Ms. Ellory Holland,*
>
> *Congratulations! It is my pleasure to offer you admission to Portland State University and the School of Art + Design. I am happy to offer you a place in our incoming class. As a distinctive arts community within a major university, we take great pride in our students' commitment to artistic achievement and academic excellence. I want to congratulate you on your accomplishments, and I look forward to welcoming you to our campus community in Portland this fall. . . .*

You know that feeling when you've been waiting so long for something to happen that when it finally does, you almost don't believe it? I print it out and read it again. Somehow, it looks more real on paper. I start to believe it. This is the letter that says I'm going to get my new start. In spite of what I did, everything I lost. I'm not sure I deserve this. Maybe what I deserve is to be stuck on the West Shore forever, pushing my guilt up the mountain over and over like Sisyphus and his stone.

I push the thought aside.

I am not a terrible person. I earned this.

Mom makes my favorite dinner on Saturday to celebrate—buttermilk chicken, Caesar salad, and ice cream for dessert—and calls the aunties to share the news. Dad walks around the house with this big, goofy grin on his face, bursting with pride.

All weekend, I dream about forwarding the acceptance to my former friends, Principal Keegan, the whole school—as if it would matter, prove something about my worth. *Look at me, Pine Brook! I'm a real artist. I'm going to Portland!*

It would prove exactly nothing. I can hear the whispers in the halls. *Who does she think she is? Ellory Holland's not just a maniac, she's a heartless bitch.*

I scale my fantasy back. There's only one person who cares, one person who I need to tell. On Monday morning, I unfold my list and spread it out on my desk. Three names are crossed off— *Bex, Jenni, Jonathan*—and two remain—*Matthias, Ret*. I print out another copy of the letter and slip it into my bag. Email opens a door, invites a response. And I don't want a response any more than I want another ambush at my car or a fresh avalanche of notes. There haven't been any new ones in weeks, ever since I told him to stop. I get the last word. The last note will be from me.

I pull into the student lot extra early. As I make my way to the second floor, my stomach lurches, just a little, and I can feel my heart start to clobber inside my chest. The past doesn't just vanish behind a screen of good intentions. All those feelings—the hurt and confusion and the deep, burning anger—they don't just go away. Whoever said that time heals all wounds didn't know what he was talking about. Time dulls the wounds, makes them bearable. But it doesn't patch you up and send you on your way, good as new.

I'm the only one who can make that happen. And it's freaking hard.

I square my shoulders and push through the doors leading out of the stairwell and onto the second-floor hallway. I walk fast, my strides long and purposeful. The sooner I do this, the sooner I never have to think about Matthias, ever again.

His locker is in the middle alcove, right next to the Smurf's. I take the email out of my bag and stare for a second at the folds of paper. My stomach heaves for the girl I used to be, the dreams I used to hold so close. Matching emails, a life together in Portland. I fought for us, and it wasn't enough. Remembering that girl—the one who believed in happily ever after—makes me want to cry or scream or disappear.

I need to get this over with. I grab a pen and press the folded paper against his locker door. *This is just one more step, Ellory. Just one more loose end to tie up tight.* I start to write.

> M—
> *This is how the story ends.*
> —*Ellory*

This is not forgiveness, not absolution. This is just a fact, an answer to the question of what happens next. I am going to Portland. Without you. Goodbye. The paper slides through the vent at the top of his locker, gone, swallowed into darkness. I click the pen shut and toss it back in my bag, and I'm done here, spinning on the heel of my boot, walking quickly toward the opposite stairwell, the one that will lead me up to my locker and homeroom and what remains of senior year.

There isn't much time left, not really. The months until graduation have melted into a matter of weeks. I've been counting them down all year, graduation day shining before me like a bright light at the end of a long, dark tunnel. But now that it's almost here, it dawns on me that I'll have to face the day itself. All the Pine Brook seniors sitting with their friends, sharing in-jokes and sentimental selfies, marching proudly across stage, cheering loud and long. Will anyone cheer for me?

I am weak for caring. But I do.

I pause for a moment on the second stair from the top and pull out my list. I press it against the wall and cross the fourth name off. As I stare at the paper, the letters waver and morph into a photograph, five glowing forms in caps and gowns, hands waving, faces lit up by the hot June sun.

Bex, Jenni, Jonathan, Matthias. Ret.

I blink. Their forms become names again, just words on a scrap of paper. I shove it back into my pocket and walk out of the stairwell, into the hall. As I spin the dial to open my locker, as I gather my books, as I walk through the door into homeroom and sit down at my desk, I think about the one name that remains. The hardest name of all. The one that makes my insides threaten to turn into smoke and ash all over again. I could say our business is finished, that I resolved things with her first.

Two roads diverged in a wood, and I— I walked away, but I never said goodbye. It was an ending, but not *the end*. And Ret, I owe you that.

APRIL, JUNIOR YEAR
(THEN)

I grabbed my bag from the seat beside me and locked the Subaru. *Beep beep.* Ricky and Rebecca were in Philadelphia for the weekend with Cordelia, visiting a grandmother or aunt. Matthias had stayed home, and this was my chance. A whole night of no parents, no distractions. I was done playing nice, done dialing it back. I was going to invite myself inside his house, and I was going to stay over. Surprise!

I walked up the steps to the front door and rang the bell. When Matthias opened the door, he looked dazed. His eyes were red, and he reeked of cigarettes and beer.

"Hi."

He coughed twice into his sleeve in response. Now that I was here, it was hard to believe I'd let him keep me out all this time. I'd allowed him to make the decisions, dictate the terms. I was so done with that.

"Did we have plans?" he asked. He didn't sound mad, just a little confused.

I shook my head no, then took a step toward the door. He took a small step back, barely letting me across the threshold.

"Can we get past this?" I asked. "I am not here to judge your house."

He ran his fingers through his hair, considering. He looked too tired to put up much of a fight. Then he stepped aside, making a sweeping gesture toward the living room. "Behold. The Cole habitat in all its glory."

The carpet was worn and stained in spots. Cordelia's toys were all over, and the coffee table was a landing zone for mugs and stacks of mail. In the middle of it all sat the couch, the room's bizarre focal point. Upholstered in a loud red and green plaid, it looked like a giant, forgotten Christmas gift, still waiting to be unwrapped.

The room was a little dusty, and a little dark. The heavy brown drapes and wood-paneled walls weren't doing it any favors. But it wasn't like it was a hoarder house or filled with trash or anything.

"It just needs a little light," I said.

"Or something. We've been meaning to replace the couch." He lifted the bag from my shoulder and set it down on the floor. "What's this?"

"I thought I'd stay over."

He didn't respond right away. It was as if he hadn't heard me, was somewhere else entirely. After a minute, he said, "I went to this amazing show last night. I stayed out really late, walking along the river, and the music just stayed with me."

I recognized the look on his face—it was how I felt in the shop sometimes, totally lost in creating. I imagined that was how music made Matthias feel.

"Anyway, I just got home a few hours ago. I guess I fell asleep."

Right. So that explained the unshowered look. Matthias coughed again and rubbed at his eyes. He looked hungover.

"Are you hungry?" I asked. "We could order Rosa's."

"I need to write, while the show's still fresh. I guess you can hang out, but I'm not going to be the best company." His palms were open, take it or leave it.

In retrospect, just thinking about the whole pathetic scene makes me cringe. I should have turned around, walked back out to the car. But staying was so easy to justify, when going home meant giving up. I still thought we had something to fight for.

"You write, I'll be down here. I have eight chapters of Faulkner to get through by Monday."

He reached behind me to close the front door. "Just don't go in the TV room, okay? Or the kitchen." He looked torn between apologizing and running away.

"Scout's honor. I will stick to the living room."

It was six. I resolved to make myself scarce and actually get some homework done. We had all night. Things would turn around.

But when Matthias still hadn't emerged by eight, I put Faulkner down and stood up to stretch. My stomach was growling, and the lumpy Christmas couch was starting to leave permanent plaid imprints on my butt. Being alone down here was getting weirder by the minute. It *had* been two hours; how long could it possibly take to write a blog post? I passed the TV room on the way to the stairs. I didn't have to go in to see that it was Ricky Cole's territory, a disaster zone. The stale booze smell wafted out into the hall. I headed up to Matthias's room.

"Hey." I stood in the open doorway, waiting for him to notice me.

Matthias glanced up from the wooden workbench that served as a desk, where he was hunched over his laptop. His bed was half made in a hasty, spread-up kind of way. Otherwise, the room was neat, almost spartan. No clothes on the floor. No piles of records. He had exactly two posters on display, both framed, both hung perfectly straight. Next to his laptop stood a single framed picture of Matthias hanging out with Dave and the Smurf by the Franklins' pool.

This was not the bedroom I had imagined. Dark and poster plastered. Cluttered, messy.

What else had I been getting wrong?

"I need to ask you something, about Ret and Dave."

His eyes narrowed. "What?"

"Did you tell her what you told me, about the stuff with your dad?" Last week, I'd found them all together in the woods by school. Drinking, hanging out. Doing whatever they were doing without me. I kept seeing Ret, collapsing in giggles into Dave's lap, liquid sloshing out of her cup and into the pine needles. She was still keeping him close, her little secret. I hated the thought of them together, but Ret did what she wanted.

"No one knows about that except you," he said. "And you'll keep it that way?"

"Of course," I said. And I meant it. Telling Ret the truth would only make Dave more appealing, his dark side even darker. I could see that now. It was better if she didn't know.

I stared at my boyfriend for a long moment. Then I took a step into the room, and another. Things had been terrible for weeks, but it didn't have to be that way. Fighting for us did not mean sitting downstairs with a book. It meant reminding him of the way we used to be. The way we could be again. I slid into his lap and pressed my lips against his. I could feel my throat tighten with need—*I need you, Matthias. I need us to be okay.*

"Ellory, stop." His voice was edged with something rough. He leaned all the way back in his chair, away from me. He looked at me like he didn't even know me, and suddenly, it was perfectly, terribly clear. I'd been fooling myself all night. There was nothing to fight for when he didn't want me here. Not at all. Not downstairs reading and definitely not in his room, not kissing him.

I felt sick. If I didn't get out of there immediately, I might actually throw up. Somehow, I was moving, pushing myself up from the chair, onto my feet. Everything was unsteady, my legs were wobbling, but I was standing, backing away toward the door.

"Ellory, I'm sorry." Something I couldn't quite place crossed his face like a shadow. For a second, it was like he saw me as a vase teetering on the edge of a shelf, and if he reached out fast enough, he could still keep me from falling. But then the moment passed. He turned his head, his eyes latching back onto the computer screen. He might want to save me, salvage this moment, but more than that, he wanted to get back to his blog post. He wanted me gone.

"Ret texted me," I said, a lie, an excuse. "She needs a ride to

Jenni's." It may as well have been true. Everyone was probably already there, or would be soon. I'd get in the car, and in ten minutes, I'd be there too. I'd just go join my friends like everything was normal, and then it would be. I felt a sick twist of pride. If there was one thing I'd mastered over the last few months, it was faking normal.

"We should talk. . . ." His voice trailed off. This time, I understood his words for what they were. A thin offering he hoped I wouldn't take. They were the words you said when you were trying to be polite, but you didn't mean it. I should have understood that two hours ago. *So naive, Ellory. So fucking naive.*

"No." I just wanted to get out of there and forget I'd ever come. When I got to the doorway, I stopped, just for a second. "You're busy. We'll talk later."

I didn't wait for him to say anything. I took the stairs two at a time and grabbed my stuff, and I couldn't get outside fast enough. It wasn't until the door clicked shut behind me and the early spring air whipped against my face like a chilly sheet that I finally let myself breathe. I gasped, leaning forward, clutching the Coles' porch railing, sucking in gulp after gulp of air.

When I could move again, I hurried down to the driveway and unlocked the Subaru. I didn't look up to Matthias's window. I didn't check to see if he was watching me. I'd never felt so glad to slide into the driver's seat, to feel the cool cushion press against my back and legs. I started the car and switched on the lights and backed down the drive, not stopping to pull over until I was three blocks away and the house was completely out of sight. Gone. Like tonight had never happened. Then, I texted Ret.

What are you up to?

At Jenni's. Obviously. You with
Matty?

Change of plans. On my way.

We're about to order pizza. You in?

Absolutely.

My fingers trembled against the screen. Ret had no idea how messed up I felt. No one did. I resolved to keep it that way.

MAY – JUNE, SENIOR YEAR
(NOW)

Ret hasn't been in English all week, the last week of senior year. The days until graduation tick by fast, and now that I need her, she's gone.

On Friday, Mr. Michaels helps me load my sculptures and bins of materials into the back of the Subaru. There's a lot to carry. Ever since January, I've been on fire, completing piece after piece, the last few months more than making up for my lackluster fall. I promise to look for him tomorrow in the stands, then I start up the car and drive to the break in the guardrail. I haven't been here in months, not since that day over winter break when I came back to clean up our trash, alone. Now it's warm, bright. The sun is like a soft blanket against my bare arms as I slip between the metal ties, scramble down the bank.

Even before I reach the rough tangle of weeds that conceals our usual spot, I know she's not here. Hasn't been in months. The grass is thick and undisturbed in the places our feet used to tamp it down, and the few pieces of litter I step over belong to a stranger. The straw from a juice box. Car ads in a faded newspaper. One purple shoelace.

I push through the weeds, and our spot is just as I left it in December, except greener, filled with dandelions and thick, uncut grass. I sink back into the empty hollow in the bank, Ret's hollow, and let my head fall softly against the weeds and dirt at my back. There's no flask to pass back and forth, no memories to unearth and hold up to the light. No stories to tell each other, to make ourselves feel better about the girls we were. The girls who tore each other apart.

Instead, I dig my fingers into the damp earth near the shoreline and uncover a handful of pebbles. I rinse them off, then lean back and toss each tiny stone into the river. I watch the water swallow them, one by one, and my mind drifts back to Wednesday, to my last school-mandated session with Dr. Marsha. We talked about Portland, about all the good progress I've made with my list.

Then I said the first truly honest thing I've said to her in months.

"I just don't know how to resolve things with Ret. Not without a time machine. Without a total redo."

I waited for her to contradict me, to tell me I'd find a way. It was the last time we'd meet in that gray and navy room. Maybe she'd even hand me the answer, a parting gift.

"Sometimes," she said, "life gives us problems that resist easy solution. This isn't one you get to fix, Ellory. Your job is to keep moving forward."

Of all the possibilities, I'd never imagined a free pass: You don't have to find a solution because *there isn't one*. Let the sheer impossibility set you free.

I toss the last pebble into the water and watch it disappear. If I'd been telling her the whole truth all along, not parceling out bite-sized morsels week by week, she wouldn't have let me off the hook so easy. Sorry, Dr. Marsha. I didn't like lying to you. But what choice did I have, when I knew what you'd say? You would have called my behavior unhealthy. Drinking, sneaking around, living inside the past—Ret & Ellory against the world, one more time.

And you would have been right.

I look around the deserted bank, my only company a mama duck and her seven ducklings bathing in the shallows beneath the bridge. Now that I'm here, Ret's nowhere to be found.

I stand up, dust the dirt off the back of my jeans. Suddenly, I know what I have to do. There's one place Ret and I can be alone, one place I know she'll meet me. If I'm honest, I've known it all along. The answer wasn't in therapy, it wasn't at Pine Brook, and it's not here at the river either. Graduation is tomorrow, and after that, I'll finally be ready.

APRIL, JUNIOR YEAR
(THEN)

It was remarkably easy to avoid someone at Pine Brook when the only period you had together was lunch. I knew the halls Matthias took between classes. I took a different route. I had no idea I was developing skills that would get me through senior year, skills I'd come to live by. I just needed to get through the week.

On Monday and Tuesday, I skipped the sky dome and clocked extra hours in the metal shop, working on a new sculpture. This one was different than any I'd attempted before. Bigger. Angrier. Sometimes I heated piece after piece of steel scrap and twisted until it threatened to snap. Sometimes the metal broke and I threw it away. Kept going. Twist, coil, twist, coil. Figure out later how the pieces fit.

On Tuesday night, Matthias texted me.

> You sick? Haven't seen you in school.
> Was hoping we could talk.

I waited an hour to text him back. My fingers were heavy typing out the words.

> Not sick, just need some time.
> Talk later, OK?

> OK. Let me know.

On Wednesday, I braved lunch. Matthias waved at me from across the sky dome, and I lifted my hand in response, barely waving back. He didn't push back his chair to come over. Good. I let my arm drop back down into my lap. It weighed a thousand pounds.

"What's going on with you this week?" Jenni asked. "You've been kind of quiet."

Jenni had been kind of quiet herself, ever since Ret and Jonathan had split. I wasn't sure if she was actually into him, or if she was just letting Ret burrow deep under her skin. If I hadn't been so entirely absorbed in my own problems, I might have thought to ask. But I stayed silent, and Ret wouldn't let it go. *Remember that time when Jenni liked Jonathan? Remember that time when Jenni thought she had a shot?* It was Ret's favorite new joke.

"It's nothing," I said. Everyone was looking at me from around our little table. Three pairs of concerned eyes passed over my tray of barely touched tacos and rested on my face. "I was thinking about this new project I'm working on. I must have zoned out."

Bex turned to Jenni. "You have to let the artiste work. You have seen *Frida*, right?"

Jenni shook her head, no.

"*Basquiat*?" Another no from Jenni.

Bex sighed. "We have films to watch."

The tortured artist act seemed to satisfy Jenni, at least for the moment. I picked up a taco and took a big, deliberate bite. I could feel Ret's eyes still burning into my face long after the others had moved on to discussing Lizza Kendrick's new pixie cut. (Daring, but all wrong for her face.) I knew Ret wasn't buying what I was selling, but she didn't press. For some reason, she was letting me off the hook.

The week dragged. I ducked into the bathroom on Thursday after French. When I came out, Ret, Dave, Matthias, and the Smurf were standing together, leaning against Dave's locker and laughing at some joke I told myself I didn't want to know. *Ellory. Hey, Ellory.* I shoved my hands in my pockets and kept my head down. I pretended not to hear his voice. Talking meant admitting that Saturday had actually happened. That it had really been that bad. My mind looped back and back and back to that moment. My weak, rubber band legs. The look on his face: how he wanted me gone. Every time I saw him across the sky dome or leaving class or closing his locker door, that look was all I could see. Every time, I felt sick all over again.

On Friday, I forced myself to wait at his locker after school, my stomach churning, my boots like lead weights against the hall floor while droves of Pine Brookians ran toward the stairwell. It was the last day of school before spring break, and eighth period had officially let out. The halls were filled with shouts and high fives and hands banging against locker doors. I had never felt so uncelebratory.

But I couldn't put this off any longer. I needed to talk to him today, right now. I'd waited until the last possible moment, and I couldn't let this silence drag out into break. Not talking was starting to feel worse than talking. By three fifteen, the building was clearing out. Still no Matthias. I fiddled with my phone, pretending to check Instagram.

"He skipped last period." My head jerked up. The Smurf was standing in front of me. "He's downtown, I think. Preparty supply run."

"Hey, Steve." I shoved my phone into my bag and forced a smile. "I must have forgot. Thanks."

"No big. See you at Franklin's?"

"Wouldn't miss it." I waved and started down the hall toward the stairs.

Shit. Dave Franklin's spring break kick-off party. I had completely forgotten. If things were normal, I'd be going with Matthias. We'd make it a throwback to last June, spend the entire night on the living room couch. But things were far from normal.

I pushed open the big doors at the front of the school and the bright afternoon sunlight wrapped itself around my skin. It felt pretty, soothing. It felt totally wrong.

Five hours later, the dinner table was clear, and Dad and I were loading the last of the dishes into the dishwasher.

"Important call?" He glanced at my phone, and I slipped it

back into my pocket. "You've been looking at that thing every five seconds."

"Sorry." I lifted the big pot, the one we always loaded on top, and fit it snugly over the tumblers. "I thought I might go out, but now I'm not so sure."

"To Jenni's?" Dad dried off his hands with the dish towel and folded it back over the bar on the stove door.

"Yeah, Jenni's," I lied. "I'm just not feeling so hot." Truth.

"You know your mom and I would be happy to have you stay in for a movie night. She just raided the video store that was closing on Market."

"The Rent-a-Flick is closing?"

"It's official. We are the last family in America to still collect DVDs. She brought home two shopping bags, you should pick something out."

"I might still go out. I'll decide soon, okay?"

I gave my dad a kiss on the cheek and headed to my room, Bruiser emerging from nowhere to follow me down the hall. I needed to turn off, chill out. My room meant no need for big smiles. No pretending everything was just super. I closed the door and flopped across my bed, and Bruiser settled in a ball at my feet. The comforter was soft and cool beneath my skin. I pressed my face into it and exhaled.

A minute later, I checked my phone, again. Nothing. After this week's vow of silence, what would I say? *Want to meet me at Dave's party, start over? By the way, about last Saturday. Can we pretend that never happened?*

Right.

Maybe I'd text Ret. She'd definitely be going to Dave's tonight.

If we went together, maybe it wouldn't be so weird. And not that she really needed the moral support, but I knew Jonathan would be there. A few days ago, after weeks of moping around the Pine Brook halls like a discarded teddy bear, he had started hooking up with someone new. A pretty strawberry blond freshman with perfect skin and perky breasts and shiny pink nails.

Ret swore she didn't care, but I had seen her watching them together, seen the lapis blue of her eyes harden into ice.

I checked my phone again, opening up to our group chat, Spraaang Break. Bex was already over at Jenni's, and they were promising daiquiris with fresh peach nectar to Ret and me if we showed up.

> **ELLORY HOLLAND**
> Putting in some QT with Mom and Dad. Let's make a plan for midweek!

> **JENNI RANDALL**
> Boo. Ret with you?

> **ELLORY HOLLAND**
> Nope, probably at Franklin's party.

I closed our chat and scrolled back through my messages, to my last exchange with Matthias, four days ago. **Talk later, OK?** I'd written. He'd said, **Let me know.** The ball was officially in my court. He had stopped calling, stopped texting, stopped trying to get my attention in the halls, because I had told him to. I'd told him we'd talk later, and then I'd left him hanging all week. I clicked on the new message icon and started to type.

Hey. Delete.

Can you talk now? Delete delete.

What's up? Ugh. Delete delete delete.

I tossed my phone down to the end of the bed, and Bruiser raised his head to look at me.

"Don't judge," I said. I pushed myself up to stand in front of the mirror. My hair was a mess. My cheek had a web of lines pressed into it from the comforter. I walked across the hall, into the bathroom, and splashed water on my face. It felt cold, sharp. I gasped.

"Everything okay, honey?" Mom called from the family room.

"I'm fine," I lied.

"Your dad said you're not feeling well. Did you take your temperature?"

"I'm just a little tired," I lied again. I buried my face in my bath towel. Even after my skin was dry, I kept it pressed to my face, my breathing muffled against the soft fabric.

"Do you want to watch a movie with us? You should see everything I picked up."

I walked back into the hall and stared through the doorway into my room, where my phone was still lying face down at the foot of the bed. Bruiser had stretched one paw across it, as if claiming it, or daring me to pick it back up. "Be right there."

I could have texted Matthias. I could have texted Ret. I could have even gotten in the Subaru and driven over to Jenni's. Instead, I slipped off my shirt and jeans. Then I dug around in my dresser until I found a clean pair of sweatpants and a big, soft T-shirt. When I walked down the hall to the family room, I left my phone behind.

JUNE, SENIOR YEAR
(NOW)

I walk onto the field and allow myself to blend into the sea of maroon and gold. Groups of kids gather at the thirty-yard line where row after row of plastic chairs have been set up, stretching toward the end zone. On stage, Principal Keegan is adjusting the mic and trying to tamp down a stack of papers at the podium. Someone emerges with a paperweight. Someone shouts, "After party at Maria's!" and Maria Hidelman looks like she's going to have a heart attack. Someone does an impressive series of cart-wheels and flips across the grass.

This morning, I almost told my parents I didn't want to go. You don't need to go to graduation to graduate, after all. But the year is over. I made it. I owe it to myself to acknowledge that officially, even if I have to do it alone.

"Hey, Ellory!" Up toward the front, in a sea of senior Rockettes, Abigail is standing on her chair. She sweeps her arms back and forth in a big wave, then points toward an empty seat next to her. I haven't seen her much this spring, though we've taken to waving in the halls and saying *hi*. I never imagined sitting with the Rockettes at graduation, but I return Abigail's wave and start walking, grateful for the offer.

I take my time walking down the field, and my eyes roam across the rows. I find Jenni first, in the back with her boyfriend, Elliot, the lead vocalist in Pine Brook's only Christian rock band. I wonder if he's wearing his trademark brown leather jacket under his graduation gown in this heat. The boys are sitting a few rows further up: Matthias, Dave, and the Smurf. They all have *PBJ* spelled out across their caps in bright yellow tape. *Pine Brook Jesters. Peanut Butter & Jelly.* I don't know them anymore. I don't know their jokes. I keep going. Bex is somewhere in the middle-right rows, snapping selfies with the senior dance team. All the planets, flung far apart.

I find Ret last. I wasn't sure she'd be here, after her disappearing act last week, but she's perched in a seat on the end of the aisle up front. Alone. As I get closer, I wait for her to sense me. *Three, two* . . . She turns around and stares. I force myself to look back at her, stare straight into the sun. She raises her hand toward me; she's going to wave.

She takes aim and shoots me straight through the heart with one slender middle finger. Then she bursts out laughing, doubling over into the aisle.

She is toying with my heart. She is serious as death.

My hands are shaking, and I tear my eyes away, up to the rows of teachers in their suits and dresses seated on stage. Safe territory. I can't tell who looks stranger: all of us in our caps and gowns, or all of our teachers in their too-fancy clothes. When I look back, Ret's slouched down in her seat again, her back a solid wall of maroon fabric. She reaches into the folds of her gown and slips out her flask, then takes a long drink. No one seems to notice, or care.

I suck in the warm spring air and keep walking. Abigail is waiting. I press into her row, and her friends make room as I pass by. No one hassles me or gives me a hard time. When I slip into the empty seat beside her, Abigail smiles. She takes my hand in hers and squeezes, one quick pulse. I squeeze her hand back, *thank you*, and then we all turn to look as the marching band enters the field and begins to play the Pine Brook anthem.

After the valedictorian address, Principal Keegan makes some sappy remarks about seizing the day and we all shuffle onto the stage to shake his hand and take the blank scrolls that we're promised will be replaced with our real diplomas in two to three weeks. When they call Matthias's name, I look away. When they call my name, I can hear my parents and Mr. Michaels cheering from the stands. No one boos. No one objects. The voice that says everyone is talking about me, pitying me, judging me finally shuts up. At least for today, I've been granted a reprieve. And after this, I never have to come back. I walk across the stage and shake Principal Keegan's hand like everyone else.

And then the air is filled with a thousand caps and tassels that flare like stars, and it's over. Abigail is hugging me, and then my parents are hugging me, and there are camera flashes everywhere. The light stings the back of my eyes. As the field starts to empty out, I look around for Ret, but she's gone.

THEN, THEN, THEN . . .

APRIL, JUNIOR YEAR
(SPRING BREAK, SATURDAY)

I burrowed deep into my comforter and pressed the phone icon on my screen. *Calling Ret . . .* It was ten in the morning, the first full day of spring break. I was too lazy to get out of bed, but after my night of chamomile tea and *You've Got Mail* with Mom and Dad, I needed an update from the real world, bad.

"Morning," she mumbled.

"How was the party?" I slid the phone between my shoulder and chin.

"Huh?" Ret's voice sounded rough, like I'd woken her up.

"Dave's party? Any gossip to report? I haven't left the house in almost seventeen hours, so please humor me."

"Sorry, still waking up." I could hear her stand and walk across the room, the sound of the blackout curtain scraping against the window. "Jesus, Dave's. Ellory, why did I go to that party?"

"What happened?" I sat up, letting the comforter bunch down around my waist.

"The typical shit. Jonathan was there, of course. With his strawberry skank. Since when are freshmen even allowed into Dave's parties? They spent the whole night making out on the white couch, right in the middle of the living room. It was disgusting."

My stomach lurched. The living room couch. Our couch.

"Was Matthias there?" There was a long pause on the other end. "Hello?"

"Yeah, Matty was there, and the Smurf." Ret made a noise through the phone that was half moan, half growl. "Dear Maude, I drank so many wine coolers. I think I will vomit if I ever have to look at another Keylime Berryade or Coco Colada."

"Jesus, Ret."

There was another long silence on the other end. "I think I did something really wretched last night." Ret's voice was small. "If you'd've been there ... Ellory, why weren't you there?"

"Why didn't you text me?"

Ret didn't answer. I could hear her moaning softly. "I might need to puke."

"Do you need to call me back?"

"No, wait. It'll pass." There was a long pause, and it sounded like Ret was pulling a sweatshirt on over her head. "Christ, it's all coming back. I saw Jonathan, and then I drank all the sugar drinks, and then we were all over each other, in front of the whole party. In front of everyone."

"You and Dave? I'm sure it wasn't that bad." I wanted to ask about Matthias, had he been there with anyone, had he asked about me, but Ret had clearly been too distracted to notice. I sank back into the pillows. "Were you planning to keep him a secret forever?"

Ret stifled something that sounded like either laughter or a sob. In a minute, I could hear her breathing even out. "Maybe I'm still under the influence or whatever. I'm overreacting."

"That's the spirit."

There was another long pause. When Ret spoke again, her voice was serious. "Ellory May, I need you to listen to me. Here's the takeaway: High school boys, they suck. They drive us to do brainless shit, and they don't deserve us. I am cutting myself off."

"Okay." It was hard to take Ret seriously. She'd just find a college guy in no time. "Sounds like a plan."

"Doesn't it? Listen, I have the most amazing idea. Epic. We'll put a moratorium on dating, until college. You and me together, starting right now. Wouldn't that free up so much space in your head? Like, for art and stuff? We will be desired and unattainable."

"Hold up, don't drag me into this." I laughed, sharp and short. Classic Ret, assuming I'd blindly follow her into the abyss.

"He's all wrong for you, Ellory. You've been miserable for months."

"Did something happen with Dave?" I asked, redirecting. "Should we call someone?"

"No, it's nothing like that. Swear."

"Okay." We sat in silence for a moment, and I tried to wrap my head around Ret's drama. She'd embarrassed herself at the party, and now she wanted to swear off men. Maybe she would end up ditching Dave, but she'd change her mind about the moratorium by next week, and I'd be the one left alone.

"You were with Jonathan for a long time," I said. "You should try being single. But I am not breaking up with my boyfriend in solidarity. Sorry." Whatever problems Matthias and I were having, those were between us. I wasn't about to make any hasty decisions to humor Ret.

She didn't respond for a long time. Too long. But when she spoke again, her voice was cheerful. "I just hate to see you in pain, Ellory. Think about how much fun we would have senior year. You and me, single. Totally free. Promise me you'll think about it."

I swallowed. There was a lump in my throat, and I wasn't exactly sure why. "Fine, I promise."

"I'm going back to bed. Let's get lunch this week, girls only."

"Sure, I'll text you."

I clicked the red icon on my phone. *End call.* I needed breakfast. I needed to think. I knew Ret inside and out, and there was something she wasn't telling me.

APRIL, JUNIOR YEAR
(MONDAY AFTER BREAK)

But we didn't get lunch. On Tuesday, I drove Bex to the Capezio store in Camp Hill for a new pair of pointe shoes, and that was the last time I talked to anyone aside from my parents, Bruiser, and Matthias for the rest of break. Wednesday night, I turned off my phone and deactivated my Facebook account. It was easier not to know what anyone was saying.

When I got to school on the first day back, it was obvious
that everyone knew what had happened over break. Lying low
had delayed the inevitable, but word had spread without me. A
thousand eyes latched onto me in the halls, waiting to see how
I'd react. At lunch, I skipped the sky dome and retreated into
the shop. I thought about skipping French too, but I couldn't
hide forever. When I walked into class, Ret and Jenni were there
already, sitting on the other side of the room, across from our
normal seats. So they were avoiding me. Nice. Ret was staring
intently at the top of her desk, but Jenni looked up at me with
this weird, totally unblinking stare. She didn't have to say it; lines
had clearly been drawn. Jenni was out of the doghouse and soaking up the sun. Just like that, she'd traded my friendship for a
ticket back into Ret's good graces.

I sank down into my usual chair and I didn't say anything
because what could I possibly have said that wouldn't have come
out in a stream of knives and flames and pure, unfiltered venom?
I kept my head down and bored rage holes through the top of the
desk with my eyes. She had been lying to me for months. She had
let me lie to myself. I *hated* her.

When Bex showed up in the doorway a minute later, it was
like someone was forcing her to choose between Mom or Dad
after the divorce. She was only in this class to brush up on what
she called "textbook French" for the AP exam, and suddenly I
resented her deeply for taking the easy path. She should be in
Spanish, or Mandarin. Was she going to make the easy choice
now too? But then the choice was made for her because the people
who normally sat where Ret and Jenni had parked it showed up
and slid into the seats next to me instead, and so she wound up
on the other side of the room. And suddenly it was Team Ellory

against Team Everyone Else, and I knew that this was going to get ugly. This wasn't going to be about rallying around poor Ellory, and how bad she must be hurting. No. This was going to be about forgive, or get out.

APRIL, JUNIOR YEAR
(SPRING BREAK, SATURDAY)

For the rest of the day, Ret's words were a jumble in my head. I couldn't add them up. Something else had gone down at that party, something more than a living room full of people watching two kids pawing at each other. Who cared? Certainly no one would by the time we got back to school.

It wasn't like Ret to be shy about a fling. To be shy, period. Boys were her weak spot, her one insecurity, but this drama felt manufactured to hide something else. Dave had done something, said something. I started to seethe. Maybe I should have warned Ret away from him, after all, but even as the thought crossed my mind, I knew she wouldn't have listened.

I cleaned my room. I drove to CVS for my mom. Whatever had happened, I could have stopped it. If I had just gotten in the car, gotten over myself, gone to that party. *Ellory, why weren't you there?* Finally, after dinner, I picked up the phone and broke my week of silence. I texted Matthias.

APRIL, JUNIOR YEAR
(MONDAY AFTER BREAK)

I wanted to scream and throw my desk across the room, smash it through the window, turn the classroom into a war zone of explosions and broken glass. I wanted everyone to see what I was feeling inside.

But we were in class, and I was not a violent girl.

So I sat and seethed while Madame Clement launched into a cultural lesson on the Parisian school system, and Bex threw me a series of worried glances from across the room, and Ret looked like she was going to burst into tears at one point, and then Jenni gripped her hand and squeezed it hard, and that's when my insides lit on fire. It was like my entire body was engulfed in flames. The anger was hot and white and pure, and I couldn't let it go. It was the only thing keeping me silent and in my seat and pretending to listen to Madame Clement's assessment of the French testing system.

At the end of class, Ret dropped a note on my desk before Jenni grabbed her by the shoulders and rushed her out into the hall. *You do what you have to do, Jenni. Don't even worry about me.* Bex stood in the doorway for a moment, hovering between me and the other girls. She wanted to say something, but she was afraid. Choosing me meant losing Ret. I shoved my books in my bag, and when I looked up she was gone.

Lemming.

APRIL, JUNIOR YEAR
(SPRING BREAK, WEDNESDAY)

For the first part of break, he was busy. Extra shifts at the restaurant, Cordelia, the usual. He couldn't meet up until Wednesday, so I waited. I took Bex to get new dance shoes, I hung out at the library with my mom. Ret wanted to get lunch, but I put her off. I had to talk to Matthias first, had to know the truth. I had pushed my way into his house, just like I'd pushed him into talking about the future before he was ready. I pushed, and he pushed me away. We didn't use to do this to each other. He took me to the restaurant. He took me to the Crow. He took me out with Cordelia. He used to invite me in, not shut me out.

And then I'd shut him out with my silence. If there was anything left to salvage, I had to know.

On Wednesday, I waited for him to come over. Finally, there was the soft grind of truck tires against the curb out front. The muffled slam of the door. It was almost two; my parents were at work and Matthias definitely wasn't supposed to be there, but I didn't have time to care about the rules.

I opened the door and took him by the hand. His palm felt a little clammy. He was wearing a shirt with little ivory snaps, jeans, his scuffed-up loafers. I took it all in. I hadn't looked—really looked—at him in days.

"Ellory."

I guided him into the family room, into the early spring sunshine that stretched across the floor like a big, bright tongue. This was it. The moment of truth. I hooked my thumbs into the front pockets of my shorts and lifted my chin.

APRIL, JUNIOR YEAR
(THURSDAY AFTER BREAK)

I tore up Ret's note without reading it, and I kept my phone powered down, and I pretended not to hear when she called after me in the hall. I didn't want to talk, and I sure as shit didn't want to listen to anything she had to say.

There was nothing to say.

I could feel Bex's eyes linger on me in class, but she still sat with Jenni and Ret in the sky dome and she still took shelter behind the sacred walls of Jenni's house after school, so fine. Her priorities were clear.

The three of them were dead to me.

Each day after school, after the shop, I retreated into my room. I hadn't gone out all week, or last week, for that matter, but by Thursday I desperately needed to leave my bedroom. I couldn't be here trapped in this cage of hurt and anger and complete and total treason for one more second. By ten, I was going to fucking explode if I didn't do something, so I ransacked my room and packed everything I could find of Ret's inside a cardboard box. Records and photos and bottles of nail polish and a mod dress from Hot Topic that I used to really like. Nothing was spared. Anything that Ret had ever given me went in that box. I lingered a moment over her Nirvana T-shirt, but then I shoved it inside. Fuck it. Finally, I grabbed a bottle of hairspray and a box of matches and waited for my parents to go to bed.

APRIL, JUNIOR YEAR
(SPRING BREAK, WEDNESDAY)

I couldn't drag Matthias into the future. That much was abundantly clear. Instead, I was going to take us back. It was a little silly, but if he'd come with me, let me take us back in time, it would be something. A first step toward a new start for us.

"You have to close your eyes."

When his eyes were shut tight, I reached out and took his hands in mine.

"I want you to think back to Christmas Eve. Okay?"

He nodded.

"You were wearing jeans and a sweater. I had on that gauzy green shirt. Remember? I gave you gloves, and you gave me this ring." I moved his hand over to the metal band, guiding his fingertips across the three interlocked stars.

The corners of his mouth twitched up into a smile.

"After that night, everything changed. I don't even know what happened, but what if we could just erase everything since January?"

I kicked off my sandals and dropped his hands from mine. Then I grabbed the remote and switched on the DVD player, where *It's a Wonderful Life* was queued up.

"You can open your eyes now."

I crossed my arms in an *X* and grabbed the hem of my shirt. Before I could overthink it, before he could say anything, I lifted it over my head. I was wearing the same underwear set I'd had on that night, violet and lace. Matthias looked at me, unblinking. I unbuttoned the top button on my shorts and pulled the zipper down. With a little shove, they fell around my ankles.

APRIL, JUNIOR YEAR
(THURSDAY AFTER BREAK)

Once I had a plan, I felt better. I waited until it was pitch black outside and the light went off in my parents' room, around eleven thirty, and I crept down the hall and pulled my boots over my pajama bottoms. I started up the Subaru and held my breath until I was sure Mom and Dad didn't hear the car, and then I eased it slowly down the driveway. As soon as I was in the street, I switched on the lights and put my foot on the gas pedal before I could change my mind.

When I got to Ret's, most of the house lights were out. She had the blackout curtain pulled across her bedroom window, but I could see thin blades of light shooting out from around the edges. I parked the Subaru a couple of houses down from the Johnstons' and grabbed the box and my supplies from the trunk.

It wasn't that spectacular of a fire. The smoke was thick and choking, but the flames were totally contained by the soaking grass, and I could tell right away that it wasn't even going to burn through to the bottom of the box. It didn't matter, though. It was *symbolic*.

For the record, if I had really wanted to burn down their house, I would have soaked the box with gasoline, not spritzed a little hairspray across the top. And I would have put it on the porch, right in front of the door, not on the front lawn, well away from the house and trees. And I probably would have waited until summer, when the grass was dry and brittle, not picked a night after four days of rain, when the ground was soaked through.

I also would not have run back to my car and honked the horn to warn her after watching every lingering scrap of Ret and me leap into flames on her front lawn.

After I'd slid into the driver's seat and tapped the horn three times, I craned my neck around to watch Ret pull aside the curtain, her face a dark shadow in the window, then gone. Then seconds later, she was on the front lawn, dragging the hose across the grass, barefoot in a black T-shirt and flannel pj pants covered with little glow-in-the-dark skulls. She was coughing and tripping over the hose. By the time she got there, only about half the box was still lit, but whatever. I'd made my point. I started the engine and peeled off down the street, relishing the squeal of the tires, not waiting to see Ret's head jerk up to watch the Subaru speed away.

APRIL, JUNIOR YEAR
(SPRING BREAK, WEDNESDAY)

I felt very beautiful and very alive standing in front of Matthias in just my bra and underwear. On the TV, it was Christmas Eve in Bedford Falls, and an angel was watching over George Bailey. I could feel the echo of that other night all around me. It was working. I thought about the bad stuff. The drinking and the shitty parents and the secrets he refused to share with me. Even now, even after all this time.

I didn't care anymore. Maybe it was weak of me. But I was done waiting for something to change or break or fall apart. I just wanted things to go back to the way they were before.

His eyes flickered toward the TV, the soft glow of black and white.

"There's peppermint schnapps in the kitchen," I said, motioning toward the door with my chin.

"No, thanks." Matthias encircled my wrists in both his hands, keeping me close. The black band dug into my skin beneath his fingers. He wasn't smiling.

"No shots?" I asked.

He was silent for a moment.

"No, to all of this," he said. "I'm sorry."

APRIL, JUNIOR YEAR
(FRIDAY AFTER BREAK)

When I pulled into the student lot on Friday, I felt almost good for the first time in days. Some kind of cautious peace settled around my body as I pushed through the main doors and walked down the hall to homeroom. I could still see the surprise on Ret's face, her frantic stumble for the garden hose, the licking flames. My lips stretched into a thin smile. For the first hour and a half of my day, I felt like I could make it through the rest of junior year.

I didn't usually have to see anyone until lunch, but today everyone was in the hallway after second period, waiting to pounce as soon as I got out of math. Ret and Jenni and Bex. Everyone except Matthias, who'd been avoiding me all week. For the first time in months, he and I were on exactly the same page.

"What the actual fuck, Ellory?" Ret said as I stepped out into the hall, her small body suddenly huge in front of me, a wall of spite and anger. She was wearing those ridiculous snakeskin heels from Hot Topic, the ones she could barely walk in. Teetering, she managed to back me against the wall, and Jenni was right there next to her, almost as tall as I was in big platform boots, her eyes flashing with more passion than I'd ever seen Jenni give anything before.

"You could have burned down my house. What the hell were you thinking?" Ret's voice was thick with anger or something even stronger.

"What are you, some kind of arsonist now?" Jenni asked. "You're lucky Ret didn't call the cops."

"Back off," I spat at Jenni. "This isn't your fight."

"The hell it's not," she growled, stepping closer to me, her nose almost touching my nose. I stepped back and hit the wall. "At least Ret's been trying."

"What?" My question was directed at Ret.

"I left you a note." The anger had drained out of her voice, and she was almost pleading. "And about ten voice mails. I waited for an hour on Wednesday."

"Yeah, I didn't read that. And in case you haven't noticed, my phone's been off."

"I told Veronica it was some losers from school. I didn't rat you out, okay? But you have to talk to me."

Of course Ret hadn't told her mom. Then she would have had to tell her what she had done to make me so mad that I would set a box on fire in their front yard. No one was telling parents or calling the cops.

"I'm supposed to *thank* you now? Is this some sick kind of joke?" I was almost screaming. I stepped forward, my shoulder digging into Jenni's arm, shoving her out of the way.

"Everyone, please stop!" Bex pleaded. I had almost forgotten that she was there, she'd been such a pathetic wallflower standing lamely to the side, her hands shoved in her pockets. It was the most she'd said all week. Too little, too late, Bex.

She reached out to tuck a strand of hair behind my ear. It was a mom gesture, calming, diffusing. It didn't work. I flinched away like her fingers were burning. In reality, I was the one on fire.

APRIL, JUNIOR YEAR
(SPRING BREAK, WEDNESDAY)

For a moment, everything was completely silent. Matthias was still holding my wrists, resting my hands lightly against his chest.

"There are some things I need to tell you," he said. He let go, and my hands fell limply down at my sides.

I didn't say anything. I walked over to the couch and sat down, my back stretching into a long arc, my elbows resting against my knees. Suddenly I felt very, conspicuously naked.

"There's stuff I should have told you a long time ago. I just wasn't ready." He sat down next to me, his leg not quite touching mine.

I nodded. Was this it? I had been ready forever.

"I don't even know where to start." He paused for a moment. I bit the inside of my cheek and waited.

"Remember the stuff I told you about my dad?"

I nodded again. Of course I remembered.

"My dad's an asshole. He's an addict. He buys more than he can afford. Like, all the time. If Dave was a decent human being, he would cut Ricky off. But Dave's a greedy motherfucker, and Ricky just keeps running up a tab."

I swallowed. I wasn't sure what to say.

"Remember Frank? Bouncer at the Crow, lots of tattoos?"

"Sure."

"Frank and this guy Rob over at Sally's Pub, I sell to them. For Dave."

I looked at Matthias blankly. I was cold, and I wanted to get up and get the blanket from the end of the couch, but I didn't want him to stop talking.

"It's how I pay off Ricky's tab. He always owes. Always. And there's good business in the clubs. Dave doesn't know the guys downtown, not like I do. So it works out perfect for him. I do the work, he takes a cut. Ricky buys more coke. World without end."

All those shows. All those nights when he wouldn't take me along. "You said it was for Cordelia. The errands downtown."

"Who do you think pays for her phone, and her clothes, and gymnastics and dance class? It's sure as shit not Mom and Dad, and the restaurant's not enough. Don't you get it, Ellory? *Everything's* for her."

"You could have told me."

"Sure. Oh, by the way, just thought you should know, I deal coke for Dave. Your boyfriend is the youngest, hottest drug dealer on the East Shore. And that's not going to change any time soon. Not until Cordelia turns eighteen or Ricky gets locked up. So let's go to the movies on Sunday. Let's plan our future. Let's plan our fucking cross-country adventure to *Portland*, for Christ sakes."

"Give me a little credit!" I shouted. "I didn't know things were so bad because *you never told me*!"

APRIL, JUNIOR YEAR
(FRIDAY AFTER BREAK)

I dodged Bex and shouldered Jenni out of the way. I was completely and utterly consumed by white hot anger, and as pissed as I was at them for being such goddamn lemmings, this anger was all reserved for Ret. How dare she try to use this little drama to bury the fact that she completely and utterly betrayed me? So I burned some shit in her yard. Big freaking deal.

"You need to grow up and take some responsibility for your actions," I spat out, stepping toward Ret, making sure that she was the one stepping back this time. She wobbled in her heels, but kept her balance.

"Don't be mad at me," she wheedled. Her breath was sugar sweet. Whiskey sweet.

"Are you *drinking*?"

Ret grabbed protectively at the straps on her bag. I knew without looking that the flask was inside.

"That's none of your business," she breathed.

"Great," I spat. "Real classy, Ret. Did he give it to you, or did you pick it out yourself?"

"Ellory, please. Just let me explain. This is all a big misunderstanding." Her words were watery, wavering.

"Unbelievable. I have never met someone so freaking selfish. And joke's on me, because I thought we were really friends. But you only know how to care about yourself."

Ret's face went from pale to white. Jenni gasped, and I whipped around, glaring.

"I shouldn't have to defend myself here." The words were coming out of my mouth in a rush of hot steam. I looked from Jenni to Bex. "You're both freaking cowards."

Ret wobbled again in her heels. It was ten fifteen. How much had she had to drink? Whatever. Let her play her little game of Sid and Nancy. Let them all go up in flames.

The second bell rang, and we were late to class. Mr. Ren poked his head out of the math room to throw us some serious teacher shade for loitering before closing his door. I broke away and headed for the stairwell before I completely lost my shit in the middle of the hall. I was so done there.

APRIL, JUNIOR YEAR
(SPRING BREAK, WEDNESDAY)

I was freezing. The afternoon had taken a sharp, careening turn, and I felt like the world's biggest fool sitting there in my underwear. I wanted to get dressed, but I didn't want Matthias to watch me putting my clothes back on. Giving up. Instead I reached for the blanket and wrapped it around myself, tight.

"There's more," he said.

"Lay it on me. Really, go wild."

He grimaced. "I really don't know how to say this, and I don't think . . . Ellory, I'm so sorry."

My head snapped up, my eyes locking into the slouched frame of my boyfriend next to me on the couch, his usually perfect posture folded in.

"I should have ended things in January. I should have just let you go."

"What do you mean?" I couldn't keep the shake out of my voice. "Are you breaking up with me?"

"I've been hanging out with Ret a lot, ever since Cordelia and I saw her at the mall over winter break. We drink, shoot the shit, vent about our messed-up families."

"I know," I said softly. He was dodging my question. I clung to it like a tiny scrap of hope. "I saw you that day in the woods, remember?" And those other times you don't know about. "I know about Ret and Dave."

He looked confused. "What does this have to do with Dave?"

I raised my eyebrows at him. "It's not exactly a secret anymore," I said. "They've been hooking up for weeks."

He sank his face into his open palms. I could hear his heart beating. Or maybe it was my heart. The blood started to rush to my head, pounding against my skull like waves. I knew what he was going to say before he said it. She had lied to me. She had lied *through her teeth*. And I'd let her get away with it. Before he even opened his mouth, his voice was ringing in my ears, growing louder with every pulse, with every beat of blood.

"Not Dave. Ret's been hooking up with me."

APRIL, JUNIOR YEAR
(FRIDAY AFTER BREAK)

Ret pushed in front of me, weaving, sloppy. It was embarrassing. She reached for the stairwell door, which smacked against my hand.

"Watch it." My words were shards of glass. I hoped they would slice her into a million pieces.

"Sorry." She raised her hands in front of her chest. "I didn't mean to hit you. But you have to listen to me."

"No, I don't," I said through gritted teeth, pushing through the door and into the salmon pink stairwell. Ret followed behind me, Jenni and Bex right on her tail. I started for the stairs. This conversation was over before it started.

I was on the top stair when Ret grabbed my wrist, her fingers closing in a tight circle. Our band burned into my skin like dry ice, a reminder of who we were supposed to be—best friends, Ellory & Ret.

"Let go." I stepped down as far as her grasp would allow. I twisted halfway around to face her and gave my arm a shake, but she held on tight. She stood three stairs up, wobbling in those heels, swaying back and forth, her eyes two deep, lapis wells of confusion and hurt.

"I said let go." My voice was a warning bell; it rang out clear and sharp. Heat coursed through every inch of my body, threatening to erupt into white, hot flame. And when that happened, it was probably best for Ret and everyone there if they weren't within a good five-foot radius.

"He was all wrong for you, Ellory. He was making you miserable, and you were never going to end it. I was *helping* you. We were supposed to be single together, remember? That was the plan."

Did she even hear herself? "Maybe that was your plan."

"Ellory, come on," Ret whined. She tugged on my arm, her fingers digging the band further into my wrist. "It wasn't supposed to happen like this. I didn't mean to get drunk at that party, for everyone to see us."

"So you didn't mean to get caught."

Ret's mouth twisted down. "I thought we'd hook up a couple times, he'd feel guilty, and he'd finally break it off with you. I was doing it for you, Ellory May. You were letting him drag you down, and he was being such a wimp. I just wanted the old Ellory back. My Ellory."

I'd had enough. She was delusional. She was drunk. And once the words started, I couldn't make them stop. "You're a lying, selfish whore, Margaret Johnston. You were only helping yourself, and you know it. You are not my friend. You're a narcissistic, back-stabbing *slut*."

The words were horrible, mean. I didn't care. I just wanted to get away from her, to forget this terrible week ever happened. I was so done. I held on to the railing with my free hand and wrenched my other arm back, yanking hard, freeing my wrist from Ret's grasp.

One second, she was peering down at me from the top of the stairwell. Those ridiculous shoes. Whiskey rotting her breath.

The red knot of her lips, a Three Alarm Fire. The next, she was tumbling fast down an entire flight of fifteen hard, vinyl stairs. Ret's scream filled the stairwell with the echo of a thousand blades while I gripped the railing and the three of us let out one awful, collective gasp.

APRIL, JUNIOR YEAR
(SPRING BREAK, WEDNESDAY)

"Say something, please."

"Do you love her?" I asked.

Silence. Oh my god.

I stood up, then staggered back against the couch. The blanket slipped off my shoulder and down my back, exposing my skin. I felt unsteady on my feet, but I wouldn't fall over. I wasn't going to faint like some poor, scorned ingenue.

"I wanted to tell you, but she made me swear I wouldn't." Because she knew I'd never forgive her. Because then her fun would have to stop.

All of a sudden, everything Ret had said on the phone made so much sick sense. Two kids pawing at each other in the middle of the living room floor. Not Ret and Dave. Ret and *Matthias*. The room was crashing down around me, or maybe I was the one crashing. I snatched the fallen blanket and clutched it tightly around my shoulders, stepping away from the couch, away from him. Who *was* he?

"Are you okay?" Matthias stood up and reached for my arm.

"Don't touch me." He jerked his hand back like I'd bitten him. Maybe I should have. "I need you to get out. Right now."

He ignored me. "She offered to help, that's how it started. She knew you better than anyone, said she knew how to fix things. I don't know why I trusted her." He said it like it was some kind of excuse, like I'd asked for an explanation.

"And hooking up factored in how exactly?"

Matthias grimaced and folded his arms across his chest. I couldn't tell if he looked more defensive or scared. "It just happened. She was easy to talk to. It was *fun*, okay? Remember fun? It didn't mean anything."

"Please."

"God, fine, that's such a cliché, but you know what I mean."

"No, I don't," I said, my voice hard. If he was trying to hurt me even more, mission accomplished.

His eyes narrowed. "Right. Everything's serious with you, isn't it? Look, I fucked up, but I guess it's for the best. She made me realize how not ready I am for this. For you."

His words were sharp, designed to cut to the bone. I sucked in a gasp so fast it burned my lungs and tears pricked my eyes.

"I'm sorry," he said, more softly. "I didn't mean that."

"Save it." I scrubbed at my face with the blanket. *Get ahold of yourself, Ellory.* For a moment, neither of us said anything. I just wanted him to leave, for this nightmare to be over.

"She said she was hooking up with Dave?" he asked finally. Had she? Had she ever really said it was Dave Franklin? There was a tinge of jealousy in his voice, and I almost laughed at the bitter irony of it all.

"She let me believe what I wanted to believe," I said. "Now get out."

He still didn't move.

"I don't know if I love her," he said finally. "I don't expect you to forgive me."

Was I supposed to *thank him* for letting me off the hook? Fuck that. I straightened my shoulders, and the blood started flowing back down into my chest, my limbs, my feet. "You have to leave, Matthias. Now."

He wouldn't meet my gaze. He started to back toward the family room door. I knew that feeling. Those wobbly legs. That slow backing away. For an instant, I saw him like a vase teetering on the edge of a shelf. I wanted to watch him smash into a million little pieces.

APRIL, JUNIOR YEAR
(FRIDAY AFTER BREAK)

It was over so fast. One minute, she was flying down the stairs. The next, she was still. I screamed. I never meant for any of it to happen. I didn't mean for her body to end up twisted on the landing, her forehead split open into a red gash, her face and shirt streaming with blood. I didn't mean for something to snap when her back crashed hard against the stairs, something vital, something at the base of her spine.

I didn't mean it, I didn't mean it, I didn't mean it. But I'd be straight up lying if I said that before I knew how bad it was, before I knew that she wasn't going to get back up, before all that, when it was just her hair flashing past me in a fan of black and green streaks, one snakeskin heel flying off and careening all the way down to the first floor—I'd be lying through my teeth if I said that in that one quick second, I didn't enjoy it.

I will never, ever forgive myself for that second.

Then, everything was a blur of noise and motion and slick, deep red. I was screaming and everyone was screaming and teachers were pouring out of classrooms and I was on the landing, my hands and knees against the cold, tile floor, and everything was slippery with Ret's blood. It was in my nose, my eyes, everywhere. I pressed my face into her chest and screamed and screamed until someone pulled me off her, and the street outside the school erupted into a roar of sirens.

I looked up at my friends, frozen at the top of the stairs. Bex clutched at her stomach, her mouth hanging open in a silent O of horror. Jenni's eyes were a steel flash. An accusation, a blade cutting me in two.

She'd heard every word I said to Ret. Every unforgivable, mean thing. Bex might absolve me in time, but not Jenni. She knew what I felt in that quick second. She saw straight through me.

I wanted to tell Jenni that I didn't mean it. That Ret probably did believe she was trying to help me, in her own twisted way. I was only trying to get away from her. I definitely didn't mean to hurt her. But Jenni was all the way at the top of the stairs, and the words wouldn't come.

Then, there were paramedics everywhere, and we were all being hurried away from the stairs.

Then, Ret was on a stretcher and I was back in the math room, my face pressed against the window. I got blood on the pane. I couldn't even see Ret, there were so many people and machines hovering around her like a swarm of bees.

Then, Ret was gone.

Somehow, I was downstairs, in Principal Keegan's office. The clock said 10:47. I should have been in third period. I was getting blood on the orange fabric. They'd have to replace the chair. It had soaked though my shirt, streaked my hair. My hands were covered in a deep red brown. It looked like a thin coat of enamel. I turned them over and over, transfixed by the dark half-moons beneath my fingernails. They were somebody else's fingers, somebody else's hands. In the hallway outside, everyone was sobbing and talking and I couldn't figure out why my mom was there, wrapping me in the old flannel we kept in the back of the car in case of a breakdown. The receptionist had to tell me over and over that they had called her, that I could go home now.

APRIL, JUNIOR YEAR
(SPRING BREAK, WEDNESDAY)

I willed myself to stay standing until he was in the hall. Don't cry. Don't move a muscle. I stood perfectly still until I heard his footsteps stop ringing against the flagstone, the thud of the front door. I clutched the blanket around my bare skin until the slam of the truck door, the sputter of the engine, the hum of the tires told me he was really gone.

Only then, only when the house was entirely silent and there was no trace of Matthias left anywhere, only then did I collapse onto the floor, the blanket falling in a heap around me, the sobs heaving out of my lungs in frantic, painful waves of water and sound.

APRIL, JUNIOR YEAR
(SUNDAY)

Everyone agreed it was an accident. I was told over and over and over. *No one blames you. It was a terrible accident.* There were so many witnesses. Bex and Jenni, and two seniors ditching class. Three sophomores watching the commotion from the base of the stairs. Everyone saw. Everyone agreed. It was an accident. It would take time for the full toxicology report to come in, but they had found her flask in her bag at the hospital. Her blood alcohol level was 0.11—about three shots of whiskey. Enough to smash through reason, depth perception, reaction time. In combination with hard, vinyl stairs and five-inch heels, enough to be fatal.

On Sunday morning, Mom sat on the corner of the bed and told me that Ret's funeral would be later that week. I didn't have to go. She'd lived for almost two days in the hospital, if that dark place where Ret's brain had gone could be called living. Traumatic brain injury. Severe damage to the spine. The part of her brain where Ret had lived—real, breathing Ret, my Ret—had been gone from the moment she'd hit the landing.

No one would press charges. She'd been drinking, a lot. I'd been careless, yes, but it was a freak accident. It wasn't my fault. I was told over and over. My mom started calling what happened *the fall*. It was a kindness, a shortcut, a way of taking something hard and shaping it into two little words that can slip off your tongue. As I lay in bed, my brain riffed on the possibilities: *fallout, fall from grace, fall guy, fall apart*. There was a piece of truth in each and every variation. But of course what she actually meant was much more literal.

Principal Keegan suspended me for the rest of the year. He made it very clear that the suspension was for fighting in school—not because they blamed me for Ret's death. My parents might have fought it, but everyone agreed I needed time away from Pine Brook after the accident. They said the word over and over and over. Accident. But they didn't know what it was like in that moment. How *good* it had felt to say those terrible things. How for an instant, I'd *enjoyed* watching her fall. *Accident, fall.* The words rested like a hot stone on my tongue. I gagged. I swallowed. The stone was on fire. It burned straight through me, leaving a charred-up, blacked-out, gaping hole inside my chest. *Crackle, pop.*

I pick Tuesday because Tuesday doesn't seem like a day people visit cemeteries. You go on a Sunday or holiday, not on a spring evening, three days after graduation. I pick Tuesday because I don't want company. Because if I am going to really do this, I need to be alone.

I drive through the entry gates, past the shop selling artificial wreaths and bright orange and yellow pinwheels. There's nothing there I can imagine being loved by the living. Why would we choose it for the dead? There are only a few cars parked along the wide asphalt drive. Good. I drive past the older parts of the cemetery, the ones that have graves with looming stone angels, the ones with crumbling headstones and lush grass.

There's only one part of Saint Aloysius where she could be. The part with fresh dirt and glossy, new stones. The part at the end of the drive. I pull the Subaru up along the shoulder and step out of the car into the low-hanging sun. What if she doesn't show?

I force my feet to move away from the car, onto the grass. She'll show. As much as I don't want to be here, to see the new grass, to stand in front of her stone, I need to say goodbye. It's been a year. One year, one month, and two weeks to be exact. I am a coward. I am overdue.

I start at the end of the first row and walk along, reading the names. It's been a long time since I've been in a cemetery, since my grandpa's funeral. I don't remember a lot about it. We were in Maryland. I thought we'd all throw a shovelful of dirt on the grave, because that's what happened in movies, but no one did. I remember it had rained the night before, that my shoes were caked in mud.

Some of the stones have intricately etched portraits of the deceased, or the whole family. Some have poems, songs, memories. They look almost painted on. The patches of grass in front of the graves are decorated with artificial sunflowers and bright streamers and wreaths shaped into black and gold Steelers helmets and red, white, and blue Phillies diamonds. I guess there are a lot of sports fans among the dead. I keep walking.

One grave has an entire Barbie tea party set up in front, complete with little yellow and white teacups and saucers. I stop to read the headstone. The girl who died was only four. Her stone is etched with a detailed likeness of the Magic Kingdom. It makes my stomach twist. I keep going.

Then, in the sixth row back, I see her. She's wearing her

graduation gown, sitting on top of her headstone, her legs swinging in the wind. Her shoes peek out from the bottom of the gown, a pair of snakeskin heels stained with deep, red blood. I shudder. Even in death, Ret still knows how to make a scene.

"Ellory May," she calls, waving to me like nothing has happened, like we're just two friends hanging out in a graveyard on a sunny afternoon. "About time you showed up."

You're in my head, I think, but she's still there, the maroon gown fluttering around her. *You're not real.* She kicks off the bloodstained shoes and grins.

"Poor taste, right? Veronica sued the shit out of Hot Topic, not that it was their fault. Wouldn't want to disappoint her from beyond the grave." She laughs, then slides down from the headstone, bare feet sinking into the grass.

She's different today. This isn't the girl in AP English that only I could see, the pair of lapis eyes following me down the hall, the shadow waiting at the riverbank, where no one was around to watch me slip a fresh bottle of my mom's amaretto out of my bag, unscrew the lid, and try to forget. This Ret knows she's dead, knows our dance is over, the lights have come up. Which means, of course, that I know. That I'm ready to face the truth. Because there's no moving on unless I let her go.

I will my legs to carry me through the grass.

When I reach her headstone, I'm surprised to see how simple it is compared to so many of the others. Ret's is unadorned with etchings or quotes. Carved into the sleek face are simply her name and the dates that bookend her short life. *Margaret Sara Johnston*. It looks wrong written out in full. A plain name for a plain girl, and Ret was never plain. The grass in front of the stone is freshly trimmed, and two pretty pink wreaths rest against the base of the stone. They're the pink of little girls, of party dresses, of ballerinas. They're all wrong for Ret.

I look over at her. Her head is tilted to one side, her arms folded across her chest. Her hair is streaked bright cherry red, and falls almost down to her waist. She looks me up and down like I'm an antique at auction, and she's appraising my worth. Then her lips part into a smile. They're coated in her favorite Three Alarm Fire gloss. God, I miss her.

"You're not real." I force myself to look her in the eyes. She purses her lips and slides a pair of red plastic sunglasses down across the bridge of her nose, blocking me out.

"Damn, Ellory. Haven't you already hurt me enough? You don't have to go hurting my feelings too."

Ret. You were wild and bold and absolutely maddening. Selfish and demanding and more scared than you'd ever admit. You were adrenaline rushes and tested limits and fierce, bright light. And now we have to say goodbye.

I feel the tears coming all at once, and there's nothing I can do to stop them. I don't want to stop them. I hate Ret for dying and I hate myself even more. I sink onto the ground in front of the wreaths and sob and sob until my breath is a hard, chafing rasp against my throat. Until there are no tears left.

When I look up, she's still standing there, looking embarrassed for me. I reach into my bag and pull out her red leather notebook. Then I hold it out, an offering.

"Don't you know ghosts don't read books?" she mocks me.

"We both know you're not a ghost." My voice is steady. "I made you, and now I need you to leave so I can say goodbye to Ret."

She takes a step back. "I *am* Ret," she says.

"No," I say through gritted teeth. "Ret died last April. Ret is buried beneath this stone." I know, on some level, that I'm talking to a figment of my imagination, but that doesn't make this any easier. This figment has a face and a voice and a name. And I need her to leave.

"I made you up because I wasn't ready to forgive myself. And because it was easier than admitting you were really gone. I needed you, and you were right there, waiting."

"I'm still here," she says. Her voice is a whimper.

I reach out and take her hand in mine. "I love you. And now I need you to let me say goodbye." Then I let her hand go.

She takes another step back. She wavers. Through her maroon robes, I can see rows of graves. I can see grass and sky.

I close my eyes and count to ten, fifteen, twenty. There's no magic number here. There's only me. I'm the only one capable of moving on. Ret's death was a terrible tragedy. A horrible, ugly thing. She was drunk, and I was angry, and Matthias was a coward. We were all responsible.

For over a year, I haven't been able to forgive myself. I said awful things. The last words I said to her, the last things she ever heard. And for one second, before I knew how bad it was, before I knew that she wasn't going to get back up, I enjoyed her pain.

But I am not a criminal, hideous. I hate the word, but it was an accident all the same. I can admit that now. I didn't mean it, and that does mean something after all. It means I deserve my own forgiveness. I picture my face on a giant balloon. Sharp features, sharp chin. Fine blond hair, fluttering in the wind. I twist the string around my hand, and then I release it into the sky.

When I open my eyes, you'll be gone. When I open my eyes, you'll be gone.

I open my eyes. I'm alone.

I turn back to the grave and rest the notebook at the base of the stone, between the wreaths. Then I reach into my pocket and pull out the black band I never used to take off my wrist. Veronica wears Ret's now. And now mine will be with her. I open the notebook and slip it between the pages.

"You hurt me too," I say to the empty air. "You took Matthias, and you expected me to thank you for it. And you know what? You were right." I laugh, and it feels good. Really good. "He really was terrible for me. But you lied to me, Ret. You thought I'd give in, like I always gave in to you. And then you went and died on me, and I couldn't even hate you, I was so busy hating myself."

I sink back against the side of the stone. My voice is quiet this time. "I am going to live with your death every single day, and it's never going to get easier or better or go away. I am going to miss you and mourn you, and some days I'm still going to be mad at you. But I'm finally ready to say goodbye. I forgive you. I forgive us."

No one responds because there's no one else here.

My Ret. Reckless and brash and full of light. The star around which the rest of us were in constant orbit.

You have to get used to living with it. I can hear Dr. Marsha's voice ringing in my ears. *You can't go back, Ellory. You have to find a way forward.*

The air around me is completely silent. I feel like I should be declaring some kind of victory. But there is no victory, right? There's only living, only moving on.

I'm ready to leave now. I walk back to the Subaru, slowly, daring my past to take shape again in front of me, follow me home. But nothing comes. I open the door and slide into the sunbaked car. I could come back here again, and it would be okay. It's just grass and stones and trees and sky. Maybe I'll come back again in a few weeks. Maybe I'll draw her a picture and leave it by her grave. The four of us standing together at graduation, the way it could have been, tossing our caps and tassels into the air. Me, Bex, Jenni, Ret. I take one last look around, but Ret is nowhere to be found. Fake-Ret. Ghost-Ret. Guilt-Ret. Gone.

All I feel is sadness. Regular, healthy sadness. I shift the car into drive and turn around on the road. Then I head forward, toward the gates that will take me home.

Three Months Later

The sky is wide and clear above me. The air is cool, but it's restless, shifting, bound to explode into late summer heat come mid-afternoon. I can feel the grass pressing against my cheek through the scarf we've been using as a blanket on the lawn. The air smells like long, lazy days and pool parties and third grade. Like childhood. Like a new start.

"Elle, don't fall asleep on me! I've got three chapters to get through before we occupy Waterstein, and I need the moral support."

I click my phone on to check the time. "I actually have to get to the studio if I'm going to make it there by one. You can do it. I have all the faith."

Gina groans and shifts around to grab her backpack, which she's been using as a pillow on the lawn. The bag is weighed down by a brain trust worth of bio texts, and she sways a little under its weight.

"In that case, I'm off to the library. I'm going to fall asleep out here without you to keep me on track."

I smile. It is seriously hard to separate my roommate from her books, and it's only the third week of classes. I've never met someone so dedicated to biology. Gina stands up and pulls a thick mass of curls back into a ponytail, securing her hair in a striped band.

"Meet me at twelve forty-five?" she asks.

"You've got it."

I have exactly an hour and a half to get to the art studio, make some headway on my project, and get over to our dining hall for the protest against wage cuts that just took effect for the food service employees across campus. I have a pretty sweet OCCUPY WATERSTEIN banner that I designed for the occasion folded up in my bag.

Gina waves, and I walk down the gravel path toward the art building feeling driven, inspired. For weeks, I kept his notes in a box in my room. One for each week of fall semester, until I made them stop. Then last night, I got one more note—an email, the one he waited until I was all the way across the country to send. The one that begins, *I needed you to hate me so you'd really go to Portland,* and ends, *I looked up that copper and stone guy, and he'd be lucky to have you in class.* All year, I had let his words pile up, a mystery I couldn't unravel. But now the words won't weigh me down anymore because I've found a way to put them to work.

I don't know exactly where the project's going yet, but that's okay. I have plenty of time to figure it out. The important thing is that I'm doing *something*. At the end of this tunnel of confusion and grief and pain and regret is some sort of meaning. I don't know what it is yet. But there's something in the words that have been lying fallow in my room all year, and the new words in my inbox now. In time, I'll make some sense of them.

Inside the art building, I'm greeted by a blast of cold air and a group of students staging a photo shoot in the entryway. I duck around them and down the hall, past the elevators and coffee kiosk, and then up the stairs.

I push open the door at the top and step out onto the fourth floor. The hallways are lined with flyers advertising openings around town, on-campus shows, and calls for models. I make my way to the second door from the end—the first year studio. My own little piece of Portland State. I share the space with fifteen other first-years, but they're mostly night owls. Before noon, I'm pretty much guaranteed to have the studio to myself.

Inside, I rest my bag on a worktable and pull a note from Lissette out of my cubby. It's an idea about the assignment we're collaborating on. She's seriously smart, a fierce graphic designer. But we're working on basic drawing techniques these first few weeks, and she's a little out of her digital comfort zone. I jot a response on the back of the paper and place it in her cubby before pulling my laptop out of my bag and connecting to the spotty campus wi-fi.

When my email loads, I connect my laptop to the studio printer. One sheet of paper drops into the tray, and I check to make sure the entire email is there. It is. I disconnect my laptop and press a few keys. *Are you sure you want to delete?* Yes, I'm sure.

With one copy saved on paper, I send the email to its electronic graveyard. *Permanently delete?* Yes, please.

I open my bag and remove the folder that holds all of Matthias's notes. I spread them out on the worktable. Ten unfolded triangles covered with yellow highlighter lines and question marks. I add the email to the end of the row. Eleven.

I let my eyes drift across the worktable. The pages are filled with reasonings and offerings, pretty words and ugly words infused with a charred-up, burned-out aching that I know so well. Before I came to Portland, I almost left the box under my bed to collect dust. Part of me would have been happy to leave it behind. But another part of me couldn't ignore the pain shimmering across each of those pages. I knew it; it was part of me.

I started coming to the studio in the mornings, spreading the notes out on the table, highlighting passages like evidence, like clues. Taking my own notes in the margins. At first, I was looking for answers. But then, I stopped. There are no answers here. There is no magic solution that's going to poof the last year and a half into oblivion. But there's something in the words, something calling out, demanding my focus. I might never write back to Matthias, but I am ready to make something out of all this guilt and loss.

I lean over the email and highlight two passages, then a third. I click the cap back onto the highlighter and stand back, taking in all eleven sheets, letting the words glowing yellow stand out.

if you're reading this   this will be the last letter

          genuinely cared for you   had to tell you

never stopped   sorry   is just a word

couldn't end things   so selfish   had to push you away

    doesn't capture   Ret promised a solution   here's the truth

I knew if I told you   paralyzed by indecision

                    Ret was the solution

she was messed up too   scratch that   if anyone is to blame

                                I was selfish   I let it happen

blame me   you were so willing

I couldn't tell you   to compromise   I couldn't let you stay

            here's the truth

                            don't delete this, please

I'm afraid   sorry is not just a word

I'm just like my dad   I did everything for Cordelia

            that horrible accident   blame me

        I wanted to tell you   here's the truth   because

I still loved you   I can't leave the West Shore

          Cordelia needs me   can't leave   probably ever

I fucked it all up   beyond repair

                    in public at Dave's party   a cop-out

                                                      a cliché

I needed you to really hate me   on purpose

all the way to Portland

                              no do-overs, no going back

I had to be mean   it killed me   I was so mean

                                                 on purpose

the only way to let you go   I know how it sounds

I needed you   to go to Portland

                    to really hate me

                              I knew if I told you   why

you might stay

I get lost in the pages, and the minutes melt away. I read each passage again and again, but it doesn't add up to one simple answer. This is not a package tied off with a big, shiny bow. These are fragments, thoughts, apologies. Just snippets of truth, strands of the shimmering, fragile web that will always connect me to Matthias and Ret and the West Shore.

I'm not looking for answers anymore. I'm looking for a way to create something meaningful out of these threads. Ret's and Matthias's and mine. I have ideas for a mural project or maybe something silk-screened. I pack up the papers and return the folder to my bag. I don't need to figure it out today. In fact, I have all the time in the world to create something from this sadness—something new and filled with life. I need to take my time, get things right. I owe myself that much.

I shrug my bag over my shoulder and stare straight ahead for a moment, out of the streaked studio windows and down onto the courtyard in front of the science labs. Outside, kids are gathered at the patio tables and on the grass, reading, talking, listening to music. Existing. For a moment, I am overwhelmed by how lucky I am. I get to be here. I am alive.

On my way out of the art building, I take the stairs two at a time. I have a sudden urge to be outside, to feel the sun on my skin, to feel the gravel path beneath my feet. When I push through the doors into the early afternoon light, I can feel the universe expanding just a little. It's like everything's zooming out and zooming in all at once. I am sad and lucky and alive.

The past is with me, and it will always be with me. *Two roads diverged in a yellow wood*, and I never could have known how far apart they'd take us, but how close you'd always stay. I will make something worthwhile out of everything we destroyed. It won't be perfect, and it will never be enough to bring you back. But it is what I can do.

I look up at the art building and then across the lawn, toward Waterstein. For a moment, the whole campus shimmers in the sun's bright light, and the sky looks like magic, a dance of sun spots and glittering stars. But there's nothing magical here. This is the future catching up to the past, twirling me around, urging me forward. The light changes, and the moment is gone. A girl whirrs past me on a blue bicycle, and I take off running down the path. Gina is waiting. The whole day is in front of me.

Acknowledgments

They say it only takes one "yes," but here's the truth: putting a debut novel into the world takes a whole chorus of encouragement, affirmation, and faith. Without any one of these "yesses," there would be no *See All the Stars*.

Yes: my brilliant editor, Ruta Rimas, whose expert vision and confidence in this story helped me shape *See All the Stars* into the book it is today. Without you, Ellory would still be floating through the entire first half of senior year. I'm so thankful for your keen insights and avid support throughout the publication process. Thank you also to Justin Chanda, Nicole Fiorica, Audrey Gibbons, Michael McCartney, Bridget Madsen, Elizabeth Blake-Linn, Ellen Winkler, Ellia Bisker, Natascha Morris, Rebecca Syracuse, the fantastic sales and marketing teams, and everyone at McElderry Books, present and past, who has played an indispensable part in turning this manuscript into a real, live book and ushering it into the world.

Yes: my passionate agent, Erin Harris, who saw the potential in a much earlier draft and took a leap of faith on the manuscript and on me. I couldn't ask for a better literary partner, and I'm so glad you're on this journey along with me. Your editorial acumen, industry savvy, and unflagging enthusiasm mean the world. Thank you also to Melissa Sarver White, Bobby O'Neil, Annie Hwang, and the entire team at Folio Literary Management/Folio Jr. for your support and dedication.

Yes: my husband, Osvaldo, who encourages me daily to put my writing first, even when it means letting more practical things slide. Thank you for being my biggest fan, a sharp and engaged reader, and for always being by my side. Te amo.

Yes: my parents, Pat and Tony, who encouraged my writing from the time I could hold a pencil. Thank you for never second-guessing my creative path through life and for celebrating this milestone with me.

An enormous debt of gratitude is owed as well to the manuscript's early readers and advocates. I'm fiercely grateful to the beta readers and critique partners who helped me level up my writing and Ellory's story at various stages of the process: Nora Fussner, Rachel Lynn Solomon, Bri Cavallaro, Carlyn Greenwald, and Allison Augustyn. Thank you also to Elle Jauffret and Lynda Locke for your specialized insights. And a heartfelt thanks to my heroes Tiffany D. Jackson, Stephanie Kuehn, Mindy McGinnis, Karen M. McManus, Kara Thomas, and Jeff Zentner for championing Ellory's story.

It is with absolute certainty that I say that this book would never have been written, let alone published, without the wisdom, guidance, and solace of the various literary communities of which

I'm proud and so thankful to be a part: the Electric Eighteens; the YA Binders; the Pitch Wars family, in particular my fellow mentors and my wonderful mentees; my colleagues and authors at Black Lawrence Press, Author Accelerator, and Copper Lantern Studio; my cohorts and the faculty at the Syracuse University MFA program and the Sarah Lawrence College writing program, from whom I learned an immeasurable amount; and finally the members of the NYU Department of Comparative Literature, who graciously let me leave to pursue the writing life full-time. I'm also enormously grateful to the Kimmel Harding Nelson Center for the Arts in Nebraska City, NE, where part of *See All the Stars* was written, and to the MacDowell Colony in Peterborough, NH, where I received the life-changing news that it would be published.

Last, but by no means least, thank you to the numerous family members and friends who have supported me, been excited for me, and told anyone who would listen about my book. I appreciate you deeply, and I'm so lucky to have each and every one of you in my life. Particular gratitude is owed to Sally, Sonia, Lissette, Angel, all the LSWC ladies, Debra, and Diane.

Finally, finally, thank you—*you*—for reading. This is your story now.

TURN THE PAGE FOR
A SNEAK PEEK AT

ALL

EYES

ON

US

AMANDA

SUNDAY, DECEMBER 31

Three hours into the party, I'm tipsy on more than champagne. My mother would say that's the feeling of power, but I think it's the feeling of being adored. Maybe they're one in the same. I'm standing at the top of the Shaws' balcony staircase with Carter, allowing a roomful of eyes to wash over us from below. They're looking because we light up the room. They're looking because someday, we'll run this town.

"Don't you want to go downstairs?" Carter asks. "Graham and Adele are all alone."

I follow my boyfriend's eyes to our friends in the great hall below us. The Shaws live in the most venerable of Logansville's many Victorian estates. From our vantage point on the balcony, we have an eagle-eye view of the entire party. As always, the great hall is host to Mr. Shaw's world-class antique art collection, and tonight, it's teeming with Logansville's oldest money and most auspicious up-and-comers. Graham and Adele are decked out in their New Year's Eve finest in the baroque-era corner. He looks suave in a crisp suit and forest green tie, his tight brown curls cropped close to his head. His hand rests lightly on Adele's back, and her bright gold tube dress really pops against the dark brown of Graham's skin. As usual, she's mid-brushing him off.

"Soon," I promise Carter. "Let's just take one more minute up here together." I give his hand a tight squeeze. One more minute with my boyfriend. One more minute before I have to share Logansville's golden boy with the rest of the madding crowd.

He extracts his hand from mine and trails it slowly across my back before letting it fall to the balcony rail. He's right next to me, but his mind is somewhere distant. Somewhere I can't go. The moment of tipsiness is gone, and suddenly I feel more exposed up here than adored. I let my eyes dance across my boyfriend's broad shoulders, his shock of blond hair, the faraway look in his eyes that makes my skin go cold.

Carter knocks back the last of his champagne, and a college girl in a cater-waiter tux appears to replace his empty flute with a full one. He downs half the glass in one gulp. She offers me a flute as well, but I decline. I need to stay sharp. I glance around the hall, searching for our parents, not that they'd care about Carter drinking. Ever since we became a couple freshman year, they've basically treated us like adults. After all, we're Amanda Kelly and Carter Shaw. We're their legacy. The thought makes my heart skip a beat, excitement or fear rattling inside my chest.

At seventeen, Carter's already a rising star in the community. Varsity athlete, senior class president, sharp mind for business like his father. His future is a dazzling display of success and certainty and respect. With him, so is mine.

I keep my eyes trained on the crowd until they land on Krystal, Carter's mother, who's talking to my mother beneath the Shaws' masterfully restored seventeenth-century Flemish tapestry. Linda is gesturing rapidly, a stack of platinum bangles sliding up and down her too-thin arms. She pauses to take a sip of something clear from an almost-empty rocks glass. She's probably working Krystal to secure the Shaws' large annual contribution for the upcoming benefit. The Logansville Museum of Fine Arts is one of the organizations for which my mother sits on the board. A bangle catches on the tip of one long powder-pink nail, and it takes her way too long to unsnare it. She's getting sloppy. Someone should probably cut her off.

I glance around, but I can't find my father in the crowd. If he were paying attention, he'd know the exact words to say to make her reel it in. But he's not looking. If it was me guzzling too much champagne and embarrassing myself in front of Logansville's elite, I'd be grounded until graduation. In moments like this, I can feel the scales tip another notch, the imbalance settling like so many lead bricks across my back. Watching her like this, it feels like my mother has removed herself from the equation entirely when it comes to our family's future. It's like she gets a free pass because I'm going to take care of everything.

I draw in a long breath and toss back my hair. My mother should be hosting, not boozing, but I can't tell her how to act. She leans forward and grips Krystal's shoulder, too hard. I can feel her grimace reflected on my own face. With my mother rapidly heading out of commission, I'll have to do double the hosting for us.

I turn to Carter. "Okay, let's go." His champagne glass is almost empty again, and he's running a finger absently along the edge of my dress, right where the delicate red satin meets the outline of my shoulder blades. His touch makes my skin tingle. From the great hall below us, we must look picture perfect. I glance over the rail, down to where one of my mother's museum friends is waving up at us, the gesture full of fondness for the town darlings. I wave back, then raise my eyes to meet Carter's. He's looking right at me now, but the distance is still there, thrumming right beneath the surface. I try to blink it away.

It's amazing how a change in perspective can transform the whole view.

Downstairs, I stop to exchange pleasantries with the Beaufords and the Steinways while Carter is absorbed into the crowd. Every so often, I catch a note of his rich, rough laugh or see a flash of those deep dimples, white teeth. Everyone wants a minute of his time—it'll take him all night to reach Graham and Adele. I tell myself it's fine. I have my own mingling to do. I'm in the middle of laughing at one of Mr. Steinway's terrible jokes when the cater-waiter from the balcony touches my arm.

"Sorry to interrupt, Miss Kelly, but I couldn't find your mother."

I glance around. She's right. The space below the Flemish tapestry is empty, and Linda Kelly is nowhere to be found.

"We're running low on the Kobe and Stilton toasts and crab

rémoulade, and Carla wants to know if we should run across the street to restock now or after the ball drops."

I've lived directly across the street from Carter since we moved here in second grade. The move had something to do with the fallout from the financial crisis; Dad changed jobs and my mother thought a small town would be a nice change of pace for our family. Carter and I were in school together, and our parents became fast friends. They've been cohosting the annual New Year's Eve party for as long as I can remember.

The cater-waiter clears her throat, waiting for my response. It's tradition for the Kellys to arrange the catering and host the staging area in our highly functional kitchen across the street; I don't think anyone has actually prepared a meal at the Shaws' since the Victorian era. Her question is minor, a detail. But I can't screw this up. I squint up at the giant grandfather clock at the base of the stairs. The face is so intricately designed, it's almost impossible to read.

"It's eleven twenty," she says, waiting patiently for my verdict. Her bow tie is slightly askew. It's all I can do to resist straightening it out, keep my hands busy.

I take a deep breath. My mother should really be handling this. If I get it right, she'll never notice. But if I get it wrong, I'll never hear the end of it. "Send two staff over to the kitchen and make sure they're back with the Kobe and crab by a quarter of. Tell Carla to keep the rest here circulating, okay?" I force my voice to stay steady. If she notices my nerves, she doesn't let on.

She leaves to find her boss, and I excuse myself from the Steinways to look for Carter. I just need a second of his time, a quick kiss, a reminder that he cares. That he's in this with me. Because in a few years, Carter and I will be throwing parties like this one. In a few years, no more training wheels. The torch will be passed, and it will be our arms thrusting the bright, hot flame into the Logansville night. Together.

I'm slipping through the crowd, making eye contact and smiling, when my phone chimes. Instead of the usual message preview, the words *Private Number* light up the screen. I glance around, then step out of the hall and into the entryway. Perched on the lip of the Shaws' stone fountain, my red Louboutins flashing against the blue marble floor that looks like the ocean, I open the text.

> New Year, New You. Wouldn't you look
> better without a cheater on your arm?

I look around, fast, but aside from the coat check girl in the corner, I'm alone out here with the fountain and marble floors. The very small circle of people who know the truth about Carter's one bad habit are twenty steps away, right inside the party. And none of them would send a message like this. My fingers hover over the reply box, but there's nothing to say. Someone who thinks they know something is trying to ruin my night. And I'm not about to give in to a coward hiding behind a blocked caller ID. I toss my phone back into my bag and run my fingers through my hair, smoothing the glossy strands that frame my face. When I breathe in, I'm the only one who can hear the air catch against the back of my throat. Then I walk back into the party.

"Mandy, Mandy!" Adele is grinning and waving wildly at me from the great hall's baroque corner. Only Adele is allowed to call me Mandy. Our mothers were Kappas together, and we've known each other practically since the womb. Adele's mom was a major reason my parents chose Logansville when we relocated from Pittsburgh ten years back. So Adele gets a pass. To everyone else, it's Amanda Kelly.

I make my way through the sea of satin, lace, and Jo Malone to my friends. Adele wraps her arms around me in a sloppy hug, practically lifting me off my feet with the force. The gold sequins on her tube dress bite into my skin, but she's too drunk and amped up on the gleaming, beguiling promise of New Year's Eve to notice me squirm.

"Sorry we were late getting here," she says, releasing me from the hug and locking me into some intense, boozy eye contact. Her lashes are thick with mascara, and the long, blond streaks in her hair have been freshly touched up at the roots. Adele is always immaculately put together, and people who don't really know her would never believe that just beneath her feminine exterior is a total firecracker with a passion for improv and a silly, brash sense of humor. "Ben's shitty car got a flat on the way over, and we had to wait for Triple A."

I groan and roll my eyes at Ben, who's engaged in some full-on geekery with Graham. The words *Gotham*, *DC*, and *Bronze Age* rise above the peels of laughter and clink of glasses that fill the hall in surround-sound. Ben's mouth is stretched wide into his usual dweeby grin, and he's definitely recycling the same too-short pants and too-big jacket he wore to last month's winter formal. It's something I can't quite put to words, an itch beneath my skin, but Ben brings out the worst in me. We all tolerate him because he's on varsity lacrosse with the rest of the guys, and he's actually a really good midfielder, but Ben still conducts himself like we're in middle school, like he's not part of Logansville South's most enviable group of seniors. If you hang with us, you represent us. And all Ben represents is a complete lack of savior faire. I suppose I should feel bad because his mom left them when we were in fourth grade and maybe he's been lacking in fashion and life advice, but seriously.

"Why did you let yourself be shuttled here in Ben's rattle-trap?" I hiss at Adele beneath my breath. "What's wrong with Graham's Escalade?"

I sound like my mother, but I can't help it. Just watching him hook his arm around Graham's shoulder makes the back of my neck turn hot.

Adele glances at Graham, then leans in too close to my face. "I didn't want to give Graham the wrong impression about tonight, okay? Like he's my date or something? So I said Ben could drive us, like a group thing."

"Why couldn't Graham have driven you, like a group thing?"

Adele stares at me blankly for a second. I draw in a deep breath and try to push the nastiness out. I hate when I get like this. But before I can apologize for snapping at her, Adele breaks into a slightly wobbly tap routine in her pointy heels, immediately capturing the attention of everyone around us. It's totally inappropriate, yet absolutely charming. The guys pump fists in the air and cheer her on. This is classic Adele. Diffusing the moment, choosing comedy over confrontation. Redirecting the course of the night.

I love Adele because she's been there for me forever. Because she's funny as hell. Because when my mother turns the screws too tight, Adele can just sense it, and she's at my door with mocha caramels and the latest *Vanity Fair* and *Vogue*. I should cut her more slack when it comes to Graham, and guy stuff in general.

When she's accepting a round of applause and tugging her dress back in place, I flash her a warm smile. "Sorry. I'm glad you're here."

"I love your dress," she says, tacitly accepting my apology. "Where did you find it?"

"I picked it out on a trip to the city. There are actually a few cute boutiques on Wood Street now."

The city is Pittsburgh, the closest place to West Virginia's Northern Panhandle to resemble an actual metropolis. We lived there for the first seven years of my life, but I don't really remember much before Logansville. The panhandle—that skinny strip of land nestled between Pennsylvania and Ohio—is part southern charm, part Hicksville. Logansville, naturally, brings the charm. Pittsburgh is about a forty-five-minute drive from here; my dad makes the commute every day to the investment firm where he's newly a partner. He was already a partner at his old firm, but his job kind of fell apart along with the economy. It's been a long climb back to where he is now, and we're far from the top of the mountain.

I'm totally lost in thought when Trina arrives with a heaping plate of hors d'oeuvres. I raise my eyebrows.

"What, they're for sharing." She holds the plate out to me.

Trina is tall and model-thin, and she can eat like a horse. It's going to catch up to her someday, but at the moment she looks amazing in a sapphire mermaid dress that only she could pull off and a new cascade of ombré hair. She had the wave put in

so her bone-straight Japanese locks would "flow like the ocean."
Her words. Trina's beloved Canon EOS 5D is slung around her
neck. The clunky camera kind of ruins her elegant silhouette,
but Trina would never attend a society function without it. She
would also be the first to take down any joker who makes a crack
about camera-obsessed Japanese tourists. Trina may love her selfies, but she's no hobby photographer. Or tourist. Trina's going
to be a professional.

I pluck a Kobe and Stilton toast off her plate and pop it in
my mouth. The staff must have returned with the fresh round,
which means it's getting close to midnight. It also means everything's running smoothly, not that I'll get an ounce of credit.
I close my eyes for a second, and the anonymous text message
flashes across the back of my lids. *Wouldn't you look better without
a cheater on your arm?* I shiver. Someone is trying to shake me up,
and it's not going to work.

"Where's Carter?" Trina asks. My thoughts exactly. I haven't
heard his laugh rising above the din since before I stepped out
of the hall. I glance around at our friends. Bronson has joined
Graham and Ben in the corner, although his eyes are fixed on
his phone. Any money says he's texting Alexander, his boyfriend,
who goes to school across town at Logansville North. Alexander
was invited tonight, of course, but he's still in Tulum with his
family. Graham makes a show of trying to read Bronson's texts
over his shoulder, and Bronson shoves his phone in his pocket
and joins the conversation, which has turned from comics to sky-
diving, their new obsession. Only Bronson has actually jumped
before; his dad's in the military and Bronson is kind of an adrenaline junkie. The guys all want to immortalize their friendship

by jumping out of a plane together before we graduate in five months. It's ridiculous, but not as ridiculous as Batman versus Wolverine. Anyway, Carter's not with them.

Adele and Trina are standing on either side of me, scarfing canapés. Except for Carter, that's all of us. I scan the rest of the room. Winston and Krystal Shaw are strategically positioned with my dad, Jack, near the entryway, should they need to greet any extra-fashionably-late guests. They're glowing, the royalty of Logansville. My mother should be with them, but it's probably best if I don't spend too much time thinking about where she's gone off to. Two years ago, I found her passed out in the gun room, her face pressed against a glass case housing one of Mr. Shaw's many antique revolvers. Since then, the Shaws have kept their little vintage armory locked up tight during parties. I'm sure she's found a regular bed to pass out on this time. At least she had the good sense to make an exit before she went from sloppy to fully lit.

My eyes rove through the rest of the crowd, searching for Carter. The great hall is filled with my dad's investment colleagues and their families, many of whom drove from Pittsburgh to be here tonight; the board members from my mother's organizations, the Museum of Fine Arts and the Northern Panhandle Land Trust; and the bigwigs from Shaw Realty, the largest, most successful corporate firm in the area. Carter's already slated to head up sales in one of their regional markets as soon as he graduates from college.

My eyes dart back to my friends and then around the hall one more time. I squint again at the grandfather clock. It's 11:55. I can feel my pulse spike.

"There he is." Adele's pointing up to the balcony. Carter's leaning into the wall, back pressed against the ornate cream and gold wallpaper, texting furiously. His fingers pause, and he stares at the screen for a beat. Then, his face transforms into a wide grin.

My heart sinks, blood rushing to my face. I know I don't look pretty wearing this mix of hurt and fury, but I can't help it. It's five minutes until midnight, and Carter's texting with *her*. Again. Adele takes one look at my face and turns to Graham.

"Get Carter down here. Now."

Graham glances at me, then follows Adele's gaze up to the balcony. A shadow passes over his face when his eyes find Carter. He squeezes my shoulder and presses past me. "On it."

Trina flags down more glasses of champagne, and soon everyone's crowded around me in a tight circle, guzzling bubbly and laughing hard at something Ben says that's not even funny, but it keeps me almost entertained until Graham reappears with Carter. I take a deep breath to clear my head. Whoever sent that anonymous text struck a nerve. But they're wrong: Carter belongs on my arm. I belong with him.

She is just a temporary distraction. I'm forever, and deep down, Carter knows it. He squeezes through to the center of the circle and takes his place next to me at exactly thirty seconds to go until midnight, just as the whole room starts counting down.

"Sorry, babe," he whispers in my ear. "Family stuff with my cousin. Lost track of time."

Carter thinks I don't know about her. I smile thinly and let the lie fade into the chant: *eighteen, seventeen, sixteen* . . . My fingertips glide across the gold chain around my neck until they find the small onyx heart at the end. Carter gave it to me because black is eternally classy, and it goes with everything. Because Carter knows what I care about, knows me inside and out, knows we belong together. I repeat it over and over inside my head until I believe it. Then I draw his eyes to the heart with my fingertips, remind him that he's here with me. He smiles, his eyes locked into mine.

Twelve, eleven, ten . . . All around us, our friends lift their champagne flutes toward the ceiling. Bronson scoops Adele up in both his arms, and she tilts back her head, letting her hair plunge down toward the floor in a sea of gold. Trina raises first her Canon, then her phone, and snaps a series of pictures. I smile wide. *Six, five, four . . .* Carter touches my chin and draws my face toward his. *Three, two, one . . .* His lips find my lips, and this is how tonight is meant to end. Carter and me, together, surrounded by cheering and glasses clinking, surrounded by our friends who are toasting the new year and toasting the two of us, together. We're at the center of everything. All eyes on us.

#HASHTAGREADS

Bringing the best YA your way

BECKY ALBERTALLI APRIL
NIC STONE MORGAN MATSON TUCHOLKE
ROBIN
BENWAY CASSANDRA CLARE
DARREN SCOTT
SHAN WESTERFELD
T.E. CARTER SOPHIE
MCKENZIE
STEPHEN
CHBOSKY AMY MCCULLOCH
JENN
CLARE FURNISS BENNETT

ADAM SILVERA GAYLE FORMAN
CHELSEA PITCHER ANNALIE GRAINGER
LAURA BATES HOLLY BLACK

Join us at **HashtagReads,**
home to your favourite YA authors

Find us on Facebook
HashtagReads

Follow us on Twitter
@HashtagReads